STAR STRIKER #2

TOUCH
AND
GO

MARY AMATO

HOLIDAY HOUSE • NEW YORK

Copyright © 2022 by Mary Amato

All Rights Reserved

HOLIDAY HOUSE is registered in the U.S. Patent and Trademark Office.

Printed and bound in August 2022 at Maple Press, York, PA, USA.

www.holidayhouse.com

First Edition

1 3 5 7 9 10 8 6 4 2

Library of Congress Cataloging-in-Publication Data is available.

ISBN: 978-0-8234-4912-5 (hardcover)

I love forms beyond my own,
and regret the borders
between us.
—Loren Eiseley

For Simon Amato and the Life of Gains

1.0

Through the main window of the spacecraft, the planet Jhaateez was sparkling.

Earthling Albert Kinney, Star Striker of the Zeenods, was heading to this planet and loving the view when his chaperone, Unit D3492778, activated the window shield.

"Hey!" Albert said. "I want to see where we're going."

The new robot displayed a smile. "My apologies, sir. However, we are about to pass Gravespace GJ7, and I am programmed to black out the windows for your psychological protection. Humans are prone to responses called nightmares, sir."

Full of excitement and with nothing to look at, Albert stood and began shaking out his arms and legs, bouncing around the interplanetary transport vehicle in his practice uniform and socks. "What exactly is a gravespace?"

"On page eight hundred seventy-six of the guide Kayko prepared for you—"

"I didn't read that part. Please just tell me."

"I'd be delighted, sir! Gravespaces are small moons that are like cemeteries for certain planets. Transport vehicles from these planets regularly drop off the dead on these moons. Unfortunately, some drivers save time by releasing their loads in the atmosphere above the gravespace. This means it is possible to bump into floating bodies or limbs when passing by."

"Yuck!" Albert said.

"Yuck, sir?"

"It means 'disgusting.'"

The robot's eyelids blinked. "Thank you, sir."

Albert sat back down in his chair and twirled around. "You know, you don't have to call me sir all the time."

"What would you like to be called?"

Albert grinned. "How about... Albert the Amazing?"

Unit D blinked again. "Adjustment made, Albert the Amazing."

Albert laughed, and then he started dancing around the spacecraft and singing, "*I love it! I love it! I love it!*"

"Are you having a seizure?" Unit D asked.

Albert danced around the robot. "This is called being happy," he said. "Humans sing and dance when they're happy. Try it."

Hilariously, the robot copied Albert's moves, singing, "*I love it! I love it! I love it!*"

"Thanks, Unit D," Albert said. "You just made my day."

"I don't make days, Albert the Amazing, but I am honored to

pilot and protect. You are a hero, Albert Kinney. You are Zeeno's Star Striker. You are popular."

Albert laughed, wishing he had been able to video Unit D's dance. "I'm popular?"

"Fact: since winning the johka game against Tev last week, your johkadin card is currently the most purchased and traded card in the entire Fŭigor Solar System."

Loving the sound of that, Albert plopped back into his chair.

An alert rang, and Unit D turned. "That is the signal to begin your gear orientation, Albert the Amazing." The robot pulled a metal container from a cabinet. "As I'm sure you know from the guide we provided, the planet Jhaateez has a similar gravitational pull and similar atmospheric composition to Earth, so your breathing implant will suffice there. It is cold on Jhaateez, much like your Alaska. Your smartfabric uniform will protect your core and limbs. But you will need several new items. They are approved, of course, by the Fŭigor Johka Federation. I will also need to apply this to your hands, head, face, and neck." The robot picked up a spray bottle.

"Sunblock?"

"Frostbite protection."

A layer of mist coated Albert. "*Blech*. Smells like rotten fish."

Unit D's mouth stretched into a smile formation. "As you know, Albert the Amazing, I am not programmed to smell. Please lift your chin."

As the stuff dried, it tugged slightly on the surface of Albert's skin. Next he had to put on high-tech knee and elbow pads, wrist guards, and a helmet.

"Unit D, you do know that johka is like soccer, and on Earth soccer players don't wear all this stuff, right?"

"I do know that, Albert the Amazing. All Zeenods wear protection when playing johka on Jhaateez. The Jhaateezians, however, are so agile they avoid injury." Unit D handed him one more item. "New footwear. Remember that johka fields on Jhaateez are set in craters of ice. Your cleats will allow you to run on the field, as normal. However, the icy sides of the crater that surround the field are skateable, and your boots have cleats and blades that can emerge or retract on voice command. Please practice before we land."

The fact that johka had evolved with different elements on each of the planets in the Fŭigor Solar System was overwhelming—especially because some of those elements seemed so dangerous. But this idea of a ring of sloped ice around the field that was actually used in the game just sounded fun. Albert had heard from Doz that the last Earthling Star Striker, Lightning Lee, had enjoyed playing on Jhaateez more than any other planet.

Following Unit D's directions, Albert programmed his boots to respond to his specific voice commands and chose simple words. *Blade* to make the blades emerge, *cleat* for cleats, and *flat* for just the sole. And then he put the shoes on and tried out the system while sitting.

"Blade," he said. Immediately he felt the change. He crossed one foot over his other knee to look. A blade had extended and the cleats had tucked in. "Cleat," he said, and watched as the cleats reemerged and the blade was sucked back in. "Flat," he said, and now the cleats sucked in and the bottom of the shoe was flat. So cool. He wished his shoes on Earth could transform on command.

He tried it standing up. *Blade. Cleat. Flat. Blade. Cleat. Flat.* With each change he wobbled a little, but he figured he'd get used to it.

As Unit D rambled on about the evolution of johka on Jhaateez, Albert tuned out the lecture and thought about his skating skills.

Over the years, his grandmother had given him and his sister, Erin, ice skates and in-line skates in their changing shoe sizes as birthday gifts. "Every kid should have skates," Nana had said. And when she visited, she would take them roller-skating in the summer and ice-skating in the winter. According to Nana, his dad had loved to skate, but Albert couldn't remember that. All through elementary school, Albert and Erin had hosted their birthday parties at the roller rink. But after fifth grade, he had insisted he had outgrown it.

Now the thought of being able to switch to skating mode while playing soccer sounded like an exciting challenge.

"Do you have any questions?"

Albert looked up. "What? No. I'm—I think I'm good."

"You *are* good, Albert the Amazing. I am honored to serve you. Prepare for landing."

"Wait," Albert said. "Can I see my medal one more time?"

Albert had wanted to bring home the gold medal from the first game and had promised to keep it a secret from everyone but had learned that the only item from the Fŭigor Solar System that he had permission to take to Earth was the communication device known as his Z-da.

Unit D unlocked the safe and Albert pulled the medal out and stared at it. The word *triumph* flashed, morphing into translations of the word in the different languages of the Fŭigor Solar System. Albert held the solid-gold disk in his hands, grinning at the weight of it, and then reluctantly handed it back.

The robot tapped the windows, lifting the blackout screens, and a dazzling scene leaped into view. Albert's first flyover of Jhaateez: the vast number of icy craters and dunes, the frozen rivers and dark green forests, and then the cities, sparkling as if made with a mosaic of mirrors.

Down there in the capital they were all waiting to greet him—his teammates, the officials, the reporters and photographers, and the presidents of both Jhaateez and Zeeno.

Albert pressed his nose against the cold glass and exhaled. In the white fog that formed from his breath, he wrote:

Albert the Amazing is here.

And then a chill rippled through him. He had been so excited to return and train with his friends, he had momentarily forgotten about the stakes. The last time he had played johka, someone had tried to kill him and hurt whoever else on the field had been close to him. Someone had even tried to kill Tackle. Loyal Tackle, best dog in the universe!

Whoever wanted him dead was still out there, maybe even waiting to strike again.

1.1

Nose to the ground, Tackle sniffed along the fence between the Patterson house and the Kinney house. The earth was moist and the noon air still carried a hint of the wet chill from last night's steady rain. The sun? It had been hiding out like a coward all morning. Worms and mushrooms were squirming or popping up all over the yard. As a dog, it was Tackle's job to thoroughly sniff each and every one. Couldn't be too careful. Not with Albert off to Jhaateez to practice with the Zeenods. Some kind of new threat was likely, and it could be anywhere.

The dog stopped and pushed his nose between the slats of the fence and sniffed the air near the Kinneys' driveway. He wished he could just live over there with Albert. What a thought for a dog to have. The Pattersons were nice enough. He used to be happy being a part of their family. But things were different now. While Trey Patterson had changed and wasn't interested in his old dog anymore, Albert needed him and appreciated him. Thanks to the language-translation implant Albert had received, Albert could also understand him!

A car drove by and Tackle stood still, watching until it turned the corner. He had begged to see the new planet with Albert today, the first day of training for game two. He didn't trust the new chaperone with that out-of-the-package smell, but he understood why Albert had wanted him to stay home. Albert could expect to have practices three times a week before the next big game in January. If Tackle attended them all, it would be too hard to coordinate and keep so many absences a secret. And Albert had made another good point—Tackle was needed here, to be on guard, to be on the lookout for spybots or poisons or anything that smelled or sounded or looked suspicious. And those aliens could be clever. That spy robot he had finally destroyed back in October? That had looked like a squirrel and had fooled—

Whump-whump.

Tackle's ears pricked. A sound from the north. He raced to the front corner of the fenced yard. The double *whump* sounded like a sizeable truck rolling over the speed bump on Iris Avenue, the street perpendicular to theirs. Sure enough, a few seconds later, a brown delivery truck appeared at the intersection of Iris and Oak and turned his way. The truck slowed to a stop in front of the Pattersons' house.

A delivery on the same day that Albert's training started? The dog didn't like it.

He sniffed. Even from his position behind the fence he could smell the exhaust wafting from the tailpipe. Nothing out of the ordinary. Yet.

Out hopped a woman—or what looked like a woman—with a box in her arms.

Grrr.

This human didn't smell at all like the chubby guy who usually delivered packages. Suspicious. The moment she put her hand on the latch of the gate, Tackle raced over and jumped up.

"Whoa!" Quickly, the woman slammed the gate shut and stepped back. "Okay. Okay. Calm down, dude." She set the box down and pulled something out of her pocket.

Possible weapon? Tackle growled and then sniffed the air for clues.

"Here's a treat," she said, approaching the gate slowly with a dog biscuit in her hand. "See? *Yum. Yum.*"

Mmmmnn, peanut butter…

Wait! What kind of doofus did she think he was? He wasn't about to fall for that. Someone had tried to poison him before the last game, and he hadn't taken that bait. He bared his teeth and barked even louder.

"Whatever," she said, and then she tossed the package over the gate and left.

Tackle sniffed as the peanut butter aroma walked away. See? That was the kind of dog he was—the kind to stay focused and alert, even when offered a delicious bribe!

He wasn't about to let his guard down. Not now. Not ever. He stared at the box, preparing to pounce.

Grrr. Definitely suspicious.

1.2

As Albert's spacecraft landed, he could see a crowd gathered in front of the geodesic dome of the official practice facility. The dome itself looked like a giant diamond, sparkling in the sun. Outside, the crowd was made up of Jhaateezians, accustomed to the cold. They were jumping on their thin but strong legs and flapping their winged arms to welcome him, lifting into the air for several feet and then returning to the ground. The apprehension that had swept over Albert just moments ago had now turned to wonder.

"What are those things attached to their arms called again?" Albert asked. As they grew closer, he could see that the appendages were paper-thin and featherless, as if made of iridescent silk that flowed and rustled with every movement.

"They're called froods," Unit D said. "The Jhaateezian word translates into English as 'sailwings.'"

"I'm going to be playing soccer with birds!" Albert said with a laugh.

"My apologies, Albert the Amazing, but I must inform you that you are incorrect. You will be playing johka for the Zeenods against the Jhaateezians."

"It was a joke," Albert said. "What I meant—forget it."

A second spacecraft rumbled nearby, and Albert could see the ITV carrying Linnd Na, the Liötian Star Striker who was playing for Jhaateez, approaching from the other direction.

As their ITVs touched down, the holographic portraits—the johkadins—of both Linnd and Albert were projected above the practice facility. The crowd waved flags: bright pink johka federation flags, icy blue Jhaateez flags, and the beautiful gold Zeeno flags showing a beloved ahda bird, a vacha-blossom tree, and an erupting zee.

"This is unbelievable," Albert whispered to himself.

"Albert the Amazing, this reality is, in fact, one hundred percent believable."

Albert smiled. In every direction he looked, he could see Jhaateezians skating on sidewalks of ice, each pathway lined with a vast number of sparkling glass rocks in all shapes and sizes. The sparkling rocks were also embedded in the building materials of every structure, colorful light dancing off each surface.

Unit D maneuvered the ITV to align with one of three docking doorways that opened directly into the practice facility, opened the hatch, and deployed the exit steps.

Ahead was the half-moon-shaped foyer of the facility, and everyone waiting in it burst into applause. The Jhaateezian team was on the left and the Zeenod team was on the right; and when Albert saw his Zeenod friends, joy filled him so quickly and intensely he wanted to break all this formality and sprint over for a group hug. He loved them. He loved their large, expressive eyes, their strangely color-swirled skin, and their capelike bems. He could feel the ahn radiating from them, all that positive energy just streaming out, and more than ever he wanted to help his friends win.

On a stagelike platform in the center were the Zhidorian officials from the Fŭigor Johka Federation, the presidents of Jhaateez and Zeeno, and the team tacticians, with reporters and photographers positioned in front. Even though they were indoors, the pathways leading from each docking door to the stage were made of ice. To the Jhaateezians, who were used to cold temperatures and used to skating rather than walking, iced pathways just made sense.

Albert glanced to his left and saw Linnd waving as she walked down the exit steps of her spacecraft. The Jhaateezians and Liö-tians had much in common, including sailwings and a skating culture. When she reached the path she began to skate.

Tentatively, Albert smiled and walked down until he was standing on the last step. "Blade," he said nervously, and felt the shifting to blades beneath his feet. All eyes and all cameras swiveled to face Albert as he stepped onto the ice and wobbled. Panicking, he flailed his arms to try to catch his balance, and he went down. The crowd gasped.

Linnd turned and skated back quickly. Picking him up and setting him back on his feet, she asked, "Do you need assistance?"

Mortified, Albert said no.

She bowed and turned to face the crowd. With a dramatic flair, she skated forward and then twirled to skate backward, launching into a backflip at just the right moment to land on the stage. The Jhaateezian and Zeenod athletes cheered, and she bowed. And then everyone turned to look at Albert.

The pathway of ice that led to the stage was flawless and glistening. On shaking legs, Albert skated slowly and then came to a stop by bumping against the platform. Retracting his blades with the word *Flat,* he cautiously climbed the four steps and took his place next to his coach, Kayko. So much for Albert the Amazing, he thought. More like Albert the Awkward.

A welcome speech from the president of Jhaateez followed, and during it Albert heard nothing but the voice in his own head telling him what a failure he was. Kayko's calm presence by his side was the only thing holding him together.

President Lat, the Zeeno president, was next. "We are grateful and proud to be a part of this tournament," she said with a smile toward Kayko and Albert. "After the dangerous explosion at the last game, we can only say how relieved we are that no life-forms were injured. We are confident that the Fŭigor Johka Federation's fact-finding team will soon discover the cause of the ball's malfunction."

Photos of the Star Strikers and the officials were taken and then the officials left.

The Zeenods broke into a jubilant round of fist bumping and hugging. It had only been last week that they had played together against Tev on Zeeno, but it felt like months.

"Albert!" Doz said. "Did you see everyone cheering for you? You are so populated!"

Albert grinned at Doz, Kayko, and the other players clustering around him: the emotionally intelligent Ennjy, the history-loving Feeb, the gadget wizard Giac, the anxious Sormie, the twin tanks Beeda and Reeda, and two Zeenods that Albert hardly knew, the quiet Heek and Wayt. Looking around for the other Zeenods on the roster, he said, "It's so good to see you guys, but where's everybody else?"

Kayko's face fell. "We'll be playing without the ability to sub. After our win, the Z-Tevs increased pressure against us. They managed to make up reasons to send many of our teammates to work on Tev."

Albert was shocked. "What? How can they do that?"

"You know the Z-Tevs are in power on Zeeno." Feeb shrugged. "They can do what they want."

"It's a tactic to try to make us weak, but it won't work!" Doz said. "We will play even stronger."

"Can't you recruit more Zeenods?" Albert asked.

Kayko's smile was sad. "The Z-Tevs have many ways of intimidating Zeenods who want to play johka. The players you see here,

Albert, are the ones who are brave enough to risk their lives to be on this team."

Albert glanced at the Zeenods in front of him. "Wait. Did they send Toben to Tev, too?"

"Toben?" Kayko asked, and the team looked around. "Toben was just here—ah, there he is. Toben!"

Crouched near a fountain, the animal-loving goalie looked up, smiled, and then skated over to them on an iced pathway. Clinging to his palm, looking very comfortable, was a crusty white creature about the size of a quarter and shaped like a frog. "Watch!" Toben said. He breathed on the creature, and it sprouted wings and flew back to the fountain. He laughed, his eyes sparkling. "Unique to Jhaateez!" He turned his attention to Albert. "Good to see you, Albert. How's your dog, Tackle?"

"He's mad at me," Albert said. "He wanted to come!"

The team laughed.

The Jhaateezians and Linnd were also bonding, and after a minute or two both teams gathered and started goofing off.

Doz and Beeda and Reeda did a funny dance, pretending to be as graceful as the Jhaateezians, lifting their bems like Jhaateezian sailwings. And then the Jhaateezians imitated the Zeenods doing an ahn huddle, and everybody laughed.

The Jhaateezian tactician bowed to Albert and said to Kayko: "It's a pleasure to meet your honorary noddie!"

"They call Zeenods *noddies*," Ennjy said. "It's a compliment that you are being called a noddie, Albert."

"I'm happy to be a noddie," Albert said, and bowed back. Still embarrassed by his entrance, he gave a quick glance at Linnd.

The tall Liötian grinned happily and said, "I'm happy to pick a noddie off the ground anytime!"

Everyone laughed, and Albert, feeling self-conscious, forced himself to join in.

"You'll get used to the ice, noddie," Linnd said with a kind pat on the back.

"Kayko," their tactician added, "we are sorry that you are being forced to play without subs. You know we want a fair game."

"Wow. These guys aren't at all like the Tevs," Albert blurted out to his teammates.

"Off the field we are friends," Feeb said. "On the field neither of our teams will hold back."

"Last year, we made it to the final game and lost to Tev," a Jhaateezian told Albert. "This year, we are determined to succeed."

Kayko smiled. "It will be an exciting game—"

"—for us to win!" Doz finished Kayko's sentence, and everyone laughed.

Both tacticians agreed it was time to get busy, so they headed to the doors of their respective fields. Flanking the doorways were twin fountains, each one with a boulder-sized glass johka ball in the center. Thousands of loose pebble-sized glass gems filled each basin.

"These Jhaateezians must be rich," Albert joked with Feeb, who was walking next to him. "All the rocks here look like diamonds."

Feeb gave him a look. "They are diamonds."

Albert stopped and stared at the sculptures of the johka balls and the glistening gems in the basins. "Wait," he said. "Are you telling me these are all real diamonds?" He looked up at the glass ceiling embedded with glittering pieces. "Those, too?"

His other teammates had stopped.

"Yes, Albert. Diamond quarries are plentiful here."

"Unbelievable!" Albert laughed again. "People go crazy over

diamonds on Earth. They're super valuable. For really special occasions we give tiny little diamonds as gifts, like when you propose."

Doz nodded. "We've seen it in Earth movies many times." He plucked a diamond pebble out of the fountain, got on one knee, and held it out to Ennjy. "Will you make marry with me, Ennj?"

Like a movie star, Ennjy pretended to swoon. Doz tossed the diamond back in the fountain, and everybody laughed.

Wow, Albert thought. Just wow.

The Zeenods waved goodbye and entered their own space.

As he walked in and stood on the deck, Albert was stunned by the beauty. And this was just a minor stadium. Above him rose seats on all sides, and above the seats glistened the geodesic dome of the diamond-studded ceiling. He knew that the official stadium had ten times the number of seats, which was going to be amazing. Below him was the johka field laid out on the floor of a huge, oblong, flat-bottomed bowl of perfectly smooth ice.

Albert had seen the televised game of the Jhaateezians against the Gaböqs, but that had been on Gaböq. This was his first glimpse of an actual Jhaateezian johka field.

Albert watched as his teammates activated their blades and dropped in, skating straight down the bowl, their bems rippling behind them, looking like superhero skateboarders. When they reached the bottom, they switched from blades to flats without stopping, sliding onto the johka field by taking a kind of skiing stance with knees bent. When their momentum slowed, they switched to cleats and ran like maniacs. Absolutely insane!

Still sitting on the deck, Albert looked at the bottoms of his own shoes. When both the cleats and blades were tucked in, the smartmaterial on the bottom of the shoe was slick, which would allow it to slide instead of skid on the turf. The Zeenods made it look easy, but Albert was sure he'd wipe out.

Several players hit the sloped ice again and began zipping around the bowl. On skates, the Zeenods made use of their bems similarly to the way the Jhaateezians used their sailwings, spreading a bem out to slow down, or pulling a bem in to go faster, lifting one side up to guide a turn, and even fully extending a bem to get lift on a jump. The way each bem moved on its own, like an elephant's ear, was mesmerizing.

"Let's circle up," Kayko called out from below as she jogged toward the center of the field. "Time for the ahn."

Standing on the deck above them all, Albert froze, his stomach clenching.

"Join us, Albert!" Kayko called up.

"Hold on. Just checking my suit!" Albert sat down on the deck edge and began tugging at the shoulder of his suit as if it needed adjusting.

Doz skated up the bowl and sat on the deck next to him with a huge grin. "This is awesomely, isn't it? Let's roll and rock!" He clapped Albert on the back, and the hit accidentally sent Albert sliding down the ice on his rear, the smartskin material of his suit protecting him as he kept sliding onto the turf.

Doz skated after him. "Hilarious slide, dude!" Doz said.

Albert laughed, pretending he had enjoyed the ride. If he hadn't been so nervous, he would have.

Thankfully, Kayko was all business, and they gathered in a circle to begin the ahn meditation ritual. They started by acknowledging their teammates who weren't with them. As usual the Zeenods stood with eyes closed, synchronizing their breath. Albert joined, hoping they wouldn't notice how disconnected he felt. As they continued, their bems began to gradually extend, and Albert knew that they were all tapping into that vibration of energy that connected them. Albert had felt it before, those invisible threads, the vibration of harmony, but he couldn't connect today. He was worrying about how he'd perform, and he couldn't stop.

After a few moments of increasing intensity, Ennjy gave a long, loud whoop and the players jumped forward, throwing their arms around each other's shoulders, their green-and-violet eyes now gold.

After they warmed up with their stretch routine, Kayko told Doz to start the skate-to-field drill and then said, "I'll take Albert aside and teach him to fall."

Groans of disappointment came from the team.

"Don't separate us, Kayko," Doz pleaded, putting his arm around Albert's shoulders. "Let us show Albert some moves. He can fall along the way."

Albert reddened. "I won't fall. I know how to skate. I skate all the time."

Kayko relented. "All right. Let's work on getting on and off the ice. Albert, as you know, there are no out-of-bounds on Jhaateez. If the ball goes out, it either rolls up the sides of the bowl and comes back down, or we can go after it. We can also use the sides of the bowl to move quickly and effortlessly around the field when it makes sense."

They spread out. To demonstrate, Kayko chose Heek, a winger. Cleats activated, Heek started dribbling the ball on the right side of the field toward the goal. Beeda and Reeda, pretending to be Jhaateezian defenders, advanced to try to stop him. Quickly Heek passed the ball to Sormie, who was ahead on the left, and then Heek ran and jumped off the field and onto the ice, blades emerging, bem fluttering. Using the bowl, he skated toward the goal with more speed and less energy than it would have taken him to run.

While play continued with the ball on the turf, Feeb pretended to be a Jhaateezian defender and took off to try to keep Heek from advancing toward the goal on the ice. Feeb skated up the bowl way in front of Heek, did a 180, and then slid down, trying to knock Heek out on the ice with a slide tackle. But Heek jumped over him by tucking up his legs and pulling in his bem and kept going. By this time, Sormie had passed the ball to Wayt on the turf, who had passed to Giac. In the perfect position, Heek headed off the ice, sliding onto the turf first on flats and then switching to run on cleats without pausing. Giac passed him the ball. Heek shot and scored.

Albert cheered. "That looks so cool!"

Kayko called out positions to demonstrate the next move. "If the ball rolls onto the ice, sometimes it's better to cradle rather than kick it. Watch. We can move the ball forward on the ice with a special trick."

To demonstrate, Sormie took a position with the ball at the right top of the box.

"Imagine that Sormie couldn't find a way to shoot," Kayko said.

Immediately Beeda and Reeda ran in to pressure Sormie, blocking the goal.

"From right midfield Giac sees this and hits the ice," Kayko went on.

Giac took off skating on the right side toward the goal. Sormie kicked the ball onto the ice in front of Giac, and then as Giac approached the ball, she squatted all the way down on one foot while extending one leg straight out in front of her, stretching out both arms for balance. The ball kept rolling forward, but it stayed in her possession because it was loosely held in her squat between her skating skate and the knee of her extended leg.

"That skating trick is called shoot the duck!" Albert said. "Except I've never seen it done with a ball."

With the ball safely cradled in that position, rolling along, Giac zoomed around behind the goal, and when she reached the left side, where Feeb was ready on the field, Giac stood up, tapped the ball onto the field, and skated out of the way. On solid ground, Feeb got the ball, dribbled, and kicked the ball into the net.

"Goal!"

"As you can see, Albert, you have to know when to use the ice. We can show you other moves later. Right now, let's do our on-off practice drill." Kayko called out for everyone to start the drill, which was to do six laps around the field, getting on and off the ice at least twice for every lap, practicing how to transition from turf to ice or ice to turf and how to fall safely if a fall was unavoidable. If they'd been jogging each of those laps on turf, it would have been exhausting, but that was the beauty of the ice: they could travel quickly without using up much energy.

Immediately, Albert's teammates took off.

Scared of falling, he hesitated.

"Let's break it down step by step, Albert," Kayko said.

"No. That's okay, I've got it." Albert jogged on the right side to the center line. Wanting desperately not to look like a beginner, he didn't stop when he got to the ice. "Blade," he said, activating his blades. He jumped, and when he landed he lost his balance and freaked out. Arms flailed, legs went out from under him, and he toppled backward, throwing back his right arm, elbow locked, to break his fall.

His teammates rushed over, immediately noticing that his wrist guard had not been properly fastened.

Albert winced and tried to blink back tears.

His wrist was broken. He could feel it.

1.3

In the Pattersons' yard, Tackle sniffed the cardboard box. The thing hadn't exploded when the delivery woman had chucked it over the gate, and he couldn't smell anything clearly dangerous. But vigilance was key. Assume the worst. That was the only way to go.

He started by nosing the thing around a bit. Just pushing and then tipping and then knocking it around more violently. Didn't make a noise. Whatever was inside was either well wrapped or wasn't made of metal at the core like that squirrel machine that had turned out to be a robotic spy. *Grrr.* That squirrel had really made his life miserable. The way it had kept outrunning him. *Grrr.* But he had finally gotten that chump between his teeth.

Riled up just thinking about his old nemesis, Tackle pounced on the box. In a fury, he pawed and clawed at the top until a piece of the tape pulled loose. With his teeth clamped on the tape, he shook his head back and forth, whipping the box. The momentum ripped the tape off; the box hit the ground and a creature tumbled out.

The next thing Tackle knew, he was face to face with another set of eyes. Black, beady eyes.

Grrr!

The dog attacked—and only when the yard was covered with fake brown fur and stuffing did he stop.

Strewn around the yard were the pieces of a small teddy bear, a "lovey" much like the "loveys" that Trey's little cousin Maya brought whenever she and her family came over. Confused, Tackle moved from piece to piece, sniffing the polyester fiber to see if anything suspicious had been embedded in it.

He had a sinking feeling that his instincts had been wrong about this one. Maybe this bear was just a kids' toy after all. *Grrr.*

1.4

While Albert was dealing with his broken wrist on Jhaateez and Tackle was dealing with his misplaced aggression on Earth, countless other stories were playing out, not only on Earth, but also on the planets in the Fŭigor Solar System. The brilliant botmaker Mehk, for one, was experiencing a moment of joy on Zeeno. And now his story requires attention.

Mehk was alone, of course, in his small, barely furnished apartment. He had just received a phone alert from his bank. Seven million lorts had been deposited into his account.

"Ha! This is good news indeed!" The botmaker laughed.

His pet, the spiderlike robotic gheet that was perched on his shoulder, responded by rising onto its eight legs and jiggling for three seconds, one of the happy dances Mehk had programmed it to do.

The botmaker rubbed the top of his gheet's hairy head, and then he pulled out his log and began to record his thoughts.

```
Money has appeared in my bank account. No doubt from Presi-
dent Lat. She said I would need to purchase the supplies for
the new mission to eliminate Albert Kinney on her command,
but I have other plans....
```

He glanced out the window. The sky over the capital of Zeeno was soft and pink.

```
I am done taking orders from the puppet president of Zeeno.
Her primary goal is to serve the Tevs and Z-Tevs who want
to make sure the Zeenods don't gain support. I don't care
about any of that.
```

21

He paused. The only thing he cared about was protecting the advances he had made in robotics and artificial intelligence. Now that Lat knew about the alternate Star Striker—his extraordinary robotic masterpiece waiting in the wings—he believed she wanted to get her hands on it before he could show it to the solar system. If she did, she'd give it to the Tevs and Z-Tevs and they'd pretend they had created it, and he couldn't let that happen. He turned back to his log.

```
When I was creating my masterpiece I had to spend so much
time and energy stealing resources. Now here is Lat putting
seven million lorts in my hand! With seven million lorts, I
can buy an ITV and retrieve my masterpiece. Ha! The trick
will be to move fast, before Lat even knows I am gone.
```

He stopped writing. Out the window, a Z-Tev police vehicle flew by on its usual patrol with its torpedo-like DRED strapped to its side. Mehk imagined himself zipping out of Zeeno's atmosphere in his own ITV. He imagined traveling to Earth, kidnapping Kinney, and putting him safely in hibernation. He imagined blowing up Kinney's empty ITV and faking Kinney's death. He imagined the Zeenods calling Kinney's alternate into play, unaware that the alternate was, in fact, Mehk's robotic masterpiece! He imagined the game against the Jhaateezians, how thrilling it would be to watch the Zeenods win the game. He imagined walking out onto the field after the game and revealing that the talented new Star Striker was *his* creation—the most sophisticated and intelligent robot ever designed. He imagined releasing Kinney to prove that he was no murderer. He imagined showing how Lat and the Tevs and Z-Tevs were the true murderers. Everyone would be in awe of his brilliance. Every planet would want his technology.

He touched the embedded microbot on the side of his head that sent a positive thought-loop to his mind. *Believe in your brilliance. You will succeed.*

The gheet crept down his arm and into his hand. Mehk held it up. "The new plan begins," he said, and exhaled a gentle puff of air into his pet's face. Each of the creature's six eyes sparkled blue.

1.5

Holding his broken right wrist, Albert followed Kayko out a special trapdoor in the johka field that was known as the emergency exit, feeling as if his heart had been fractured, too.

"We'll get you into your ITV and Unit D can fix your wrist, and then you can pop into your hygg," Kayko said. "You will feel better by the time you arrive home. Next time, we'll start by teaching you to fall properly. And don't forget to keep up with the lessons I created for you."

Barely listening, Albert followed the underground corridor to the lobby and then back to his waiting ITV.

"Hello, Albert the Amazing." Unit D greeted him at the threshold. "Allow me to run a medical scan."

Before Albert could blink, he was seated inside and a drone was humming as it zipped from his head to his feet while Unit D organized medical supplies.

"The scan is showing that the distal radius bone of your right arm is fractured," Unit D said. "You will need an injection to—" The robot plunged a needle into Albert's arm.

"Ouch!" Albert yelled. "What was that?"

"A fehkhahting injection containing engineered proteins, apatites, and osteocytes. Zeenods use the term *fehkhahting*, which is loosely translated as 'bone knitting.' To *fehk* means to knit, and *haht* is bone. Do you know what knitting is, Albert the Amazing?"

"Yes, I know what knitting is," Albert snapped. "My grandmother knits."

"Ah, your grandmother is a fehker!" Unit D's face smiled. "How does it feel? I added a pain-numbing medication because life-forms are known to dislike pain."

"It feels terrible. Everything is terrible." Albert slumped back in his chair.

"My apologies, Albert the Amazing, I will—"

"Stop calling me that!"

"Yes, Albert the Amazing, I will make the modification. Would you prefer *sir*?"

"Just call me Albert! You know, if Unit B were here, she'd be calling out all my shawbles! She pointed out every time I was impatient or ungrateful or...whatever."

The robot blinked. "I am not programmed with the same customizations as Unit B. I am Unit D at your service, Albert."

The spacecraft fell silent.

Albert looked out the window.

"I detect an emotion," Unit D said. "I believe it may be anger. Am I correct, and, if so, why are you experiencing it? Are you angry at your own behavior or at external circumstances?"

Albert closed his eyes. "I don't want to talk about it."

The medical drone completed another scan from head to toe, and then Unit D wrapped a medical sleeve around the injured wrist. "Blood pressure normal. The distal radius fracture is almost healed. You will look and feel wonderful after your hibernation in the hygg." The robot ratcheted up to a standing position and turned to face the spacecraft's controls.

"This whole practice sucked," Albert said under his breath. He walked to the rear of the spacecraft and changed into his Earth clothes and shoes. As he did, he noticed that a diamond about the size and shape of a chocolate chip was stuck in the bottom of his cleat. Quickly, he pried it loose and stuck it in his jeans pocket. After such a bad practice, he thought he deserved to get something good out of it, and who would ever know?

He crawled into his hygg and fell asleep.

1.6

Although Albert had traveled to and from the Fŭigor Solar System many times to train for the game against Tev, the way time-folding worked was always disorienting. Whenever he reappeared in the bathroom stall of the boys' bathroom at school after days of being away, he had to remind himself that only twenty-seven Earth minutes had passed.

When he returned to Earth on this particular day, after having had such a disastrous first practice on Jhaateez, the thought of having to get through his afternoon classes turned his foul mood fouler.

Feeling guilty that he hadn't kept up with his ahn lessons, he decided to do one during history class. Kayko had suggested that he review the first three lessons, but Albert was impatient to move forward. Careful to keep his phone hidden, he opened the new lesson. Bypassing the need for earbuds, he chose to send the audio straight to his implant.

Welcome to the fourth lesson: Always Learning. Take a few moments to focus on your breathing and to be present and we will begin.

Albert turned to a blank page in his notebook so that he could pretend to write his history assignment while listening. A thought occurred to him: Maybe instead of walking to and from school every day, he could skate. It was that ten-minute thing his nana had taught him last October—spend ten minutes a day practicing what you're *not* good at and you'll improve. And on the weekends, he could also hit the skate park, practice skating around in the big bowl and run some dribbling and shooting drills there.

There were only two issues. First, he had outgrown his skates and would need a new pair. Second, if anybody from school saw him with skates, he'd be roasted. In middle school, any change in behavior or appearance would get noticed and ridiculed, and he just didn't need the commentary. But both issues were solvable. He could buy skates, and he could carry them in a pack every day and put them on or take them off a block or two from school. That routine would make it less likely that he'd be seen by anybody.

He sat up straighter and felt a smile coming on. Okay. He could skate everywhere. Practice 24/7. It wouldn't be the same as having more time to practice on Jhaateez, but it would definitely help.

Ding! A bell signaled the end of Kayko's lesson.

With dismay Albert realized he hadn't even listened. In one ear and out the other, as his nana would say. Angry at himself, he tried starting the lesson back at the beginning, but his teacher began checking their work.

As it happened, he couldn't find another opportunity all day. Finally, when the last class was dismissed, he hustled to his locker, grabbed his phone, and texted his mom.

Can I please get some in-line skates? I know the ones Nana gave me last year are too small. Today, if possible?

The answer came back in seconds.

No. You didn't even use those skates last year. And you still owe me money for the phone.

He called her and she picked up immediately. "Mom. This is important. I need them. I want to start going to this skate park and—"

"Albert, I can't believe you're calling me while I'm at work to beg for a new toy."

"Not a toy! I need—"

"The answer is no. And don't beg Nana. I have to go." She hung up.

He slammed his locker door and was suddenly face to face with Jessica Atwater. An awkward yelp came out of his mouth, and he jumped back, embarrassed.

She laughed in a sweet way. "Sorry! I didn't mean to scare you."

He straightened up and stammered, "You didn't—I wasn't—

I—never mind." He started walking, and since school was out and they were both leaving, she followed.

"Did I hear you say skate park? You know I'm there with my board, like, every day after school." She turned around so Albert could see the skateboard she had attached to her backpack with a bungee cord. "If you don't have a board, I have an old one you could borrow."

"Hey, wait up!" Trey's voice came from behind as he rushed through the busy hallway to join them. "What's this? A secret meeting?"

"Yes," Jessica said, continuing to walk. "We're plotting our takeover of the planet." She smiled. "Actually, I heard that Albert is thinking about taking up skateboarding and I was just offering my old board."

"Skateboarding isn't really my thing," Albert said quickly. "I mean, thanks, but—"

"I'm interested," Trey said. "I think I'd be good at it. I did a lot of skimboarding at my summer camp and nailed it." He looked at Albert. "That was the camp you decided not to go to. It was awesome."

They turned down the main hallway and headed out the double doors. The grounds of the school and the street itself were pretty, lined with towering old-growth trees. Just after noon, the November sun had burned through the clouds and had warmed the air and dried the grass. Although some of the trees had lost their leaves, there was still gorgeous autumn color in the branches.

Trey turned back to Jessica. "What tricks can you do?"

Jessica brightened and started to talk with her usual passion, and Albert winced. Why couldn't he have thought to ask her that?

"Those tricks sound amazing," Trey said. "I still have a lot of travel team practices and games. But now that school soccer season is over, I have time to learn something new."

The way Trey talked made Albert want to vomit. He missed the old Trey. Everything Trey said now just showed how full of

28

himself he had become. They had reached the wide curved side-walk that wound around the front lawn of the school, and Albert was about to pick up his pace when Jessica stopped.

"This is a perfect stretch," she said, getting out her board. "The first thing is just to learn how to roll from your bails. You guys know what that means, right?"

"Yeah," Albert said, even though it was a lie.

"I don't know," Trey said. "Is it a trick?"

Jessica smiled at Trey. "It means knowing how to fall. I can teach you how to do it here on the grass."

"I'm in," Trey said. "I should pay you."

She shrugged. "Pay me in chocolate. I'm a chocoholic."

Albert quickly made up a fake excuse and hurried ahead, trying to block out their voices behind him. When he reached the street, he turned back to see Jessica step off the board and roll across the grass in a somersault with knees and arms bent. As soon as she popped back up, Trey did it, and Albert could hear Jessica's encouraging cheer.

1.7

Albert! Tackle raced to the fence the moment he saw him turn onto their street. *How was it? Tell me everything.*

The sight of the Ridgeback with his paws up on the Pattersons' gate, his tongue hanging out and his tail wagging, was, without a doubt, the best part of Albert's difficult day. He jogged the half block, dropped his backpack, opened the gate, and hugged his friend. After a few minutes of wrestling and chasing and rolling around together, they settled down, and Albert confessed that he hadn't had the best practice. He didn't like revealing anything that would lower Tackle's opinion of him, so he moved on quickly and focused on how mean his mother was being for not allowing him to get skates.

Then he noticed small tufts of stuffing on the ground.

Uh-oh, Albert said. *What did you do?*

Me? The dog tried to look innocent.

Albert followed the tufts like bread crumbs and there behind the Pattersons' sweet gum tree was a bigger mess. Under a ripped and flattened cardboard box were the pieces of a shredded teddy bear. A card, still attached by a pink ribbon to one dismembered paw, read *For Maya.* Albert knew Trey's little cousin Maya. Over the last summer, when Trey was away at camp, the Pattersons often had Maya and her parents over for backyard barbecues. She was about three years old, and sometimes Albert's sister Erin would invite her over to jump on their trampoline, which she loved.

Let me guess, Albert said. *The Pattersons ordered a present for Maya and you ripped it up?*

Tackle's forehead wrinkled and his tail lowered, and then he sank to the ground. *I thought it was like that squirrel. I thought it was a machine for spying on you or hurting you.*

Albert smiled.

Why are you smiling? the dog whined. *I'm going to get in trouble.*

I'm smiling because I can actually fix this, Albert said. *Come on.*

He took the *For Maya* tag and ran into his garage, and the dog followed.

I don't see how you can fix—Tackle stopped talking as Albert lifted the lid of a large bin labeled GYM BEARS on a storage shelf and revealed a selection of stuffed bears in perfect condition, each with a glittering silver star embroidered on its chest. *Ta-da!*

What the—Tackle stuck his nose in the bin.

Albert's smile got even bigger. *Erin's gymnastics team gives these bears out like trophies. Bears for achievement, bears for attendance, bears for attitude. Erin doesn't even like them.*

Brilliant, Tackle said.

Albert picked one out and attached the card to its paw. *I'm sure the one they ordered for Maya didn't look exactly like this, but they'll probably think it was a mistake and won't care.*

He found a box in the recycling bin and repackaged it. Luckily the packaging label could be retaped on the new box. *Looks great,* Albert said. *Don't attack this one.*

Tackle snorted.

As Albert replaced the box at the front door, Tackle fetched his leash. Albert had sweet-talked Mrs. Patterson into giving back his dog-walking job—very hard to refuse since he offered to do it for free. Right before they were about to go, Albert got a call.

"Hey, kiddo," his nana said. "I'm at the park. Heading home soon. Your mom called to check up on me and she mentioned that you wanted skates. Isn't there a box of your dad's old skates in the garage? One pair might fit."

Albert brightened. "Nana, you're a genius."

"I was sorry when you lost interest," she said. "Skating is fun."

He thanked her, and he and Tackle ran back to the garage. The second pair he tried worked. *This will be so great, Tackle. Come on!*

With the leash in his hand, Albert began to skate, and Tackle trotted along beside him. The sidewalk was wide and level for a

31

few blocks, and Albert's control felt good. He knew how to skate. He just hadn't had the chance yet to prove it to the Zeenods.

Doing great, Tackle said as he picked up his speed to match Albert's steady rhythm.

After the third block the sidewalk began to slope downward, heading toward their favorite park. At the bottom, Albert could see his grandmother walking up the hill on the sidewalk with her cane, easily identifiable by the hand-knitted bright orange cap she was wearing. Now that she was out of her wheelchair she walked every day to improve her mobility after her broken hip.

At first, he was happy to see her. But that changed as the pavement angled more sharply downward and he suddenly picked up speed. One way to slow down was to zigzag, but the sidewalk here was too narrow. The busy street was on his left and there were hedges, prickle bushes, and fences on his right. Nowhere to go but straight ahead.

Slow down, Tackle said, racing beside him.

I can't! he said, letting go of the leash.

Nana was a short half block away. Because the city bus was coming, she couldn't step into the street.

"You're going to crash!" she yelled, waving her cane.

"I know!" Albert was flying now. He realized that if he had sailwings like the Jhaateezians he could use them to slow down, and then he realized how ridiculous it was to think about that at a time like this.

Tackle stood still and barked at the bus in a vain attempt to scare it away.

"Jump over me!" Nana yelled, and then, amazingly, hit the pavement, tucking in like a turtle.

Albert couldn't believe it. He leaped into the air and pulled his feet up, missing the top of her head but taking her orange hat along for the ride. With a clatter, he landed on the sidewalk and jolted back. And that was when he began a spectacular wipeout, slamming back onto his right wrist.

He knew instantly. Same wrist. Broken again.

Tackle ran to his side.

"You alive?" Nana said, standing up.

Albert nodded. "I think my wrist is broken."

"Uh-oh," she said. "Let me see."

After an examination, she agreed that there was probably a break but said it could have been worse.

Albert closed his eyes, waiting for the pain that he knew was going to hit after the shock wore off. Weakly, he managed to say, "I can't believe how small you got. That took guts, Nana. I almost sliced your head off."

"Funny what we'll do under pressure, right?" She smiled and picked up her hat. "I guess I knew that wanting to not kill your nana would motivate you. That was a good jump, kiddo. Now all you have to do is learn how to fall."

He winced. Every muscle in his body was starting to hurt.

While Tackle kept Albert company, Albert's unflappable grandma called his mom and explained what had happened. Then she called for a ride to take them to the emergency room.

As Albert cradled his throbbing wrist, a heavy feeling settled over him. He was brick-headed for thinking he could be an asset to the Zeenods. He got lucky on Zeeno, he thought. There was no way he could play well on Jhaateez.

2.0

The sun was just peeking over the violet-tinged horizon on Zeeno as a robotic voice on Mehk's phone repeated, "The ITV you have requested is ready for purchase. Please verify your Z-Tev identification and scan your payment now."

The botmaker scanned the identification code he had stolen from a Z-Tev and then gave the voice command to transfer the payment from his account. Buying a getaway ITV certainly wasn't what President Lat had in mind for this money, Mehk thought with glee.

After a few seconds, the reply came. "Congratulations! Your payment has been successful. Your activation code is being forwarded."

"Thank you," Mehk said with a laugh. He wanted to tell the inferior robot clerk on the phone that if he had designed this purchasing software, he would have made sure it could detect that he was using a false name and a stolen ID. Ha! This escape plan was going to be easier than he had thought.

"Please submit the location at which you'd like the vehicle to arrive."

"With pleasure," Mehk said, and gave the address of an abandoned factory, which he thought would be a safe place.

The gheet on his shoulder jiggled. Mehk smiled, logged off, and walked into his small bedroom. The last things to pack were the only things he really needed—the tech essentials he kept hidden in his wall safe. He pushed his bed aside and crouched down. About one foot up from the floor, a bloodsucking flatworm called a yit was clinging to the wall. Nothing unusual in this; these worms liked to crawl up surfaces. Except this one wasn't real. It was, in fact, one of Mehk's custom-designed synthetic creatures. Years ago, he had been given the task of fabricating fake yits to be sold as gag gifts to celebrate the Tev holiday Haagoolt Eve, and he had gotten the idea to use a few for different purposes.

Mehk leaned in and breathed on the fake yit, and the warmth of his breath activated the elastic properties of the material it was made of, causing its edges to curl up. Mehk peeled it off like a reusable sticker, and in doing so he revealed a small lock embedded in the wall. He pressed his thumb against it and the secret compartment's door sprang open.

Just then, an alert came from his phone. "Front-door surveillance system reporting two figures approaching."

2.1

When Albert woke up, his right wrist—now in an ordinary cast—was throbbing with pain, and as soon as he tried to roll out of bed, more pain shot through the rest of him, first his core, then his back, then his thighs, no doubt from the fall.

Feeling like an old man, he groaned as he cradled his arm and gently eased his feet onto the floor. His dad's old skates were sitting by the door.

"Albert," he heard his mom call. "You're going to be late."

Ouch, ouch, ouch, ouch, he thought as he dressed. Glancing at himself in the mirror when he was done, he said, "What's the point, Albert? What's the point?"

He could hear Erin in the kitchen arguing with his mom about something. Erin never had trouble waking up on school days. She practically cartwheeled out of bed. He, on the other hand, had never been a morning person. And he had slept worse than usual, bothered by both wrist pain and regret. He had made so many mistakes and couldn't stop replaying them in his mind. Now the thought of another practice on Jhaateez filled him with dread.

When he left the house for school, Tackle greeted him as usual, jumping up on the Pattersons' fence. Albert opened the gate and gave the dog a rubdown with his good hand.

I'll get my wrist fixed on my way to Jhaateez, Albert said. *But I'll have to keep the cast on here so that nobody gets suspicious.*

Good thinking, Tackle said. *And Albert, I can smell your fear. Don't worry, man, you're a Star Striker. The Zeenods picked you for a reason. You're going to get this skating stuff down.*

Thanks, Tackle. Albert gave the dog a hug and took off.

At school, everyone was curious about his cast, and he made

up a story about a bike accident. Saying he wiped out after jumping over his grandma just didn't seem like a good idea. Somehow he got through the morning and then headed to a boys' bathroom just before noon to activate the szoŭ. To make sure that no one would notice that he was disappearing during lunch every Monday and Wednesday, he was varying his szoŭ locations. This time, he chose the bathroom in the music hallway, which was almost deserted. Right now, only one girl was in the hallway. She was at her locker, her back to him, on her phone. Not a problem. But halfway there, he heard a familiar voice behind him.

"Hey, Albert!"

Albert's stomach clenched. Sure enough, Freddy was running to catch up.

"I wanted to ask you after band. Which bone did you break? Or did you break more than one? My sister broke her ulna two years ago."

Ever since that bonding moment at the band concert, Freddy was back to bestie mode, following Albert between classes, always wanting to talk about something—grades, assignments, the symbolism of the Arkenstone in *The Lord of the Rings*.

Albert didn't want to brush Freddy off, but if he didn't, Freddy would have a thousand things to say. Just as he was trying to think of an excuse to make a getaway, the girl at her locker ahead of them turned and walked toward them. She was the new girl who had just moved from Seoul, South Korea, named Min Jee. Albert and Freddy had both seen her coming out of the music room this morning when they were coming in and had overheard Mr. Chaimbers asking another student to show her to her next class. Now she was finishing her call and approaching like she wanted to ask them a question.

Freddy froze. "Oh no."

Albert could see the crush all over his face. And, thanks to Albert's language-translation implant, he could understand Min's Korean as she ended the call. "Got to go," she said in Korean into her phone. "I can't figure out how to open the stupid locker, and I'm going to ask these two guys." She glanced up at them. Assuming they couldn't understand, she added, "They're both really cute."

Albert smiled. It was a little thing, but it lifted his spirits. He was dying to thank her and tell Freddy, which would be hilarious, but there was no way he could do that without arousing suspicion.

Just as she started to ask them for help, Freddy blurted out that he had to go, and he turned and ran down the hall faster than Albert had ever seen him run.

"I was going to ask for help with my locker," Min said in English.

Quickly, Albert showed her how to work the lock, and as he was walking away, the Korean words for "See you later" popped out of his mouth before he could stop them.

"You speak Korean?" Min asked.

Albert laughed nervously. "No! I just heard that one phrase on Netflix." He repeated it and hustled away almost as fast as Freddy had.

The bathroom was empty, and as soon as he locked the stall door, he activated the szoŭ. The familiar icy prickles came first, then the warmth, and then the falling up instead of falling down until everything went black.

As Albert materialized on board the ITV, Unit D was waiting with the usual unblinking and unnatural smile. Albert explained the fiasco with the wrist, asked for treatment, and, for once, welcomed the sight of the medical drone. Before he knew it, the fehkhahting of his wrist was complete. Under his now-useless cast, the bone was healed. At his request, the robot created an ingenious hidden hinge in his cast that would allow Albert to remove it whenever he wanted.

"Please don't tell Kayko or any of the Zeenods about my wrist," Albert begged.

The robot's head tilted. "I am programmed to tell the truth if asked."

"Well, don't tell the truth if not asked. Just keep your mouth closed," Albert said, and then, for good measure, he added, "That's an order."

"Yes, Albert." With a clank, Unit D slammed its mouth closed.

Albert sighed and climbed into his hygg. All he had to do now was try to get through another practice without breaking his wrist again.

2.2

From his bedroom, Mehk heard the screech of his front door being forced open. Quickly, Mehk tossed his phone into the secret compartment built into the wall, closed the door, slapped the fake yit over the lock, pushed the bed back into place, and faced the door just as two Z-Tev guards walked into the bedroom, weapons raised.

"What is this? Why—"

"Hands out." One of the Z-Tevs stepped forward. "You are under arrest."

"But there must be a misunderstanding." Mehk tried to look innocent. "I work for—"

One guard pulled the trigger of a device. From it flew a smart-cuff, a strand of fabric that curled around Mehk's wrists, pulling them together tightly and cinching automatically.

The other guard grabbed the suitcase of clothes Mehk had packed and began searching the rest of the apartment, stuffing what little else he could find into another bag. It didn't take long, and then Mehk found himself being prodded out the door.

As he walked down the corridor toward the main entrance, his fear worsened. Yes, he had stolen all those resources and committed crimes when he was working on his masterpiece, but President Lat had promised she would pardon him for those crimes. And yes, he had caused the explosion at the last game, but Lat had blackmailed him to do that! Why would she have him arrested? Could she know he was planning to take the money and run?

"What am I being arrested for?" he turned to ask.

As he was pushed out the apartment building's doors without an answer, he wondered why the guards hadn't beamed him directly from his apartment to a spacecraft. Then he saw the media. A dozen reporters with drone cameras on the street began recording his exit as the guards hustled Mehk into the waiting ITV. The media had gathered, knowing he was being arrested. President Lat had wanted a photo op. Stunned, he sat in silence as the spacecraft took off.

Shivering and sweating simultaneously, he tried to think of a way to escape. After five minutes of fruitless rumination, he finally noticed a sensation—a tickle under his bem, right between the shoulder blades—and recognized it immediately. His gheet! Long ago, he had programmed the gheet's foot sensors to monitor his heart rate and to respond to changes by hiding under his bem. When the officers had come to the front door and Mehk had stood, the gheet must have quickly crawled there.

The corners of Mehk's mouth lifted in the tiniest of smiles.

2.3

Although the hibernation in the hygg helped him to heal, Albert's mind was a mess when they landed on Jhaateez. He was already planning to stay away from the ice and avoid the skates, but he couldn't do that forever.

When the hatch opened and he was hit with a blast of cold air, he grumbled, "Why does it have to be so cold? I hate cold."

Unit D began a scientific lecture on the reasons for the planet's atmospheric and geologic features.

"Oh, stuff a sock in it," Albert said, and left, knowing that the poor robot would be mystified by his command and probably literally start looking for a sock. He missed his old chaperone Unit B and decided he would ask Kayko if she could customize more of Unit B's mannerisms into Unit D's system. Maybe that would help.

Kayko and the team were arriving, and as Albert nervously skated into the foyer to meet them, he could feel a fake smile spread on his face. He wished he could be excited for another practice, but all he felt was anxiety.

In the next moment, an entourage emerged from another doorway and the atmosphere shifted radically. President Lat, four Z-Tev police officers, two Fŭigor Johka Federation officials, and reporters and cameras from various planets converged.

"What's going on?" Sormie asked.

"It feels tense," Ennjy said, her bem pulsing.

The police officers approached, and just as Kayko was about to address them, they cuffed her and informed her that she was under arrest. The team was shocked.

"I don't understand," Kayko said as the press swooped in, cameras rolling. "Why am I being arrested?"

By now, the Jhaateezians had arrived for practice, and a crowd was gathering.

A Z-Tev officer spoke. "Kayko Tusq, you are being arrested for the attempted murder of Albert Kinney."

Kayko staggered back, her bem stiffening, her eyes turning gray.

The crowd was speechless.

Doz stepped forward, glaring, and Albert could feel his friend shaking with anger.

Before Doz could speak, Ennjy was at his side. "This isn't right, Doz, but be careful. If you are arrested for speaking out, you can't help us."

President Lat spoke to the crowd with an FJF official standing at her side. "The Fŭigor Johka Federation has completed its investigation, and it has been determined that the johka ball that exploded at the end of the Tev-versus-Zeeno game was not an accident. It was deliberately programmed to explode."

This was expected. None of the Zeenods had believed it was an accident.

Lat went on, staring directly at the cameras. "Z-Tev police have found evidence showing that a Zeenod robotics engineer named Mehklen Pahck designed the explosion with the intent to kill Albert Kinney. He was paid to do it by Zeenod team tactician Kayko Tusq, who—"

"I have no money!" Kayko protested, and the officers strengthened their hold on her.

The president kept going. "We have traced money from Kayko's bank account to Mehk's bank account," she insisted. "We have also discovered Kayko's diary, which outlined her motivation in detail."

Kayko looked back at Ennjy and Albert and the team. Albert could tell by the expression on her face that there was no diary. None of this was true.

As the team began to voice their support, the police officers forced Kayko toward the doorway leading to where their vehicle was docked.

Ennjy ran to her side. "Stay strong, Kayko. We will right this wrong," she whispered before being pushed back.

The Jhaateezian security arrived.

Several reporters asked for information about the botmaker. As the vehicle flew away, the Zhidorian FJF official spoke. "Mehklen Pahck is also in custody. Through Kayko's diary, we learned that the explosion on the johka field wasn't Kayko's only murder attempt. The two worked together to try to kill Albert on several occasions."

Cameras zoomed in on Albert, and he felt his face grow hot.

"Lies. All lies," Doz blurted out.

If they had been on Zeeno and if no cameras had been rolling, that outburst would have earned Doz an electric shock from the police.

Zeenods were not allowed to speak against the Z-Tev police in public. Since they were on Jhaateez and since the Zhidorians were present, the Z-Tevs held back. Albert knew from what the Zeenods had told him that Doz's outburst would be deleted from the news videos.

The two-headed FJF official went on. "Under the circumstances, today's practice session will be canceled. Instead we will need to question everyone on the Zeenod team."

President Lat bowed. "Certainly the Zeenod team will cooperate. Although we are saddened to discover that Zeenods would betray Zeenods, we are relieved to have the guilty parties arrested. It means that our beloved team and our guest striker will be safe from harm, which is more important than anything else."

Doz opened his mouth to voice his anger, but Ennjy put her hand on his bem and addressed the officials. "We are certain that there is a misunderstanding and will cooperate fully," Ennjy said calmly. Albert knew she wanted to say more.

The FJF official led the team to the Zeeno spacecraft, where they were each given a lie-detector test.

"Do you know Mehklen Pahck?"

"Did you know that Kayko Tusq was planning an explosion?"

"Did you know that Kayko was working with Mehk?"

Albert answered, worried that his nervousness would mess up the test.

After the FJF official left, President Lat entered.

"You'll give Kayko a lie-detector test, too, right?" Doz asked. "She'll pass it. We know she will."

Lat's face was stern, her gaze steady, her bem hanging motionless. "Kayko will receive a test. I will make sure of that. Your job is to stop asking questions. Do not defend Kayko or make accusations against the Tevs or Z-Tevs. This will only cause unrest. My job is to protect as many Zeenods as possible, and the best way to move forward is to stay quiet. If you become demanding or aggressive, you will make Zeenods look bad in the eyes of the security forces and in the eyes of the media." She looked especially at Doz. "Do you understand?"

Doz did not reply, and Ennjy quickly placed her hand on Doz's shoulder and answered for him. "Yes, we all understand."

"I know Kayko's betrayal is hard for you to accept," the president continued. "It was hard for me to accept. Kayko became overwhelmed by her own shawbles. She thought that if Albert Kinney was killed, she could blame it on the Tevs and Z-Tevs and gain more sympathy and support for herself and for you. She thought sacrificing Albert was worth it."

No one said a word. The room vibrated with even more tension.

"When the news gets out, every Zeenod will feel betrayed," Lat said. "Fans will turn against the team. No one will support a team whose coach has brought such dishonor to the game. I'll understand if any of you decide to quit the tournament—especially you, of course, Albert."

Albert felt a chill run down his spine. He was sure that Kayko was innocent and sure that Lat knew it.

As he returned to his ITV, the crowd of reporters and Jhaateezian onlookers snapped his photo and threw out questions.

"Albert Kinney, what does it feel like to be on the team of a coach who wanted to kill you?"

"Albert Kinney, do you still feel that you're in danger?"

"Albert Kinney, are you going to quit?"

2.4

The warden of Mehk's prison unit was a Z-Tev bully known as Blocck. And when he greeted Mehk, two things burned in his red eyes: a love of power and a hatred of Zeenods.

He had a long, ragged scar that sliced down the side of his thick neck; and since every Z-Tev had access to a medical office with smartskin technology, it was obvious to Mehk that Blocck kept his scar as a way of showing off his survival skills.

"So, here's the brilliant robotics engineer," Blocck said. "I'm honored you've chosen to stay here with me."

"I was not told why I was arrested," Mehk said, keeping his voice calm.

The warden informed Mehk about the so-called evidence that had been "found" linking Kayko Tusq and him to the attempted murder of Albert Kinney.

As he spoke, Mehk's brain connected the dots. President Lat's main goal was to do whatever the Tevs and Z-Tevs wanted. They had wanted to make sure Zeeno lost their first game and had thought that killing Albert Kinney was the key. That plan had failed. Now the pressure was on. The Zhidorians, who were neutral, had to investigate the explosion, and they must have discovered that it wasn't an accident. So Lat must have thought up the idea of blaming the explosion on two Zeenods—Kayko and him. She must have created a fake account to make it look like the money in his account came from Kayko and then forged a diary. What a scheme! A way to turn public opinion against the Zeenods. A way to make everyone—including their own Star Striker—distrust the Zeenods. He had to admit, it was clever.

"As you'll see, the service here is excellent. And if you're ready, I can personally escort you to your room. Kayko Tusq is being processed on another floor here in the prison. Too bad you're separated."

Mehk kept his mouth closed.

"Can't think of anything to say?" The warden laughed.

"I'm waiting until I'm introduced to someone with enough intelligence to understand me," Mehk replied, and Blocck gave him a swift electrical shock.

"I guess you're not smart enough to know how to avoid pain." Blocck smiled. "Don't worry. I'll help. I'll tell you when to speak from now on. Let's go."

Without another word, Blocck led him to his prison cell. Quickly, Mehk scanned the space, which reminded him of the punishment cell he'd spent so much time in at the orphanage when he was young. It was small, of course; he had been expecting that. A depressingly low ceiling, a cold floor, both red in color, four solid-gray walls, one door. Two air vents in the walls on each side, low to the floor, caught Mehk's eye. But unfortunately, they were only large enough for a hand to pass through, not a body. A hygg and a toilet were the only items inside. All hyggs on Zeeno float, and this one did, too, but this was an inexpensive version, a flat bed, instead of a tent. It floated about three inches off the floor. Without the tent there would be no hydrating mists, no tissue massaging, no privacy. Waiting on the hygg were a thin blanket and a prison uniform, the latter of which Blocck ordered Mehk to put on.

The gheet hiding under his bem twitched.

For a moment, Mehk fantasized about activating the stun setting of his gheet and tossing it into Blocck's face. One bite from the gheet and Blocck would fall into a coma. Ha! Tempting. But putting Blocck to sleep would only raise the alarms, and his gheet would probably be destroyed in the process.

Calmly, Mehk picked up the uniform and focused on keeping his gheet from being discovered. Fortunately, he had designed his robotic pet's exterior with sensor-blocking coating technology, so he didn't have to worry about it being detected by drones. But that technology wouldn't prevent actual eyes from seeing the tarantula-sized gheet if it came out of hiding.

Without appearing to be concerned, Mehk slipped off his regular clothes, careful not to disturb the gheet, which was clinging to his skin under his bem. Then he pulled on the new uniform, adjusting his bem over the back of it like a cape, hoping the gheet wouldn't be dislodged and fall to the floor.

All good.

A small scanning drone started at his feet and revolved around him, moving upward incrementally, scanning for weapons, illegal materials, suspicious substances. It passed right over the hidden gheet and kept going.

By the time the drone finished, Mehk was practically grinning. "I'm as clean as a baby gnauser," he said.

A good head taller than Mehk, Blocck leaned in. "I don't believe I asked for your opinion, so I suggest—" He leaned closer. "And what do we have here?" With the tip of a long fingernail, the warden tapped the coin-sized metallic disk half embedded in the side of Mehk's skull. His breath was moist and hot. "Sneaking in a little secret? Microbot of some kind?"

Mehk had completely forgotten about his experimental thought-loop microbot. It, like his gheet, was coated with sensor-blocking film, but he should have thought to take it out the moment he had been arrested. It would have been better to drop it along the way rather than have them get their hands on it. "I'm obviously not hiding it." Mehk tried to keep cool and lied. "It's a medical device. Just a little invention to address—"

Tapping the disk again, Blocck said, "Take it out."

"That's not so easy. I would need a special tool—"

Gripping Mehk by the shoulder with one cold, strong hand, the warden ripped the disk out with the sharp fingernails of his other hand.

Mehk winced, more at the loss of the resource than the pain.

The warden dropped the disk into his pocket and smiled. "I think the authorities are going to love finding out what this is. I think I'm going to get a bonus."

Two short beeps came from outside the door, and the warden brightened. "We have a surprise of our own. Your new roommate is here!" He opened the door and in flew a quadcopter drone. Sleek and gray, the drone's body was about the size of a flattened johka ball, with two arms in addition to its four blades and a fully automatic camera in its belly.

"Let me introduce you to your very own paired-entity enhanced robot, known as your PEER," Blocck said. "We're very proud here of our robotics. We've been combining the best discoveries from many sources—maybe even your own work—to create the ultimate prison companion."

The drone zipped over to Mehk and whirred in front of his face, sensors flashing and beeping. A computerized voice from the PEER's belly spoke: "Biometrics complete. Connection of PEER Number 417355 to Zeenod Mehklen Pahck successful." The thing zoomed over to his side and hovered there at eye level, the camera in its belly staring at him.

"There you go," Blocck said. "Now you're a team. Isn't that nice? If you behave, your PEER will be happy to give you a little space and dock outside your door while you're in your cell. You can sleep in peace and privacy. But if you don't behave, your PEER will be worried and want to be with you day and night." Blocck shrugged. "I think it's sweet, but that constant, in-your-face attention has been known to drive prisoners insane."

Mehk didn't respond.

"See those little arms there?" Blocck gestured to appendages on the drone. "One fires nets. The other fires bullets. Don't even think about touching your PEER." Blocck began to leave and turned around. "Oh. One more thing. The thousand other prisoners here are all Zeenods, and they all know that you are a traitor to the Zeenod team." The warden smiled. "Too bad you don't have an eye back here." He tapped the back of his head. "It's helpful when you need to watch your back." The Z-Tev walked out, staring at Mehk with his rear-facing eye.

Mehk's mind raged. He had to escape. He needed to know if the Z-Tev police had searched his apartment and found the drive in his secret safe. If so, they would know how to retrieve his masterpiece, and everything he had worked so hard to create would be stolen.

2.5

On the trip back to Earth, Albert was quiet. The thought that the botmaker who created the explosion was in prison gave him some comfort. But he was worried about Kayko. To be arrested without having done anything wrong! Clearly, someone was trying to frame her—and the Zeenods couldn't trust the police. They couldn't even trust their own president! Other Zeenods were being shipped off against their will to work on Tev. And that was just the stuff Albert knew about. There had to be so much more.

Yet somewhere deep inside Albert, a little bubble of relief was forming—not the good kind of relief that comes after a good kind of closure, but a cowardly relief that Albert didn't want to face or own. Inside that bubble, a voice whispered: Use this as an opportunity and quit...you are sure to fail playing against the Jhaateezians on Jhaateez, Albert, but if you quit now, no one will know what a failure you are.

Just as Albert was about to enter into hibernation, a video call came through.

Ennjy's face appeared on-screen. "Albert," she said, the colors on the surface of her skin deepening. "There is bad news. Supposedly Kayko failed her lie-detector test. But we believe it was faked, and we are not giving up. We have—"

"Wait," Albert said nervously. "Should you be talking like that? How do we know no one is spying?"

After the last game, Kayko had done another search of the ITV and had discovered a stinkbug spybot embedded in the ceiling. She had said it was the most sophisticated bot she had ever seen. Although she had destroyed it, Albert couldn't help wondering if whoever placed the first had managed to sneak in another.

"We have been doing regular checks on the ITV, Albert," Ennjy said. "We believe it's safe to speak openly. As I was saying, we had a team meeting and we have decided we must do whatever we can to prove Kayko's innocence. Giac is going to secretly devote all her time to finding out as much as she can about the botmaker Mehk. The rest of us intend to keep training. We hope you will join us, but we understand if you need to quit. If so, we ask that you give us your decision in time for us to initiate the recruitment and training of the alternate Star Striker."

Albert's thoughts were jumbled, and Ennjy, sensing it, told him to go home and think about it.

"One more thing," Ennjy said. "Unless Mehk has been acting alone, there is someone still out there who may want to kill you. We are all in danger until we determine exactly who framed Kayko and can safely get that information to our allies who can help us. Be extra vigilant. Pay attention to unusual sights or sounds en route and on Earth. Report anything directly to me."

When Albert returned to school, he couldn't focus, which meant he didn't get his work done, which meant he had more homework to do that evening. After school, he dragged himself home. He wished he could talk with Lightning Lee. Lee had been in his situation. Lee was wise. How frustrating that the only other human being who might be able to give him some advice couldn't be revealed to him.

He was almost too depressed to stop at the Pattersons' for his ritual after-school visit with Tackle, but Tackle was waiting and ready with questions.

How was it? What's wrong? You look terrible.

Albert opened the gate and sat with Tackle in the grass, petting the ridge along Tackle's back and scratching behind his velvety ears. He explained Kayko's shocking arrest and the discovery of the bot-maker and the warning that they should all remain extra vigilant.

Albert took a deep breath. *I think I should quit.*

Quit? the dog asked, his forehead wrinkling with compassion.

Shame burned inside Albert. He thought the Zeenods would have a better chance at winning with whoever was their second choice, but he didn't want to admit it even to Tackle.

Sometimes, the head will come up with a story to cover up what the heart is feeling if what the heart is feeling is too painful to bear. Albert didn't want to acknowledge his lack of confidence, so his mind handed him a terrible thought: Maybe the Zeenods were being naïve and Kayko did betray them and this whole tournament wasn't worth the risk.

I have to go, Tackle, he said quickly, standing up. *See you later.*

Albert, the dog called out. *Wait. Let's go to the park. You'll feel better if we run around.*

Thanks. Maybe tomorrow, Albert called back, hoping Tackle couldn't hear the break in his voice.

Okay, I'll patrol tonight, Tackle called out. *You can count on me.*

3.0

The next morning, an unfamiliar sound outside Albert's window woke him. *Clack clack.* Pause. *Clack clack.* Pause. *Clack clack.* Pause. The repetition had a violent quality to it that sent a chill down Albert's spine. His room faced the driveway, and the sound was right outside his window.

As he held his breath and listened, images of what might be causing the sound snapped through his mind: the doors of a spacecraft opening, the heavy metallic footsteps of a robotic hit man, Tev weapons being primed.

With increasing dread Albert wondered why Tackle wasn't barking. He couldn't hear sounds coming from his kitchen, either, which was unusual. The thought occurred to him that everyone he loved might have been kidnapped or killed while he was sleeping.

Heart pounding, Albert slipped out of bed as quietly as possible and tiptoed to the window. Bracing himself to see an alien assassin, he lifted the shade slightly and peeked out.

It was Trey practicing a skateboard trick over and over. His phone, propped on the garbage can, was recording his efforts. No doubt he was using the Kinneys' driveway because the Pattersons' didn't have enough space. Tackle was there, watching through the fence slats, not barking, of course, because it was just Trey making the noise, not a robotic hit man from planet Tev.

Feeling ridiculous, Albert glanced at his clock. There were thirty minutes before it was time to leave for school. Of course Trey would have gotten hold of a skateboard. Of course Trey would be up early, grinding to gain skills. Trey had never been afraid to work hard when he was trying to learn something new. Albert had always been that way, too. Their old coach had affectionately called them Gainers. A pang of sadness shot through Albert as he watched his old friend nail the trick and ham it up for the camera. Once upon a time, they would have done this together. Since that summer camp, Trey had changed for the worse.

Albert dropped the shade and walked over to look at himself in the mirror. He had made huge gains since he had begun to train with the Zeenods. He had gotten physically and mentally stronger. Yes, Trey was physically stronger and more coordinated. But Albert, not Trey, had been chosen by the Zeenods to be a Star Striker. The Zeenods believed he could connect with his teammates through the ahn and knew that this connection was as important as physical strength. Albert took a breath and let it out. He couldn't quit.

Careful to keep up the pretense of having a broken wrist,

Albert hurried through breakfast and slipped out the door, not letting his mom see that he was bringing the skates. She'd freak out to think of him skating with a broken wrist.

The moment he was out, Tackle was running to the front of the Pattersons' gate for the ritual morning hello.

Tackle took one look at the skates and guessed that Albert was not going to give up.

I have to try, Albert said.

That's the spirit, Tackle said.

In the next moment, Trey walked out of his house, ready to head to school, too, and Albert hid the skates.

"Check it out," Trey said, holding up the skateboard. "Got it from Jessica yesterday. Last night I watched a bunch of skateboarding videos and this morning I practiced and now I'm going to start posting videos of my own tricks. They're going to go viral. Check this trick out. It's called the Cave Man." Holding his board in his back hand, Trey ran out into the street, then jumped into the air and threw the board directly under his feet. While still in the air, he landed on the board and then used his legs to slam the board down on its wheels. Board and boy zoomed forward effortlessly. He glanced back. "Cool, right?"

Albert almost choked with envy, feeling the confidence he had gained this morning slip away.

Brag, brag, brag, Tackle said under his breath. *It's all he does these days.*

As Trey pushed off toward school, Albert popped inside the Pattersons' gate to give Tackle a hug. *I just wish he weren't so immediately good at everything he tries to do,* Albert said. *He makes me feel like dirt.*

Don't worry, Tackle said. *One step at a time. Or should I say, one glide at a time. Are you skating to school?*

Maybe after school, Albert said.

Sounds like a plan, the dog said, nodding.

School was painfully slow. Finally, when the last bell rang, Albert hurried out. His mom had informed his clarinet teacher, Sam Atwater—Jessica's dad—that he had a broken wrist, but Mr. Sam, as he was called, said Albert should come to his lesson as usual. He had texted Albert to say that every great musician learns how to adapt to injuries and that it can create a "beginner's mind" state, which is conducive to learning. That was Mr. Sam. Always looking on the positive side.

Albert left school quickly, jogged to a quiet street, and changed into the skates. His goal was to make it to Mr. Sam's house and take off the skates before Jessica even left the school grounds. He had no desire to be seen by her.

The street was basically level, so he got a rhythm going. He practiced skating on one leg for a while and then on the other, keeping that other leg free to kick. A piece of cake, or as Doz would say, a piece of cookie.

Not a single cloud was visible in the whole expanse of the blue sky. Although the air was cool, the afternoon sun burned bright, as if it wanted to get in extra shine time before the evening kicked in. Albert looked at the splashes of autumn color in the trees and had a thought: The Earth was just as beautiful as Jhaateez, in its way. A Jhaateezian would probably think the red and gold of the oaks and maples on this street were astonishing.

In no time, he was turning onto Jessica's street, and their house with their crazy painted door was in sight. On the street, he was pushing himself to pick up speed when Jessica whizzed by on her skateboard, eating a bar of chocolate. She glanced back to see who was on the skates and, recognizing him, called out, "Hey!"

His mind went foggy with panic and he veered up a driveway to his right in a last-minute attempt to…what? Turn around? Hide? Pretend it wasn't him? He didn't even know. Somehow in his fog he didn't notice the parked car in that driveway until it was right in front of him and he couldn't stop and—*BAM!*—he slammed against the car's trunk. The car alarm went off.

"Whoa! Albert, are you all right?" Jessica came flying over. "That must have hurt!" She hopped off her board and yelled over the blaring of the car alarm. "Is your wrist okay?"

Mortified, Albert lifted the arm with the fake cast and wriggled his fingers. "Nothing's broken—I mean, nothing new broke. Obviously I have a broken wrist here. Ha ha." He laughed nervously and began to walk, awkwardly in his skates, toward her house and away from the noise.

Jessica followed. "When you were talking about the skate park, I thought you were talking about getting a skateboard, not skates."

"I don't have anything against skateboarding," Albert said quickly. "It's just—I mean, I found these in the garage and I'm just messing around—I mean, I'm thinking it will help my coordination and everything for soccer, too. I mean, everything helps everything, right?" He knew he sounded ridiculous, but he couldn't stop. "I thought the skate park would be a good place to—you know, no chance of bumping into any parked cars there! Ha ha!" His laughter was pathetic.

They reached her driveway and she gave him a funny look. "You sure you're okay, Albert?"

He nodded. They heard a chirp and the car alarm stopped, and they both turned back to see the owner of the car coming out of her house to inspect the scene.

"Nothing's wrong!" Jessica called out with a wave. "We just touched it accidentally."

Her neighbor waved back, and Jessica and Albert went inside.

"In-line skates are cool," she said, putting her skateboard by the door and kicking off her shoes as Albert sat down in the waiting-for-a-lesson chair and started taking off his skates. "It would be fun to see what I could do with them at the park."

"That's—um—that's exactly what I was thinking," Albert said. He was finding it difficult to talk with her standing so close.

"Can I try your skates while you're taking your lesson?" She stepped next to Albert and put her foot next to his to see how much smaller hers was. "Never mind, too big," she said, and stepped back. "I promised Trey I'd show him some things at the park sometime. I'm there almost every Saturday afternoon. You should bring these and come."

Hanging out at the skateboard park with Jessica and Trey at the same time sounded like a recipe for humiliation. Happily, he had an actual conflict—practices on Jhaateez. He smiled then, thinking about how incredibly cool it would be to tell Jessica Atwater that the reason he couldn't come was because he had to travel to another planet, where he was an actual sports celebrity. He couldn't do that, but he could at least let her know he was playing on a team. "Sorry, but I've got this *really* big practice I have to go to," he said, pretending disappointment, but the whole thing came off wrong. He sounded conceited and uninterested in Jessica—he could tell by the change in her expression.

"No problem," she said quickly. "See you later."

Before he could try to fix it, she was gone.

Cursing at himself, Albert put on his regular shoes as the sound of another student playing a song drifted from the back hallway. Then he looked at the time on his phone. He had fifteen minutes before his lesson.

59

He recalled listening to one of Kayko's ahn lessons while sitting in this exact chair back when he was training for the first game. One part of that message had been to forgive himself and send himself kind thoughts. He shook his head. Obviously, that one hadn't stuck.

He pulled up the lesson he had failed to pay attention to in history class on Monday. As it began, he recognized that the narrator was Kayko, and he realized that he was just now making that connection.

The warm, rich tone of her voice hit him hard. He thought back to how it had felt when he'd been kidnapped and had been sent hurtling toward that black hole. His old chaperone, Unit B, had advised that Kayko and Ennjy save themselves and retreat, and Albert had been sure that there was no hope. But then Kayko's voice had streamed into his ITV. *Don't worry, Albert,* she had said. *We are not surrendering the fight.*

Kayko had saved his life—and now she was in prison. Ashamed that he had lost his confidence, ashamed that he had doubted her, he vowed to focus his attention. He wanted to stay on the team, help prove that she'd been framed, help the Zeenods win the next game and the whole tournament. If the botmaker Mehk was in prison, he couldn't be framing her. So who was? Who wanted to see the Zeenods fail? Vatria? Hissgoff, the Tev coach? A rabid Tev fan? Whoever was framing Kayko had to be connected with whoever had tried to kill Albert during the Tev game. Clearly, Albert was still at risk.

He noticed that his mind was galloping away and turned his attention back to Kayko's voice.

Welcome to the fourth lesson: Always Learning. Take a few moments to focus on your breathing and to be present and we will begin.

Albert took a breath and let it out. *Focus,* he said to himself as he closed his eyes.

Everyone falls. If you are not falling, it means you are not trying anything new. If you were afraid of falling when you were a baby, you would never have learned to walk.

Albert laughed. He had never thought about it that way.

Practice the art of falling. To do this, you must embrace the ground. Do not try to resist it. But once you are down, get up quickly. Practice this over and over. Embrace the fall and get up quickly. Embrace the fall and get up quickly. We must be willing to be beginners again and again, and we must seek many different teachers. The only thing to know is that there is always more to know.

A bell signaled the end of the lesson. Albert opened his eyes. He flashed back to Kayko's offer to teach him how to fall at the first lesson. Jessica had offered to teach him to fall, too, and, come to think of it, even Nana had said he needed to learn to fall. But being told that had felt like being told he needed to ride a bike with training wheels or to ski on the bunny slope, so he hadn't listened. That was definitely a shawble. In his mind, he could see the faces of his teammates all looking at him during that first practice; and, as if it were happening now, he could feel the desire to impress them rise again like a wave surging in his chest. With that desire came a fear of failure like a heavy weight pulling him down.

He started to berate himself and then stopped. The wisdom

from two of his earlier lessons came to him: Acknowledge what you're feeling without judgment and be kind to yourself. Shawbles that are met with shame, anger, denial, or fear will just get worse.

Albert closed his eyes and took a breath. *The only thing to know is that there is always more to know.*

He looked at his phone. Nine minutes left until his music lesson. Using his phone, he searched *how to fall on skates* and watched a video. An in-line skater was mimicking different kinds of falls and different ways of falling "right" and falling "wrong."

The basics: Don't panic. Don't flail. Don't stiffen the arms and legs. Don't try to stop the fall with your arms locked. All things Albert had done.

If you're skating forward, fear can make you jolt back, which is exactly what you don't want to do. Keep the core tight and the limbs loose. *Bend your knees and lean into it,* the athlete on the video said. *Melt into the fall and then get up.* The athlete did a shoulder roll on the grass the way Jessica had.

Embrace the fall and get up quickly, Kayko had said.

Albert ran out into the Atwaters' yard. He tightened his core and melted into a shoulder roll, then jumped back up. Tightening his core but keeping his limbs loose definitely helped. "Embrace the fall and get up quickly," Albert chanted as he ran and fell and rose again.

Already he could feel a difference. He did it again and again.

A window on the second floor opened and Jessica stuck her head out. "What are you doing?"

Albert looked up. He felt the familiar wave of embarrassment rise and was about to make up a lie. Then he shrugged. "I'm learning how to fall," he said.

"Nice." She laughed.

The door opened, and Mr. Sam's other student stepped out. Feeling good, Albert grabbed his clarinet case and waltzed in. That afternoon he had what Mr. Sam said was his best lesson yet.

"I would have thought a broken wrist would have slowed you down, Albert," Mr. Sam said. "But that was some good work."

Delighted, Albert skated home, actually enjoying the movement of his muscles, the feeling of the crisp November breeze on his face, the beauty of the sun, low on the horizon, sending its last light of the day through the branches of the trees.

When he rolled up the driveway, Tackle ran to the gate, tail wagging.

Hey, looking like a pro, Albert, the dog said.

Thanks, Albert said.

After taking off his skates, he grabbed Tackle's favorite rubber ball and played a game of catch with him until his mom and Erin arrived and he had to follow them in for dinner.

By the time he walked in, the kitchen smelled amazing, thanks to Nana.

"Good evening, everybody! Did everybody have a great day? I did!" Albert plucked three onions from the bowl on the counter and began trying to juggle them, dropping them immediately with a laugh.

Nana laughed, and Erin and his mom gave him funny looks.

"Who are you? I was expecting to have two grumpy kids," his mom said. "Last night all you did was complain, Albert."

"Me? I'm Albert the Amazing, famous throughout the universe for my good cheer." Albert picked up an onion and put it on Erin's head.

She swatted it off, and he asked her why she was grumpy.

"She's mad because she wants to stay at the gym until eight on Thursday nights," his mom said. "And I put my foot down and said that a family dinner at least once during the week was more important."

"Brittany is training until eight every night," Erin said.

"I'm not Brittany's mom, and we're not going to keep arguing about it." Their mom sat down and looked gratefully at the plates of pasta and broccoli and garlic bread that Nana was setting out on the table. "Thank you. I, for one, am starved."

"Me too," Albert said. "Thanks, Nana."

"My pleasure," Nana said. "If I'm going to keep staying, I might as well earn my keep." She patted Erin's hand. "Family dinners are important. You gotta eat!"

"Brittany says I'm getting fattish," Erin whined.

"I say Brittany is getting brattish," Albert said. "Tell her to put a sock in it. Preferably one of mine because they stink."

Erin laughed.

3.1

In his cell, Mehk paced. Although his PEER had stayed outside the door so far, it had been a long night. Through the small air vents, he had to listen to the prisoner in the cell to the left snoring and farting and the prisoner in the cell to the right humming and chanting to himself. The night would have been worse if the PEER had been in his face as he tried to sleep, so he made a vow to behave.

Out of habit, he paused and listened for the positive thought-loop in his mind and then remembered that the microbot was gone. He missed it. His own thoughts were as dark and slippery as the giant eels in the under-rivers of Gaböq. Had Lat somehow found a way to get her hands on his masterpiece or was it still in place, functioning as usual, he wondered? Before he had been arrested, he had checked the data every day to make sure there were no system alerts. How maddening to be stuck here without any way of knowing what was going on.

How frustrating to think he had come so close! If he had left before the police had arrived, he could have taken care of Kinney, and then his robotic masterpiece would be in place as the alternate Star Striker. How thrilling it would have been to watch that unfold! How satisfying to stand up after the game and reveal to the entire solar system that the player was a robot and that he had created it! Every planet would be begging for his technology.

The gheet hiding under his bem squirmed, and Mehk quickly climbed into bed and pulled the blanket over himself. He had to get out of here.

To escape would mean hacking into the very thing that was doing such an effective job of guarding him—his PEER. Every system had its flaws, Mehk knew. He just had to figure out the weaknesses of this system.

Under the blanket, his gheet crawled down Mehk's arm and into his hand. With gratitude, Mehk patted its hairy head and felt it nuzzle into his palm. His only consolation. His companion. This little guy was at least a handful of proof that he was a brilliant engineer. He wanted to talk to it out loud, the way he did when he was in his apartment. Without that ability, without his log to write in, without his work, the minutes crawled.

In the next moment, the cell door was opening. Mehk left the gheet under the blanket and quickly stood up.

The PEER zoomed in first and hovered, eye level.

Telda Lat walked in next, followed by Blocck, who set a chair down in the center of the cell and then left. The door slammed shut.

President Lat sat down, adjusting her bem. The PEER took a surveillance position, hovering directly above Mehk's head.

"Mehk, let's speak honestly."

"Speak honestly?" Mehk took a step toward her, and immediately his PEER emitted a warning.

"Behavior change. PEER on alert."

"Calm down, Mehk," Lat said. "I am not your enemy."

He forced his anger down and took a step back. "You promised that if I helped you with the explosion, you would help me unveil my masterpiece."

She nodded. "Those plans had to change."

"What do you want from me now? Let me out, and I'll happily get rid of Albert Kinney once and for all."

"I'm taking care of Albert Kinney," she said. "You need to hand over your masterpiece. The Tevs and Z-Tevs want it."

Mehk's mind whirred. Her statement revealed some good news! She must not have been able to find his secret drive. His biggest fear had been that she'd find it, hack into it, and learn the location of his masterpiece. Instantly, he decided to lie and convince her that his robot was gone—that was the only way she'd stop searching for it.

He looked at her without blinking. "I destroyed it."

She stared back. "You what?"

He smiled. "I activated the code for destruction the moment I was arrested. I thought you would be smart enough to know that I'd never let you get your hands on it."

She was speechless for a moment. Then she said, "Mehk, you know that without anything special to give to the Tevs and Z-Tevs, you are nothing. They will keep you in here and make you work for them until you die."

His stare was cold. "We both know that even if I turned over my masterpiece to them, they would keep me here until I die."

Her eyes remained steady. She believed him, he could tell. When she left and his PEER docked outside the cell door, he breathed deeply. Ha! What a brilliant performance he had given. He might be in prison, but his mind was free to play her like a fool. She would leave him alone and focus her attention on destroying Albert Kinney and the Zeenods. For now, his masterpiece was safe, and that was what mattered.

3.2

The night was cold and windy. Tackle went for a pee and then circled the house six times. Nothing unusual.

He headed back in through his dog door and padded from kitchen to dining room to living room to TV room and back to kitchen six times. Up the stairs for a quick check. Mr. and Mrs. Patterson asleep. Trey asleep. Guest room door open. Room empty.

Back down the steps. He sniffed his water bowl, made sure it smelled right, and then lapped up a few good slurps. After that he headed into the TV room and rolled around on the nubbly rug. Best rug. Satisfying nubbles.

His favorite chew toy, a fake hot dog in a bun, was visible under the TV stand. He gave it a good sniff and then took it to the huge stuffed bear, an old lovey of Trey's that lay on the floor in the corner and served as his bed. Snuggle in. Chew. Chew. Lick. Chew. Chew. Lick.

Yep. Everything seemed perfectly normal. Perfectly safe.

He had one last drink and decided to go out for one last pee, and that was when he smelled it. Intruder. Kinneys' driveway. Right near the spot where Albert's first szoŭ occurred.

He barked and took off toward the smell, throwing himself against the fence.

Through the slats, he could see a shape run toward the front of Albert's house and disappear into the night.

3.3

Although Mehk had never felt like a Zeenod, he found it useful to have a bem. When he sat on the floor with his back against the wall, he could pull his bem around his shoulders and arms so that it draped into his lap. This provided the perfect hiding spot for his gheet. Even in the privacy of his cell, he was careful. Never knew when that door would open.

His hands were hidden in his lap right now, and his gheet was crawling from hand to hand. Mehk was picturing all of his information hidden in the secret compartment in his apartment. If he had worked with a partner, that partner could be retrieving the information and protecting his masterpiece.

Perhaps I should have worked with someone all along, he thought as he rubbed the hairy top of his gheet's head, someone I could count on to help me succeed. A sound halfway between a laugh and a sob escaped his throat. A partner? Anyone who knew him would know how ridiculous that sounded, which was why the allegation that he and Kayko were working together was so preposterous.

The lights flickered three times, signaling prisoners that they had two minutes before all lights would be turned off for the night.

The sound of a toilet flushing came from the left vent. From the right came the sound of the prisoner chanting to himself again. The same words and tune that had annoyed Mehk the night before: *"Come to meet me. I have a song to share."* Over and over.

Intending to tell him he'd like his fist to meet the guy's face, Mehk crouched down and peeked through the vent. He could see the Zeenod prisoner, sitting near the vent in his cell, chanting just as calmly and sweetly as could be. How irritating. Mehk was about to risk punishment from his PEER by screaming into the vent when the meaning of the words tapped open a door in his mind.

"I have a song to share."

The thought that it could be a message flitted through his mind.

Mehk pushed his hygg against the wall with the vent and climbed on. A moment later the lights flicked off. Holding his breath, he listened in the darkness.

The voice came again. *"I have a song to share."*

He didn't move.

"Sing back if you are listening."

Mehk wasn't sure what to do. Feeling ridiculous, he couldn't manage words. But his curiosity was piqued. He hummed a little of the tune and waited.

The voice chanted on. *"PEERs are programmed to disregard the sound of singing. We can safely exchange messages this way. Sing back to me if you understand."*

Aha! Mehk thought. The first weakness of the system! The engineers who created PEERs programmed them to respond to sounds or behaviors that they determined were threatening or dangerous, and those engineers had clearly made the mistake of thinking that singing could never be dangerous! The prisoners had figured this out! Although Mehk didn't like to sing, he had to admit it was a clever and simple way for the Zeenods to communicate.

"Sing anything if you understand," the voice chanted again. *"We know who you are."*

Mehk turned away from the vent, his mind churning. Actually, he wasn't sure he wanted to connect. He couldn't imagine what Zeenod prisoners wanted to tell him other than how much they hated him for being a traitor.

And then the voice went on, singing, *"I am honored to meet you. I am passing on a message from a prisoner here named Zin. He knew your parents, Mehk."*

Mehk's heart began pounding. His gheet responded by scrambling up his arm and crawling under his bem.

"Zin is your ahnparent. He needs to see you, Mehk. He will find you tomorrow."

70

4.0

On Friday morning before school, Tackle was waiting anxiously. As soon as Albert stepped out of his house, Tackle jumped up on the front gate and barked. *I've been going crazy. Are you okay?*

Yeah. Why?

The dog told Albert about the suspicious figure in the driveway. *Last night something was creeping around just under your bedroom window.*

A spy?

I don't know. I chased it away. But I expected to see you out here earlier. Trey already left for school. When you didn't come out, I thought maybe something had happened over there.

I'm late. I slept late. Albert sat and put on his skates.

I know it's getting cold, but leave your window cracked open at night, Tackle said. *You'll be able to hear me if I call out to you and I'll be able to hear you.*

Albert agreed and thanked Tackle for guarding him last night and promised to be careful.

Then he took off for school. The thought that someone or something was prowling outside his window made him nervous, but knowing Tackle was there helped.

His muscles were sore from yesterday's practice, but sore in a good way. His old coach would always say *Gains come from pains.* Tomorrow was another practice on Jhaateez, another chance.

4.1

In the morning, the door to Mehk's cell opened and the whoosh of air from the corridor rippled the bottom edges of his bem.

"Exit now. Work session." The command came from his PEER.

Mehk froze for a moment, wondering if he should leave his gheet hidden under the blanket instead of bringing it along. No, it was better to take the pet with him. Its presence, tucked under his bem, its eight feet firmly suctioned onto his skin, was comforting.

Mehk stepped out and joined a single-file line of other prisoners—all of them Zeenods, each with a PEER overhead, whirring along in a duplicate line.

The buzzing of a spy directly above, a watcher that followed every move—this was what greeted the prisoners the moment they left their cells, Mehk realized.

He kept his mouth closed and followed the line down the long hallway. About twenty prisoners were walking ahead of him in the line when an older Zeenod tripped and fell to the side. That prisoner's PEER moved with him and emitted a warning. "Behavior change. PEER on alert."

The line kept moving. By the time Mehk was near him, the old Zeenod had risen to his feet, and just after Mehk passed him, he dutifully stepped back into line, now directly behind Mehk.

This was Zin, Mehk guessed. A clever trick. He hid his comprehension, of course, continuing along as if he hadn't noticed anything. A part of him wondered if the Zeenod's statement last night about being honored to meet him was a trick. Perhaps these Zeenods were going to gang up and punish him for his part in the attack at the Zeeno game.

Inside the workroom stood ten long tables. The prisoners were lined up, twenty prisoners per table in the same order in which they had entered, which meant the old Zeenod was next to Mehk.

Mehk had heard rumors that Zeenod prisoners were forced to make all kinds of products for the Z-Tevs, and now he could see that this was true. The workroom was just one of many in the huge facility, and this prison was just one of many on the planet. Laid out in front of each prisoner was a full bin of small plastic pieces, a bottle of fluid, and an egglike object that emitted a steam of chemicals.

The moment all the prisoners were in place, the PEERs flew up and retreated to their waiting positions in docking stations on the walls, their cameras facing out. Surprised at first, Mehk quickly figured out that the drones couldn't hover directly over-head because the steam from the worktables would interfere with their cameras.

The work began. Mehk watched the prisoner next to him fit two pieces together, place one drop of fluid on the joint, hold it over the steam for three seconds, and then toss it into a bin. Mind-less work, Mehk thought with dismay, work that he could design machines to do. He didn't even know what they were making, although the piece looked like a PEER arm. Was it possible, Mehk wondered, that prisoners were being forced to create the parts for the very objects that kept them imprisoned?

Knowing that he had no choice, Mehk picked up two pieces and got to work. After just a few moments, another surprising thing happened. The prisoners began to sing a rhythmic chant.

A work song, Mehk realized, an old Zeenod chant whose pur-pose was to synchronize their work, a song whose beat matched the rhythm of their hands.

As the song grew louder, the Zeenod next to him began to whisper without pausing in his work. "We can speak here if we whisper. The Z-Tevs let us sing because it increases productivity. They don't realize that it also increases our ability to communicate with each other. I am Zin. Keep looking at your work, Mehk. I am doing the same. I am so happy to meet you, although not under these circumstances. I am sorry you have been imprisoned."

Mehk, continuing to work, replied, "I assumed you would want nothing to do with me. You must know why I was arrested."

"We do not trust President Lat. We know she works for the Z-Tevs, who work for the Tevs. We assume you are innocent, Mehk. We know that a Zeenod wouldn't harm our Star Striker or any fellow Zeenods."

Mehk took this in and stayed silent. Clearly, they didn't know about all the crimes he had committed and didn't know that being a Zeenod meant nothing to him.

The old Zeenod went on. "We have heard that you are a genius. Your parents were brilliant, Mehk. The three of us were part of a group working to free Zeeno. Right before your parents were arrested, you were born and your parents chose me as your ahn-parent. I was supposed to guide you and provide ahnic instruction if they died. But then I was arrested, too. We were all framed for crimes we didn't commit."

The work song grew louder and the rhythm of the Zeenods around him continued.

Zin whispered, "When you were in that Z-Tev orphanage, your parents were here!"

"Here?" The room grew suddenly warm, the moisture from the steam filling up the botmaker's lungs. "I was told they were banished."

"They were right here. They kept trying to escape to reunite with you, and they would receive beatings. Three years in, they tried one last time and were killed by a Z-Tev guard."

The items on Mehk's worktable began to blur. Over the years, Mehk had avoided thinking of his parents. The gheet under his bem felt a change in Mehk's posture and responded with a tiny massage, a soothing, inaudible pulsing of its footpads that Mehk had designed.

"Those of us on the main floor have been putting pieces together like a puzzle for an escape," Zin said. "We were close to being ready, and then you appeared! Poor Kayko is on the floor above us. We cannot communicate easily with her. But with you here we have hope. You are the son of my closest friends, who had the most brilliant minds! I know you can help us succeed."

The objects Mehk had in his hand slipped and clattered onto the worktable.

"Keep working," Zin whispered. "I'm sorry. This is much to process. I will leave you alone with your thoughts. We will talk more tomorrow."

"This is excellent news," Mehk said hesitantly. "But I'm curious. How do you know that you can trust me with this information?"

The old Zeenod's reply came back, his voice full of a warmth that Mehk wasn't used to hearing. "The ahn is in you."

Mehk's throat went dry.

"The ahn is here right now," the Zin went on. "Isn't it beautiful? We stay strong this way. Our PEERs can't detect it. Ahnic energy is beyond the scope of their programming. They can't stop us."

Mehk glanced up. Two hundred Zeenods singing in unison, their bems extending and billowing gently with the rhythm.

Zin whispered, "We are breathing in the ahn, sending the strength of ahnic energy to ourselves. And we are breathing out the ahn, sending the ahn to each other. Even here."

Mehk glanced up again. The eyes of all the Zeenods in the room had turned gold.

5.0

Early Saturday morning, Albert took his skates to the skate park and had the place to himself.

The park had various ramps and rails, but it was the big bowl that Albert focused on. He had to learn how to drop in. This one was only about five feet deep, but when he was standing on the deck, the drop still looked steep to him. Instead of trying, he scooted down again on his rear like a little kid, happy that no one was around to see him.

For the next two hours, he got used to skating around on different angles and practicing the shoot-the-duck move, happy to have pads and a helmet but wishing he had his smartmaterials uniform to protect him. After that he practiced falling on the grass. *Embrace the fall and get up quickly.*

By the afternoon, when he took off for Jhaateez, he was already way more comfortable.

When he arrived in the lobby of the practice facility, Ennjy and his other teammates were energized. "We have a plan that may help prove Kayko's innocence," she explained.

"Tell him now," Doz said.

"Later," Ennjy said. "I know we are excited, but our time on the field is limited and this is an important practice. Albert will tell us at the end of this session if he feels he can play with us. While we have this time together, we need to make it as productive as possible. Let's get started."

Once inside, his teammates hit the ice without hesitation.

Still not ready to drop in, Albert stood at the top. "I promise I will figure this out before the game. But for now, I'm going down the fun way." He zoomed down the ice on his rear, yelling, "Woohoo, Zeeno!" and kept sliding out onto the turf, coming to an eventual stop. Then he hopped up with a huge smile. He was upset with himself for not having the courage to try skating down, but the ride *was* fun.

To his relief and amazement, every single teammate immediately skated up the bowl and came back down the ice, sliding down on their rears, yelling, "Woohoo, Zeeno!"

"You're right!" Doz said, hopping up at the bottom. "That is seriously joyful."

Albert loved them all so much he thought he would burst.

After the warm-up Ennjy suggested a drill she called the Shadow, and she chose the quiet winger, Heek, to lead.

"What's the Shadow?" Albert asked.

"It's a response exercise," Feeb explained. "You'll see. Just do whatever the person in front of you does."

The entire team lined up, single file, with Heek at the lead. He started out jogging straight down the field, and they all jogged. He angled his run to the diagonal and the line followed.

Albert was shocked. This was follow-the-leader. He imagined Trey scoffing at the idea of using a kindergarten game as an exercise. Heek stopped suddenly. And one by one the teammates stopped. Albert didn't respond quickly enough and bumped into Wayt, who was standing in front of him.

"Sorry!" Albert said.

By this time, Heek had taken off toward the side, and when he hopped onto the ice, one by the one the team followed. Albert stopped thinking about how childish the game was and started focusing. Heek squatted into a shoot-the-duck and, in a chain reaction, they followed. As soon as Albert was down, though, Heek had already stood, turned, and skated backward. After that Heek slid onto the field, did a shoulder roll, hopped up, and kept running. On it went, every member of the team focusing intently, watching and responding so that no one player caused a break in the chain of reactions. Ahnic energy was building. Although it was challenging, Albert was loving it, the feeling of connection, the feeling that they were separate but one, like a giant, articulated beast moving with precision around the field and on the ice. Connecting to the ahn definitely gave him more control.

When it was time for a scrimmage, Albert was ready. For the most part, he stuck to his cleats on the field. But twice, he needed to get from one end of the field to the other, and he used the ice successfully. Once he slid back onto the field without falling; another time, he felt himself falling forward and successfully used a shoulder roll to keep from getting hurt.

Because there were no out-of-bounds, the action was nonstop, which made it challenging but exhilarating.

As they were doing their cooldown exercises, Giac complimented Albert on his improvement.

"We believe in you, Albert." Ennjy smiled.

"It's all hunky-dorky!" Doz exclaimed, which was one of Albert's favorite Doz-erisms.

Albert took in a breath and let it out. Even though it was cold inside, his suit and the antifrostbite spray made the temperature feel fine, and now the buzz of encouragement from his teammates made him even warmer. He was so relieved that he hadn't allowed himself to quit. Practicing in this beautiful facility with his friends was amazing. Even though it was difficult, he was improving, and he loved that feeling.

"What's the plan for helping Kayko?" he asked.

Giac's violet eyes lit up. "We've been wanting to search the botmaker's apartment to see if he left behind evidence that the police couldn't find. Evidence that would prove that Lat is working for the Tevs and that they made up the charges against Kayko. And then it occurred to me that the Skill Show could be our chance to get in. Everyone will be at the stadium, including all the guards and officers. So while you are performing, we can sneak in and search for clues."

Albert was startled at the mention of him with the verb *performing* and had no idea what a Skill Show was, but Doz spoke before Albert could respond.

"I'm going with Giac," he said to Albert.

Sormie shook her head. "It's a risk that we don't all agree is worth taking."

"Wait," Albert said. "I don't understand. What's the Skill Show?"

The entire team stopped, and Albert could tell it was something he was supposed to know about.

"You must recall this from reading about it in your guide," Feeb said. "The four Star Strikers perform in a Skill Show between the first and second set of games. This year, the FJF have chosen to have it on Zeeno."

Albert was about to lie and say he knew all about it, when Ennjy put her hand on his arm. "You didn't read that section."

"The guide is over one thousand pages!" Albert exclaimed. "I haven't read it all and—Wait. Don't tell me it's like *The Hunger Games*. Do I have to show off my soccer skills—I mean johka skills?" Albert imagined juggling a johka ball next to Vatria and Linnd and Xutu in front of judges, and just the thought made him want to jump into his ITV and never come back.

Feeb explained: "Skill Shows have been popular in the Fŭigor System for over seven thousand years. In front of a live and a televised audience, participants display a skill that they have. You won't be offering a johka skill. The idea of a skill show is to share with the audience a skill you have that isn't related to your role as an athlete."

Albert choked. "So I have to perform in front of the entire solar system?"

"Yes," Feeb said. "You signed the contract."

"But what am I supposed to do?"

"Music. Art. Cooking. Dancing. Poetry. Anything you want."

It sounded like the talent show his middle school hosted every spring, Albert thought, except this one had scary opponents. He imagined battling Darth Vader, Jabba the Hutt, and Kylo Ren for the *Great British Bake Off* prize.

"Many in the solar system believe that Kayko betrayed us with the help of Mehk," Ennjy said. "If you perform in the Skill Show for Team Zeeno, we can build back support for our team."

"It's on Zeeno next Friday?" Albert asked.

"In the stadium."

"The stadium? You'll all be there, right?"

The Zeenods fell silent.

"Albert," Ennjy said. "We're Zeenods. We're not allowed to travel outside our zone unless we have permission. Even if we got permission, we wouldn't be able to afford tickets."

Doz slapped him on the back. "Don't worry."

"You'll be great," Beeda and Reeda agreed.

For their sakes, Albert forced himself to smile.

5.1

The door to Mehk's cell opened and the air whooshed in exactly as it had done the day before.

"Exit now. Work session." His PEER whirred.

Mehk took his place in line. He was on edge, had hardly slept. Thoughts and questions about his parents, the prisoners, the PEERs, and the possibility of escape bounced back and forth in his mind. The only thing that had kept him from bouncing off the walls last night had been the presence of his gheet nuzzling into his hand. Now it was pulsing its feet under his bem.

During the walk to the workroom, Zin could not repeat the same trick to be near Mehk, so Mehk ended up standing next to the Zeenod who was in the cell to his left. But this new Zeenod was in communication with Zin, so the discussion continued once the chanting began.

Mehk whispered that he was eager to hear more, and the Zeenod began to fill him in. "We've been working independently to study how the PEER and prison system works and to study the behaviors of the various guards and technicians. Slowly, we've been developing a plan and have already managed to steal important pieces required for that plan." The Zeenod paused. "Each of these items, whether a piece of information or an object, was obtained at great risk. Some of these attempts were met with failure and punishment. But the list is almost complete."

"Very impressive," Mehk said, trying to control his excitement. "As I see it, there are two major obstacles to an escape. The PEERs and the Z-Tev guards at the main doors. Do you have plans for both?"

"Yes. For the first, we have stolen a PEER mobile control device. These are carried by service technicians for on-site repairs and reprogramming of PEERs. The device is an old one that had been put in the recycling bin, but we're hoping it can be updated."

Ha! Best news yet! Mehk wanted to do the same happy dance he had programmed his gheet to do, but he kept his joy under control.

The Zeenod continued. "As for getting past the Z-Tev guards, a disguise is clearly needed. In addition to your coding skills, we have heard that you worked at the fabrication facility and know how to program a smartskin fabricator. We believe that with our help you could use the fabricator in the medic unit to make a smartskin mask of one of the service technicians and use it to impersonate him."

"Yes!" Mehk said eagerly. "All possible. For the fabricator, I'll need digital photographs of this service technician, of course."

"We have thought of strategies for each step," the Zeenod whispered.

"But I don't understand. Are you imagining a full breakout of everyone?"

"No," the Zeenod whispered. "That would be impossible. Only one of us can go."

Mehk was about to ask why they had chosen him when the Zeenod whispered, "Kayko is the one who must escape. Kayko is the leader of the movement to free Zeeno. Once she is free, she will work to end the occupation and free Zeeno. We want freedom for everyone on Zeeno, not just for us."

Mehk's mind whirred. He wished he had his journal to write in, to help him process all this new information. They wanted him to use his brilliant mind to carry out tasks to help Kayko escape. They wanted him to be like them, to be Zeenods working together for the good of all. But he had his own goals—to protect himself and his work and to fulfill his dream of proving that he had invented the most sophisticated robot in the solar system.

At first he was going to refuse, but as he listened he realized that he might be able to work with them...and then leave Kayko behind. Once he was out of prison, he would be free to do what he wanted.

Believe in your brilliance, he thought to himself, *you will succeed.*

"I know I can help," Mehk whispered.

6.0

It's hard for any Earthling to comprehend how time works in the Fūigor Solar System. But it seemed to Albert that telling a guy that he had to perform in a talent show and then giving him little Earth time to prepare was unfair. Just when he was feeling a tiny bit more confident about skating, he got slammed with this new pressure! All Saturday and Sunday he had just wanted to focus on his skating skills. Instead he had been distracted by trying to figure out what he could possibly offer onstage.

On Monday morning, he told Tackle his dilemma before leaving for school.

Thanksgiving is this Thursday and the Skill Show is on Friday,

Albert said. *I have less than a week to come up with a skill to share, and I have zero ideas.*

I don't like the whole idea of this show, Tackle said. *It sounds like an opportunity for another murder attempt.*

I have to do it, Albert said. *Just help me figure out what to do. I'm good at juggling a soccer ball, but the Zeenods said it should be unrelated to johka.*

Why don't you sing? Tackle suggested.

Albert laughed. *I can't sing.*

Yes you can. I've heard you over the fence when the windows were open. You know. The Ba Da Dee.

Albert laughed. *You know the Ba Da Dee?*

Um, yeah. In the summer especially. You guys get loud and you keep your windows open then.

The Ba Da Dee was a bedtime ritual that Nana had started before Albert could remember.

Tackle tried to repeat the melody of it with a howl, and Albert laughed again. *See, Tackle? You sing better than I do.*

Play your instrument, then? the dog suggested.

The clarinet? No way, Albert said. *Maybe next year I'll be good enough, but I'm a beginner.*

Tackle agreed to keep thinking. And, of course, to keep guarding.

By the time Albert arrived at school, he was feeling panicky. To make it worse, school was buzzing because the posters for the seventh-grade Winter Dance had gone up. As Albert walked into his first-period Spanish class, the students who had already arrived were debating what kind of music should be played at the dance, as if that were a real problem. Albert had real problems!

"There better be good music," Camila said. Quickly, she called up her favorite video on her phone and started dancing. A bunch of girls jumped up and joined in.

Their teacher, Señora Muñoz, walked in and started dancing, too, and everybody laughed.

Albert made his way quickly to his seat and sat down.

"No, you're not doing it right, Señora!" Camila said. She demonstrated a move and Señora Muñoz tried to copy it.

"I just smile and feel the music—that's my philosophy," the teacher said. "Who's to say what's right or wrong or good or bad? Just dance."

"I just go by the beat," another girl said.

"Play me '*Oye Como Va*' and I'll cha-cha-cha the pants off all of you," the teacher said.

"Jessica's dad is the DJ," Raul said.

"¡Qué divertido!" Señora Muñoz said.

"Why aren't you embarrassed?" Raul asked Jessica. "I'd be so embarrassed, man. I wouldn't go."

Jessica shrugged. "My dad's fun."

"What's he going to play?" Raul asked. "Waltzes?"

Everybody laughed.

"The bunny hop," another student joked.

"Maybe he'll play a cha-cha-cha," Camila said.

"Are you going to the dance, Señora Muñoz?" Jessica asked.

"Ask me in Spanish and I will answer," she said. "Pregúntame en español y te responderé."

"¿Vas al…fiesta, Señora?" Jessica asked.

"¿Vas al baile escolar?" Albert corrected Jessica without thinking and then immediately regretted it.

"Correcto, Alberto. And…¡Sí! ¡Sí! Voy al baile." The teacher cha-cha-cha-ed to her desk. "Every seventh grader needs to come.

It will be muy divertido. And tell your dad to play some Cuban music for me, Jessica!"

Trey held up his phone. "Here's a video. How to cha-cha-cha Cuban style."

The teacher motioned for everyone to sit down. "Okay. Okay. This was fun, but it's time for class. Let's review."

As class began, Albert had a hard time focusing. In the row ahead and to the right, Jessica sat back, and Albert got a glimpse of the notebook in her hand. She was doodling as she listened to the lesson, and even though it was just a doodle, it looked professional. It was a line drawing of a figure playing the sax, and you could almost hear the music just by looking at it. Albert felt the snap of envy. If Jessica were in a Skill Showcase, she could draw—or play the sax. She did both insanely well.

Camila, sitting in front of him, turned around and whispered, "Hey, could you stop bouncing?"

Albert froze, realizing his legs had been jiggling, causing his desk to tap against the back of her chair.

"Sorry," he whispered. Jealousy was definitely a shawble.

And then he flashed back to the exchange between Señora Muñoz and Camila. *Who's to say what's right or wrong or good or bad?* He thought about the one-stringed instrument that Tevs played. It sounded like a cat dying to him, but Tevs liked it. He could probably squeak out a tune on his clarinet, and if he did it with confidence they would think it was supposed to sound like that. He knew that aliens were familiar with Earth movies, which meant that they were familiar with Earth music, but there was a lot of music on Earth that sounded weird and experimental. He could pretend to play that kind of music! He didn't even have to spend time practicing between now and then. He could focus on skating.

"Yes!" Albert jumped up, forgetting where he was, and everybody turned to look at him. "Sorry," he said, and quickly sat back down.

"Alberto, where is your brain right now?" Señora Muñoz asked.

Trey beat him to the punch. "Alberto's brain went adios."

6.1

Tonight Tackle was ready for his patrol. Whatever had been lurking in Albert's driveway the other night didn't have a chance.

Albert had agreed to help him out by leaving his gate unlatched as long as Tackle promised not to leave his yard unless absolutely necessary.

Back and forth Tackle paced along the Kinneys' side of the fence. Being a good guard dog meant being patient. Back and forth. Back and forth.

Hungry, he popped into the house to get a quick munch from his bowl. But when he came back out, his ears immediately pricked. A suspicious smell.

As he walked noiselessly to the gate, he inhaled a complex set of aromas. Through the fence slats on his right, he could see that a dark, squat shape had taken up residence on the driveway right below Albert's window. Was it crouching? Was it working on something? It seemed to be facing away from him, but he couldn't be sure that the thing even had a face. Tackle inhaled again. The thing was definitely biological, or at least partly biological.

Tackle padded out of the open gate and walked around to the Kinneys' driveway.

Eyes flashed. Hands appeared.

A raccoon! Or what looked like a raccoon? Maybe it was a real raccoon. After all, it had a crust of pizza in its mouth.

Tackle barked.

The light turned on in Albert's window.

The greedy little beast and the dog stared at each for a split second. Then Tackle leaped, and the raccoon took off, diving under the shed. Tackle went crazy, barking and trying to dig.

Albert ran outside, the ground cold against his bare feet.

Raccoon! Tackle barked back to him.

Tackle! It's okay. Shhh!

The dog couldn't hear, couldn't think. All he wanted to do was get his paws on that thing.

"Tackle!" Mr. Patterson and Trey were running up the driveway now.

Tackle, Albert whispered. *Get ahold of yourself. You did good. Now calm down.*

The dog stopped. *Grrrr.* Another false alarm.

7.0

Seaweed. On Thanksgiving Day, the first argument was about seaweed.

That morning, the Kinneys had done what they usually did, although they didn't usually have Nana staying with them. They cooked in the morning and then served food at St. Francis's Family Services Center at noon and then came home and ate.

Usually their meal was fun, but this year it started with an argument.

"Erin," their mom said. "You're not putting enough food on your plate. Three green beans is not a meal."

"I asked you to buy seaweed salad twelve thousand times," Erin snapped.

"What?" Albert asked.

"Brittany said it burns calories," his mom explained with an eye roll, and then she turned to Erin. "You're skinny and you're ten! Eat some turkey!"

Erin stood up and stormed off to her room.

Nana offered to talk to her, and Albert's mom snapped at Nana, and the whole meal was ruined.

After an hour of tension, the doorbell rang, and it was Albert's turn to throw a fit. "Mom!" he said. "Don't tell me you invited the Pattersons."

"Don't start with me, Albert," his mom said, her jaw clenching. "The Pattersons have been coming for pumpkin pie every year since you and Trey started kindergarten together."

"But we don't hang out together anymore," he said. "I told you that. I begged you not to invite them. Trey and I aren't friends anymore."

The doorbell rang again.

"That's ridiculous. Albert, we're not arguing. Go tell your sister to get out here and put a smile on her face. Now." Albert's mom marched over to the front door and opened it. "Cynthia! Mark! Trey! Come in! Happy Thanksgiving!"

While Albert and Erin sat, grim-faced and silent, Trey poured out news about the special soccer tournament he was going to play in the next day and showed off the skateboard-trick videos he had posted online. Albert was dying to brag that he, too, had plans for the next day; in fact, he was going to be the star of an interplanetary television show because he was a celebrity soccer player in another solar system. But he couldn't say a word.

Then came the pie and charades, another ritual.

The Pattersons had always been weirdly good at charades, and this year Nana didn't help. She kept yelling out wrong answers. What made it worse was that Trey gloated after every round they won. Even his parents called him out on it.

It's just a game, Albert kept telling himself. And then came the final round. Albert had to act out *Poor Pete,* the title of a new sitcom, and when he turned his pockets inside out to show that he was broke, something flew out and clattered onto the coffee table.

The diamond from Jhaateez! He couldn't believe he had forgotten about it.

Trey snatched it, his eyes growing wide. "Is this what I think it is? Is this an actual diamond?" He pulled out his phone to snap a picture of it, and Albert grabbed it and stuffed it back in his pocket.

"Yeah, that's right, Trey!" Albert said. "I carry extremely valuable gemstones in my pockets all the time." He felt a nervous laugh coming on, the kind that would give him away, and then Nana spoke up.

"Enough shenanigans," Nana said. "Give us your clue, Albert. The Kinneys have to win at least one round."

Albert knew she just wanted to get back to the game, but he could have hugged her.

Although Mrs. Patterson ended up winning the point, at least Trey dropped the diamond subject, which was more important, and the Pattersons finally left.

All four of the Kinneys were quiet during the kitchen cleanup. Then, rattled by the tension of the day, the whole family retired to their separate bedrooms earlier than usual.

Albert got into bed and stared at the ceiling for a few minutes. Every muscle of his body felt tight and heavy. The air in the house felt tight and heavy. The walls and ceiling felt tight and heavy.

He was thinking about how uncomfortable the quiet of a house could be when everyone went to bed with tension still in the air. He wished he had a family who didn't argue.

And then, from out of the darkness, came a soft voice. A familiar one, although Albert hadn't heard it for a while.

"*Ba da dee*," Nana sang. Albert pictured her in the dark cave of the den, which had become her room, and knew she was smiling. "*Ba da dee*." She repeated it, the sound almost glowing like a candle.

In the dark, Albert waited to hear who would be first.

Nana repeated the phrase again, and this time Erin's voice broke through the silence to echo her tentatively. "*Ba da dee*." Erin's voice sounded really young again, Albert thought.

Nana's voice came stronger, and she expanded her song just a little. "*Ba da dee da dee deee*."

This time Erin and their mom echoed the melodic phrase. "*Ba da dee da dee deee*."

This was the ritual Tackle had mentioned hearing, the one they called the Ba Da Dee. Nana would sing a phrase and each of them would join in to repeat the phrase in the dark. Ever since Albert could remember, when his nana came to visit in the summer, she would start the Ba Da Dee when they were all in bed at night. It was something, she said, she had done with her own son, Albert's dad. To Albert, the way their voices floated from their separate rooms but joined together in unison had always sounded magical.

Nana sang louder, changing the melody and phrase again. "*Ba da dee dum dee da dee dum*." The changes each time forced each person to listen carefully.

Albert took a breath and added his voice along with his mom's and Erin's, noticing the lift he felt when their voices entwined. "*Ba da dee dum dee da dee dum.*"

"*Ba da doo ba da dee deee.*" Nana's voice was even louder, more joyful now that she knew they were with her.

"*Ba da doo ba da dee deee.*" They all sang, and Albert realized that he was smiling. He knew that his mom and sister and Nana were all smiling, too. He could feel it. The walls and the ceiling had disappeared. The Ba Da Dee is like the ahn, he thought to himself. We're connecting.

"*Ba da doo ba da dee dooooooo.*" Nana let it out with over-the-top exuberance.

Albert grinned and matched it. "*Ba da doo ba da dee—*" And on the very last *dooooooo,* the sound of Tackle howling next door came through the crack in Albert's window.

Albert laughed, and a lump formed in his throat at the same time because of the strange and simple beauty of it all.

8.0

The day after Thanksgiving, Albert woke to a text from Mrs. Patterson reminding him to walk Tackle at least once that day while they were out. The fact that Trey was playing in a lot of extra weekend soccer tournaments meant that Albert's dog-walking services were in demand. Albert was happy about that. He needed Tackle to distract him from his worries. Tonight was the night of the big Skill Show.

Assuming he didn't need to practice the clarinet, he decided to take Tackle and a soccer ball to the skate park, listen to another of Kayko's lessons, and then have a good long skate session.

When he and Tackle arrived at the skate park, it was empty and calm. The early-morning sun was just peeking up. The late-November air was energizing—the right amount of chill. *You can do a perimeter check, Tackle,* he said. *I'm going to sit here and listen to a quick lesson before I get started.*

While Tackle took off, doing what he loved to do, sniffing around to make sure that the area was safe, Albert set down his helmet and pads, put in his earbuds, and called up the next session.

Welcome to the fifth lesson: The Power of Connection. Take a few moments to focus on your breathing and to be present and we will begin.

Albert took a breath and let it out. The sound of Tackle trotting in the distance made him smile. He closed his eyes and listened as Kayko's voice washed over him like the morning sunlight.

Moments of greatness come through connection, not isolation. When you connect with others, you become more powerful than you could be alone. When you connect with others, you become stronger than you could be alone. When you connect with others, you experience more joy than you could ever experience alone.

Like the Ba Da Dee, Albert thought. He wanted to tell Kayko about his nana's ritual and then remembered where Kayko was.

Pay attention and notice this. Look for ways to accept when others offer you the chance to connect with them. And find ways to offer others the chance to connect with you.

A bell signaled the end of the lesson. Eyes closed, Albert sat still, letting the message sink in. He knew Kayko was talking about connection on the johka field and much more.

Hey, Tackle said.

Albert kept meditating.

Tackle barked, and Albert opened his eyes, about to tell the dog to give him some space, but standing in front of him with a smile on her face was Jessica Atwater, board in hand.

"Sorry—were you sleeping?" she asked.

He straightened up, his face hot. "No—no. Just thinking. I came to get some skating in."

"Yeah," she said. "Great minds think alike." She held out her palm to Tackle and the dog sniffed his hello. She leaned in and rubbed him behind his ears.

See, Tackle said. *She's nice. I don't think she bites.*

Albert was happy to see her and also wished she hadn't arrived. That self-conscious part of him was rising up, the part of him that started losing confidence before even trying.

Take a breath, dude, Tackle said. *I can smell your fear.*

"Looks like we have the place to ourselves," Jessica said.

"I figured no one would be here this early," he said.

"Sorry to disappoint," she said, and laughed.

He began to stammer.

She smiled. "It's okay, Albert. I know what you mean. How was Thanksgiving?"

Keep talking, dude, Tackle said. *You're doing great.*

"Normal," he said. "If your Thanksgiving involves seaweed-salad fights and bad charades. How about yours?"

She laughed. "Normal, if your Thanksgiving involves musical chairs and ghost stories. I bet my family is weirder than yours." After giving Tackle a belly rub, she adjusted her helmet and pads.

Albert put his on. He had been feeling self-conscious about bringing a helmet and pads and was happy to see hers.

"Whenever I'm trying a new trick for the first time, I suit up," she said. "This stuff actually helps me take more risks. I hold myself back if I'm worried about wiping out."

He held up his cast. "I should be wearing full-body armor all the time."

She smiled. "How is your falling going?"

"Better," he said.

And then she noticed the soccer ball and gave him a look.

"Yeah," he said. "I was thinking of kicking the ball around."

"On skates?"

He smiled.

"That's insane," she said.

She took off on her board, and Tackle started running around, too, exploring the park. She started warming up, carving around the park's big bowl.

Albert watched with admiration until she called out, "Not fair, Kinney. You can't sit there and watch."

He felt his face grow hotter. "I wasn't watching."

"Liar."

Just skate, dude, Tackle barked.

Albert started skating. It was good. He was nervous, but it was good.

"You've definitely improved," Jessica said as she rolled past him. "Any big plans for tonight?"

I'm performing in Fŭigor's Got Talent on another planet, Albert wanted to say. Instead he just smiled and said, "No. What about you?"

"Homework," she said from the deck. And then she skated down and back up to the deck on the other side.

"Wait," he said. "Can you teach me how to skate down? I swear I'll get you a pound of chocolate if you can teach me that. Good chocolate. Gourmet chocolate."

She laughed. "You want to learn how to drop in?"

"Yeah." He felt his face grow hot, but he pushed on. "When I'm standing up there looking down, I freak out."

She grabbed her board and they met on the deck. "Everybody always makes the same mistake," she said. "When you're going down, the impulse is to jolt back, which is exactly the opposite of what you need to do. You actually need to lean in. Keep your knees slightly bent. Don't look where you're at, look where you want to go. Come on."

You can do it, Tackle barked. He was waiting on the side, tongue hanging out, tail wagging. *You got this, Albert.*

Albert glanced at the slope directly under him. "But if I lean in, I'll face-plant or land on my head."

"Nope," Jessica argued. "If you lean in and trust it, you'll glide down. If you jolt back, you'll land back on your wrist, and you'll bust it again."

She demonstrated again, gliding down and then gliding up the other side and hopping up onto the deck on that side, as Tackle barked approval.

"Okay," Albert called over to her. "I'm going to do it."

"Don't look down," she said. "Look over here. At me."

The morning sun was casting gold light on her face. Looking at her, he bent his knees, leaned in, and let gravity take him. Down he went, and the exhilaration hit immediately. A beautiful, liberating thrill.

Woohoo! Tackle was barking.

And then Albert was gliding up the other side, fast, and he

wasn't sure how to—*BAM!* He crashed into Jessica, and they both
went down.

"Oh my God. I'm so sorry," he said, untangling himself. "Are
you okay?"

She was already picking herself up and offering a fist bump.

8.1

After lights went out each night, items were passed from cell to
cell via the vents until they reached the botmaker's cell:

an old PEER mobile control device

a series of PEER protocol codes written on a napkin

a thin, flat camera

a password written on a candy wrapper

a fragment of a mirror

a syringe

a bottle of tranquilizer fluid

a battery

a pack of Z-Tev chewing gum

Mehk was told that he could keep the items hidden in the
small space just below the vent opening between the thick, forti-
fied walls. Why? Because Zeenods had discovered that the walls

had been built with an alloy that the PEER surveillance cameras couldn't penetrate. Ha! A serious mistake that Mehk would not have made if he had designed the place.

Mehk's first step was to take apart the PEER mobile control device. As the Zeenod had said, the device was old. If Mehk could update its system with the new codes a clever Zeenod spy had managed to get, they could use the device to gain temporary control over any individual PEER. For six nights Mehk worked on it, but there was only way to find out if he had succeeded.

Tonight would be the night to try using it to disable his PEER so he could photograph the service technician's face for the mask. The risky operation would require the help of the Zeenod next door.

After lights went out, Mehk hummed the tune they had agreed would be the code to begin. A few seconds later, the Zeenod's voice repeated the hum.

While continuing to sing, they each prepared by retrieving several items from the vent. Mehk took the gum and the fragment of mirror. The Zeenod took the control device. After chewing the gum, Mehk used it to stick the fragment of mirror on the ceiling in front of the door. Mehk's final step was to place his gheet on his ankle and cover it carefully with his pants' leg.

When he was ready, he stopped singing.

The Zeenod next door stopped, too.

Now or never. Mehk walked over and pounded against his cell door.

Immediately the lights turned on, the door opened, and his PEER flew into his cell. "Behavior change. PEER on alert," the PEER said as the door locked behind it.

If Mehk had been holding the control device, the PEER would

have detected it immediately. This was where the second Zeenod came in. Through the vent, the other Zeenod pointed the control device up at the mirrored fragment and activated a signal. The infrared signal bounced off the mirror and entered the optical port on top of the PEER's body.

Mehk held his breath. Although he couldn't see the Zeenod peeking through the vent, he could sense that he, too, was holding his breath. The signal was supposed to send a series of commands to the PEER's software program to disable the PEER's response protocol. This would keep it from responding to any threatening behavior changes or sending security alerts to the prison's command center.

In the next second, red lights on the PEER's body began to flash. "Disabling response protocol," the drone said, and hovered in place.

Mehk stared at it. To make sure it worked, he'd have to test it, do something that could cause it to fire its weapon or a net. He took a deep breath, and then he gritted his teeth and reached up to touch the underbelly of the hovering PEER. No response. No alerts.

Mehk's heart leaped. Great success!

The Zeenod watching from the vent sent the second signal to the PEER's optical port. Again a series of the lights flashed and the PEER sent a request to the command center.

"Requesting PEER service technician," the PEER said.

Mehk grinned. Brilliant! Quickly, he removed the mirror and gum from the ceiling and returned them to the vent, and then he withdrew the small, flat camera. At that exact moment, his hand brushed against the hand of the Zeenod who was returning the control device. Neither dared to speak.

Mehk sat on his bed and slipped the camera under his thigh.

After thirty tense seconds, the door buzzed open and the

service technician walked in with a weapon drawn and his tools in his backpack, as usual. Mehk got his first look at the Z-Tev. He had the usual Tev markings on his face and the eye in the back of his head—something that the Zeenods worried would be difficult for Mehk to re-create. He also had reddish stains on his teeth from smoking Tev cigars, Mehk noted.

"Hands where I can see them," the technician said.

Putting his palms up on his thighs, Mehk said, "Of course."

Without saying a word, the technician swiped his security badge across an optical port on the side of the drone and it lowered into his hands. Then he used his mobile control device to run a diagnostic using the top optical port. After several seconds, the Z-Tev pulled his communication device from his belt, typed in his password, and then used a voice command to send a message to the command center. "Rebooting PEER. No assistance needed."

"I admire the idea behind the PEERs," Mehk said.

The technician gave him a surprised glance. He hadn't been expecting small talk.

"I may be a prisoner," Mehk said with a shrug. "But I am a robotics engineer first. And I think the concept of using personal security drones is brilliant."

The Z-Tev grunted.

"Were you involved in designing the initial program?" Mehk asked. "If so, the software—"

"Close your mouth." The Z-Tev gave him a look and then focused back on the drone. "If you think you can trick me into giving you any information, you're—"

Keeping his hands on his knees, Mehk jiggled his leg, causing his gheet to drop to the floor. He tapped it with his foot, and it began scuttling across the floor.

"Gheet!" Mehk said, faking a grimace.

"Where?" The technician tensed and then saw the gheet and jumped into action to try to kill it. Mehk almost laughed at the predictability of the response. Tevs and Z-Tevs hated gheets as much as they hated yits.

While the technician stomped around like a fool, chasing after Mehk's nimble and swiftly moving robotic pet, Mehk secretly pulled the slim camera out from under his leg, angled it up, took a quick series of photographs, and then tucked it under his blanket.

The battle was still going on. With swiftly precise movements, the gheet escaped each stomp of the stranger's foot and then finally scampered toward Mehk. Pretending disgust, Mehk stepped on it, knowing just the right way to turn it off without damaging it. When he lifted his foot and the thing looked dead, the technician relaxed.

"Shall I flush it down the toilet?" Mehk asked. "Or would you like to?"

The Z-Tev grunted. "You do it."

Mehk picked up his beloved pet by one leg, its other seven dangling, and carried it over to the toilet. With his back and his bem blocking the view, Mehk easily slipped the gheet up one sleeve while pretending to flush it.

"This place is disgusting," Mehk said. "Where there's one gheet there's probably another."

The technician did exactly what Mehk thought he would do. He took the PEER with him and stepped out of the cell. Using his control device, he rebooted the PEER, which would mean the response protocol would become operational again. That was fine. Mehk's work was done.

The drone blinked on, docked in its usual position outside

the cell door, and confirmed, "Reboot successful. All systems are functioning normally."

Once again, the Z-Tev pulled his communication device from his belt, typed in his password, and then used a voice command to send his second message to the command center. "PEER and prisoner secure. No assistance required."

The cell door slammed shut.

Mehk waited a few seconds, listening to the retreating footsteps of the technician. When he was sure it was safe, he slipped the camera back into the vent and climbed into bed. The Zeenod next door had probably heard that all had gone as well as they had hoped, but Mehk chanted the code they had agreed he would sing to signal success.

"Our work is done. We look forward to a better day."

After a few seconds, he heard the Zeenod sing the same words to the Zeenod in the cell next to him. On and on the chant was shared.

Mehk pulled his gheet out of his sleeve, activated it, and gave its hairy head an affectionate pat.

8.2

At midnight, Albert changed into jeans and a T-shirt, put his Z-da around his neck, grabbed his coat, and crept outside. Tackle was waiting and jumped up, paws on fence to get a good look through the slats. It was time to leave for the Skill Show.

You forgetting something? the dog asked.

Albert checked for his Z-da. *No.*

Aren't you playing tonight?

The clarinet! Albert couldn't believe he had forgotten. He ran back for it and then returned.

Okay. Thanks. Wish me luck. Albert initiated the szoŭ, waiting for the now-familiar sensation of being beamed up—the prickle that started on the top of his head.

Tackle had been waiting for this moment. In fact, for ages he had been secretly knocking up against a section of the fence behind their shed to create an opening. Now he bolted through and came running up the Kinneys' driveway.

No, Tackle. No. You can't come.

I'm coming. He put his paws on Albert's chest and they were both beamed up.

When the dog unexpectedly appeared in the ITV, Unit D merely nodded and blinked. "Data in my hard drive indicates that this is the Earth canine known as Tackle. I did not know Tackle would be arriving with you."

Albert nodded and crouched down to reassure the dog. "Yep. This is Tackle. Sorry about the last-minute decision, but he's coming with me."

Recovered from the szoŭ, Tackle began sniffing the robot and then the entire ITV. After he was done, the dog was scanned and readied for the environment. On Albert's suggestion, Tackle was also given a language-translation implant so that he could understand the many languages they would encounter. Tackle was delighted.

When they landed on Zeeno, a part of the ritual was a procession from the ITV to the entrance of the stadium, where the fans who had paid extra could get a closer glimpse of the celebrities. Vatria and Xutu were being swarmed by Tevs, Z-Tevs, Sñektis, R'tinuks, Gaböqs, and Yurbs. Linnd was surrounded by Jhaateezians, Liötians, Fetrs, and Manams.

At first Albert was afraid that no one would cheer him. After all, the Zeenods from the zones couldn't afford to come, and Zeenods who had escaped from Zeeno long ago and had made their homes on other planets were hesitant to ever return to Zeeno. The fact that Zeenods from other planets had shown up at the last johka game had been a shock. On top of that, Kayko's arrest could have turned off whatever fans they did have.

But as soon as Albert and Tackle stepped out of their ITV, the crowd went wild. Some Zeenods from afar had come! Not many, but some. And all the fans of Linnd and the Jhaateezians seemed to love the Earthlings, too. Even some of the Gaböqs and Yurbs cheered on Tackle. Fans stopped them for photos and holo-autographs and tossed them gifts—small johka balls that changed colors and various candies and treats. And along the way, supporters also tossed up handfuls of tiny gold dots that sparkled and disappeared over their heads like strange miniature fireworks.

We're famous, Albert said.

It's crazy, Tackle said uneasily. It was this kind of situation—so many different life-forms jostling to get close to Albert—that set Tackle on edge.

President Lat had provided security teams to walk with each Star Striker, and that helped. The team walking with Albert carried a basket into which Albert could put all the gifts and candies after catching them. Tackle tried his best to sniff for danger, but it was impossible for his attention to be everywhere at once.

And it was in the next moment that the same Z-Tev guard who was carrying the basket secretly slipped a wrapped box from his own pack into Albert's basket. Albert and Tackle didn't have a clue. They had entered the gates and were being told they'd be going in separate directions. Tackle growled and put up such a fight, the event officials wanted to lock him back up in the ITV.

Calm down, Tackle, Albert said. *I know you want to protect me, but you won't be any help in the ITV.*

As Tackle was whisked away to the audience section, Albert was led through a series of curtained tunnels to a preparation room that was bustling with activity. Antiglare powder was applied to his face and glistening oil was applied to his hair.

Albert noticed the wrapped box on the top of the basket and brightened. A signature on the large tag was clearly visible: Lightning Lee! He plucked it out.

Dear Albert, may you perform well and bring honor to all Zeenods. This is not candy. This is a special herbal treat to calm nerves. Please enjoy this with my best wishes. —Lee.

Lightning Lee *is* here, Albert thought with excitement. Lee had been there at the last game at just the right time to give him the encouragement he needed to play. Here was Lee again, if not in person, then at least in thought—and with some practical help!

Albert opened the box to find six neatly wrapped treats, like candy balls. He took one out and was about to unwrap it when a Zhidorian FJF official arrived to lead him onstage.

Albert tucked the treat in his pocket, picked up his clarinet case, and followed the Zhidorian through another curtained tunnel to a boxlike stage that had been erected on the stadium field.

When he stepped onstage with his clarinet case in hand, he was surprised to see that his three competitors, Linnd, Xutu, and Vatria, were decked out in what Nana would call their Sunday best, already sitting in their official chairs—thrones, really. Albert had assumed he was supposed to wear his johka uniform and now felt ridiculous.

A Z-Tev news crew swooped in with President Lat. "Albert Kinney, welcome!" the president said with a smile. "We'd like to do a preshow appearance. I've prepared a little speech, which will appear on the teleprompter. Just read the words and you'll be fine."

Albert was placed in front of the crew, and the cameras flicked on.

"We're here with Star Striker Albert Kinney. What do you have to say?"

Words began to scroll on a screen to the right of the camera.

Totally unprepared, Albert began reading. "Thank you to the Fŭigor Johka Federation, to the four planets in the tournament, and, especially to Zeeno, host of the Skill Show." More words scrolled on. "I and my Zeenod teammates are grateful for the opportunity to continue playing in the tournament. We accept the sad truth that our own tactician, Kayko Tusq, betrayed us—" Albert froze. He couldn't believe he had just read that! He hadn't been paying attention. He had been tricked into saying something he didn't believe!

President Lat nodded for Albert to continue, but Albert couldn't speak.

President Lat took over and read the last line. "Our team will strive to move forward, upholding the rules and spirit of the beautiful game."

Burning with shame, Albert stumbled back to his seat. He should have spoken up to take back what he had said about Kayko. He had made a terrible mistake before the show had even started.

A director ran through the guidelines, of which Albert didn't hear a single word. He was, in fact, having trouble breathing.

Nothing was as Albert had expected. There was no live audience. Surrounded by four walls, the stage was like a small box with just enough room inside to fit the four thrones and the host. It was suffocating, except for the fact that there was no ceiling suspended above them. The bright moon of Zeeno shining in the dark sky helped a little.

After light and sound checks, the stage lights went off, an announcement for the cameras was given, and then a transformation began. With a *whirr,* the four walls of the stage folded down and the full stadium was revealed. The stage was on one end of the field, and the stands were full of spectators.

Unlike the game shows that Albert knew from television on Earth, there was no music, no applause, no flashing lights.

As the audience sat in silence, the Zhidorian host began to speak, a single spotlight illuminating their two heads. Albert and the other Star Strikers were in total darkness.

"Welcome to the Skill Show, broadcast live from Zeeno. Our participants tonight are this year's Johka Tournament Star Strikers, Xutu Nhi, Linnd Na, Vatria Skell, and Albert Kinney."

As the players were announced, blinding lights came up on their thrones and their johkadin posters were projected behind them.

Again, the crowd was silent. Albert looked into the light and suddenly felt his otherness. To know that you are about to be judged by those who know nothing about you or your culture or your experience is frightening and lonely. The other Star Strikers had friends and family in the audience. Some Zeenods were present, but his Zeenod teammates, unable to afford tickets, weren't there. He wished Tackle had been invited to sit next to him on the stage, rather than out there where Albert couldn't see him. He wished he could see Lightning Lee. He hadn't even been told that Lee would be there.

"Our Star Strikers have each brought a special guest from their home planet." The host gestured to the front row of the audience and introduced Xutu's teacher, Vatria's grandfather, and Linnd's sister, who each stood, turned to the audience, and bowed. The Star Strikers were too blinded by the stage lights to see them, but a camera beamed close-ups of them onto the huge screens on the sides of the stage. And then Tackle's name was called.

"Many saw this Earth dog rush onto the field in the attempt to save his human companion," the host said. "We are honored that he is here tonight."

On one of the screens, Albert watched his canine friend. Like Albert, the dog wasn't sure what to do. He barked a tentative greeting to the audience that was met with silence and then gave Albert an apologetic look and sat awkwardly in his chair.

"Our first offering," the host said, "is from Xutu Nhi. Xutu is from planet Yurb and is playing in this year's tournament for planet Gaböq."

The stage was plunged into darkness, and then one spotlight came up as the rhinolike Xutu walked forward. His two front limbs, Albert had learned, were legs, not arms, and the way the tripod walked was mesmerizing. Rising up from the pit below the stage was a boulder, about the size of a small Earth car. Xutu kept his single rear leg and his right front leg planted on the ground while he lifted his left front leg and struck the boulder over and over with his bare hooflike foot, grunting with each blow. As he began to hack away, chunks of rock thudded to the floor.

Albert tried to imagine what would happen if he slammed his own foot—hard—against a rock, but the feet of Yurbs and Gabōqs were like axes with two sharp points that became hard as steel when extended. Pinchers, tucked inside the main shaft, extended only when fine motor movements were needed.

As Xutu's movements and grunts grew faster, dust filled the stage. After another thirty seconds, Xutu rose up onto his rear leg so that he could employ both front feet, and he went into high gear, so fast it struck Albert as comical. Still, the audience was silent, attentive. Faster and faster Xutu pounded, and now the debris was flying and dust was filling the air. Albert looked on, confused. He didn't see the point or the skill in hacking a rock to pieces. After another twenty seconds, Xutu was completely engulfed in a cloud of dust—still the sound of his hammering continued, and then, quite suddenly, he stepped back from the boulder with a heavy thump and waited. The dust settled.

There, on the stage where the ugly hunk of rock had stood, was a sculpture of a delicate alien flower. Gorgeous, realistic—like something that would be on display in the best art museum on Earth.

Albert's throat went dry. The audience remained silent, and Xutu's wide slash of a mouth broke into a fierce smile as he, clearly accustomed to the lack of applause, blinked all three of his eyes and took his seat.

"Thank you, Xutu Nhi." The host gestured as Xutu returned to his throne on the stage.

From where Albert sat, he couldn't see Linnd's reaction to Xutu, but he could see Vatria, and she had the same fierce determination on her face that she had on the johka field.

Shaken, Albert became angry with himself for having taken this whole thing so lightly. He had assumed the show was supposed to be fun and that there was no need for him to practice. Too late, he was flooded with regret and anger.

"And now, introducing Linnd Na from planet Liöt. On the johka field, she is playing for planet Jhaateez."

As Linnd walked into the spotlight, she nodded to a stagehand, who flicked on a strange high-tech laser projector that beamed thirty strings of evenly spaced red lasers in the air like a floating harp. With intense focus, Linnd began to pluck the strings of light, first with her hands. The music she made with this harp was complicated and precise. And then she began a kind of flapping motion with her arms, which enabled her sailwings to lift her slightly off the ground. This allowed her to use both feet to pluck the strings as well as her hands when they flapped forward. The melody became faster and even more complex. It was like watching a human-sized hummingbird play Mozart with its feet and wings. When she was done, Albert was almost dizzy.

Exhausted but pleased, Linnd bowed and sat down.

Albert tried to tell himself that none of this mattered. It didn't matter how great the other players were. It didn't matter that he hadn't even bothered to practice. What mattered was that Kayko was in prison and Giac and Doz were using this distraction to sneak into Mehk's apartment to look for information that might help.

"Next is Vatria Skell from planet Sñekti." The host gestured to Albert's fiercest competitor.

Albert could feel willpower emanating from Vatria. As she walked to the center of the stage, the eye in the back of her head shifted from Xutu, to Linnd, and then to Albert.

The lights dimmed, and for a few seconds she did nothing other than tremble. Her outfit was short-sleeved, and Albert wondered if she was shivering from cold.

Mr. Sam had taught Albert that the best way to handle a performance was to wish the other musicians well and to let yourself be inspired by them instead of poisoning yourself with toxic envy—and that had worked when Albert was performing in the school band concert. He tried now, but he couldn't manage to rise above his anxiety, and he found himself hoping that Vatria would fail.

In the next few seconds, Vatria's spine straightened, and then the lights went off completely and she began to glow. Or rather light up. Speckles of light raced over her arms and legs and face. And then the pattern shifted. Albert had remembered reading that Tevs and Sñektis were bioluminescent, and he knew that this meant that they glowed under certain conditions, like fireflies do at night or like jellyfish do underwater. But he'd had no idea that they could control it in this extraordinary way. Vatria seemed to be programmed like a complex computerized projector. In the dark, her body disappeared and all the audience could see was a mechanical-looking display of colors and patterns on the stage.

When her routine was done, the lights came back up and Vatria bowed. As she returned to her throne, she refused to look at any of them.

"And, finally, we welcome the Star Striker for Zeeno: Albert Kinney."

As the spotlight hit the stage, Albert wished he had eaten Lee's nerve-calming gift, which lay in his pocket. His heart was racing out of control. Somehow he was supposed to walk into the spotlight and start playing. He stood up and reached down for his case, only to find that it was gone. Someone had taken it! Someone wanted him to fail.

The audience waited. Even though he knew the sky was above him, it felt as if a weight above him were growing heavier and heavier, slowly lowering toward him.

The host beckoned for him to come forward. Unable to see the audience, unable to see Tackle, unable to see anything but a hot white glare, Albert stepped into the spotlight. A voice inside his head was telling him to run. Another voice was telling him to stay calm and do something, do anything.

And then from the darkness came a movement.

Tackle bounded onto the stage. Nails clicking on the hard surface, he ran to Albert, turned to face the audience, and stood by his side.

The sudden presence of his friend, the sound of his panting, the familiar smell of him, were like a lifeline. *My clarinet is gone,* Albert whispered.

I know, the dog said. *Do something else. Just sing.*

Albert stood motionless, except for the banging of his heart inside his chest.

Happy Birthday, Tackle said. *Ba Da Dee, whatever.*

The distance between this moment and the moment in which Albert could imagine doing something seemed as far as the distance between Earth and Zeeno. And then an image came to him. He pictured himself in his bed in the dark. He could almost hear the sound of Nana's voice coming through the silence.

"*Ba da dee,*" Albert sang. He sounded like a kindergartener.

The place was silent. They had no idea what he was trying to do.

But Tackle sat on his hind legs and howled softly. The sound burned warmly through the silence, and Albert felt something inside him shift. The heaviness lifted a little. He looked out at the sea of darkness, sensing the waiting presence of each separate soul in each separate seat. What his opponents had done before him had been impressive but cold. He needed to do the opposite.

Okay, Nana, he thought. I can't turn back now. He took a breath and sang louder, "*Ba da dee.*" And then he gestured for the audience to sing along, not sure if they would understand.

"*Ba da dee.*" A small number of audience members sang very tentatively. Probably those brave Zeenods from other planets who had taken the risk to come. Alien giggles followed.

He smiled and nodded and sang again and gestured again for them to sing.

This time more of the audience sang. "*Ba da dee.*"

And just like that, energy stirred. Albert felt it. It was a kind of lifting up.

He changed the phrase slightly and sang again. The audience response sent a chill up his spine. They were singing it back.

Albert sang louder, altering the melody. "*Ba da da dee deeeeeee.*"

"*Ba da da dee deeeeeee,*" the audience repeated.

Joyfully, Albert invented another phrase and they repeated it.

Thousands of voices coming from so many individuals from so many different planets at the same time in the same place on the same pitch—it was electrifying. The entire stadium—all these different species of beings—was connecting.

Kayko's words came to him. *Moments of greatness come through connection, not isolation.*

With increasing energy, Albert and the audience continued. The host, standing to Albert's right, was staring at Albert with surprise, and Albert was realizing what a new experience this was for them. Yes, at johka games the Zeenods sang their anthem together and the Jhaateezians sang their anthem together and the Gabōqs sang their anthem together and the Tevs sang their anthem together, each in their own language; but maybe the species of the Fŭigor Solar System had never sung together in the same language, the wordless language of collective joy. Maybe Albert was actually making something new happen.

He kept going, imagining everyone watching and listening and singing, not just in the stadium, but all over the solar system; Ennjy and the team in Zone 3 and Kayko in prison, everyone singing together.

Then he sang a new phrase, and this time he turned to bring in the voices of his opponents, all watching from their thrones.

Linnd stood and joined in.

Xutu and Vatria sat like statues, as if afraid that to participate would harm their status.

There's no trick, Albert tried to say with his smile, *it's just an invitation to connect.* And then he turned back to face the audience, feeling a rush of affection coming from the unseen mass. He kept it going until the experience felt complete, and then he sang one final melodic line and they all joined in, Tackle howling, too.

Complete silence followed.

Elated, Albert tried to keep his cool. He bowed. *Thank you, Nana,* he thought. Then he crouched down and pulled the dog in for a hug. *Thank you, Tackle.*

I just got you started, Tackle said. *You did the rest.*

The host gestured to the screens, which jumped to a view of a voting page. With lightning speed, Albert saw the votes rack up next to his name.

"The winner is Albert Kinney...."

It was all so strange. What Vatria and Xutu and Linnd had done took much more skill than what he had done. Yet what had happened with him and the audience was special. It was amazing.

As Albert was preparing to leave, a Zhidorian assistant hustled over with a genuinely puzzled expression on one of their faces, holding Albert's clarinet case in one tentacled hand. "You must have left this in the preparation room."

He hadn't. He had set it right by this throne, but there was no time to investigate what had happened. More fans now wanted to see and photograph and touch Albert and Tackle as they returned to the ITV.

As soon as their vehicle took off, Unit D received a request to open a communication from Ennjy. Albert flashed back to the statement he had made in the televised interview about believing that Kayko was guilty. His high spirits plunged. Zeenods everywhere must have seen that interview and must hate him for it.

"I'm sorry," Albert blurted out. "I didn't know what to do. The president gave me words to say and I should have refused to say them."

Ennjy's face softened. "Albert, we understand. The pain on your face made it clear that you didn't believe what you were saying. Zeenods understand what it means to be forced by the government to support Z-Tevs and Tevs. We are learning more and more that we cannot trust Telda Lat. You performed well, Albert. Your song was extraordinary."

Albert told her about the sabotaging of his instrument and how he had to improvise. "I felt the ahn even though none of you were there," he said.

Ennjy's eyes turned from violet to gold. "We are honored to have you as our Star Striker."

Standing next to him, Tackle shook out his muscles.

"Tackle helped," Albert said.

The dog sat up and put on his most charming face, and Albert laughed.

"Our thanks to both of you," Ennjy said. "And I can share good news with you about Doz and Giac. Thanks to Giac's ingenuity, they located a secret compartment in Mehk's apartment and have found two devices, which we believe will have the information we need to free Kayko. The files are encrypted and Giac will need time to decode, but we are hopeful."

This was good news indeed. Albert felt the release first in his shoulders.

She leaned in. "We want you to know that we will do everything we can to keep you safe, Albert. Giac will be regularly checking the ITV and Unit D for signs of sabotage; she has the passcodes and will guard them carefully."

"Thank you," Albert said.

When the call ended, he and Tackle celebrated with a hug and then enjoyed smoothies and happily retreated into hibernation.

Upon waking, they returned home to the quiet of a November night in Silver Spring, Maryland, on planet Earth. After a hushed goodbye, Tackle waited to make sure Albert walked in safely before trotting to the Pattersons' backyard and entering his house through his dog door.

As Albert tiptoed through the living room, hands in his pockets, his mind replayed the evening. Even though he was proud that he'd managed to do something right tonight, he recognized that his two friends had risked their lives to try to get evidence to free Kayko, and he hoped that whatever they had obtained would be the proof they needed. And then, just as he was about to head to his bedroom, he hesitated, realizing that his fingers had closed around the wrapped treat from Lee in his pocket. This time, he hadn't even intended to bring something from Zeeno back to Earth! He pulled it out and stopped. Something wasn't right. Why hadn't Lee talked directly to Albert? Was it possible that Lee hadn't been there? Hadn't sent this gift?

Cautiously Albert sniffed it. It didn't smell bad, but maybe he should get Tackle to smell it. Careful not to make a sound, he tiptoed back outside. Often, Tackle heard him and rushed out, but he was either busy eating or already asleep. Albert hesitated. Too spooked to bring the thing back inside, he lifted the lid of their trash can and gently set the thing on top of the bags that were already in the can. There. He'd deal with it in the morning.

On his way to his room, he noticed that the door to Nana's room was ajar. He peeked in and saw her sleeping. Good old Nana. In a big way, she had saved him tonight. Without her Ba Da Dee, he didn't know what he would have done.

He tiptoed into the den, found a piece of paper and pencil on the desk, and wrote her a note.

Love you, Nana.

9.0

Tackle's bark woke him up. *Look out your window, Albert.*

Albert got out of bed. His window faced the driveway, and he saw it immediately—a dead raccoon a few feet away from their tipped garbage can. He could hear sounds from his mom's room. She was just waking up. The smell wafting from the kitchen told him that his nana was already up and making breakfast. He threw on some clothes and ran outside. Tackle was behind the Pattersons' gate, a worried look on his face.

What does it mean, Albert?

Albert stared at the stiffened corpse. *The gift. It was a trick. It wasn't from Lee.*

What?

Albert explained the treat and how he had put it in the gar-bage can.

It must have been poisoned. Tackle sniffed the air. *I should have smelled that in your pocket last night! That's my job!*

Maybe it's something you can't smell, Tackle. Don't beat yourself up. I should have been suspicious right away. I shouldn't have brought it back to Earth. What if you had eaten it?

Tackle gave him a look. *I'm not that stupid. Tell the team as soon as you get to practice today,* Tackle said. *This was another murder attempt.*

Albert felt his face grow hot. *I can't. I'm not supposed to bring Füigor items to Earth without permission.*

Tackle was silent.

I guess we both need to be extra vigilant, Albert finally said.

Tackle nodded. *I'm on it.*

Nana came out to see what the commotion was about, followed closely by Albert's mom, who freaked out, thinking the raccoon had died of rabies, and called animal control to have it removed.

Albert tried to shake off what had happened and knew that the best antidote was to grab his ball and his skates and go to the park. After a quick breakfast, he got his skates and went to the base-ment to pump up his soccer ball, which had gone flat. The pump wasn't in the main playroom, so he turned the corner and went through the doorway that led into a walk-in storage closet. As he was looking there, he heard a sound like metal rubbing on metal, and then a moment later he heard the *pat pat* of what sounded like very slow footsteps on the tile part of the playroom floor.

He froze behind the door. After a few seconds, he heard it again: *pat…pat.* Someone was in the playroom. A shiver went up his spine. If it were Nana, or his mom, or Erin, they would have called out to him. Either someone was hiding there when he came down or someone had just materialized there. His mind began racing. What if someone had tried to kill him with that "treat" and was spying on him and knew that the raccoon had died instead of him?

Heart pounding, Albert listened, hearing the innocent sounds of his mom and nana talking and cooking above him in the kitchen. He made a pact with himself. If an alien was here to kill him, he would break the secrecy vow and scream like a maniac.

Pat…pat… there it was again! And then the sound of something tipping over. Albert knew exactly what it was. The stack of games by the beanbag chair in the center of the playroom. If Albert made a break for it and ran fast, he might be able to run up the stairs before the thing could even blink.

He reached for the first thing he could find, which was a cardboard box of his sister's old princess costumes. He held the box in front of him like a shield, and then he opened the door and burst out. Yelling, he ran forward, threw the box at the figure in front of him, and turned to run up the stairs.

"Albert!" a familiar voice yelled.

Albert stopped and turned.

Erin was standing in a pile of pastel-pink costumes. "Why did you do that?"

"I thought you were an…intruder," Albert said. "You know. Like a thief."

"A thief who wants to steal playroom stuff?" She bent down and picked up her cell phone, which she had dropped. "What the heck, Albert! That's so weird."

"*You're* weird. Why were you spying on me?"

Their mom called down. "Everything all right?"

"Yes!" they both yelled.

"I wasn't spying on you, Albert," Erin said softly.

"What were you doing?"

An embarrassed look came over her face. "I was trying to get back upstairs before you saw me."

"Why?" He looked at her phone. "Who were you calling? Were you calling a boy or something?"

"No." She punched him. "Sometimes I just come down here."

"Before anybody wakes up?" Albert asked, and then he noticed the unzipped doorway of her old fairy-tale play tent, and he looked more carefully at his little sister. Standing there in her orange pajamas and the fuzzy purple socks that Nana had knitted, she looked younger and smaller than usual. Her hair was a mess and her eyes were puffy, as if she had been crying.

"What's wrong?" he asked.

"Nothing," she lied, and crouched down to restack the games she had knocked over.

He started picking up the costumes and putting them back in the box. "Sorry about the box attack. I panicked."

"You tried to kill me with little pink dresses," Erin said, and smiled.

Albert laughed. "Yeah. Well. Now I'm glad I wasn't standing next to an ax."

"What did you come down for, anyway?" she asked.

"Soccer ball pump," he said.

"I'll tell you where it is if you don't make fun of me."

"I won't make fun of you."

She pointed to a large gray tub in the corner. Sticking out of it were tennis rackets and a baseball bat. He had looked there, but the pump was in the bottom.

"Thanks," he said, and she crawled back in her old tent and from there watched him pump up the ball.

"Having a place to hang out when you're feeling bad is not anything to be embarrassed about, Erin. Sometimes when I'm feeling bad I sneak over to the Pattersons' yard and just hang out with Tackle."

"Seriously?" she asked.

He nodded. "It's comforting."

She was silent for a few seconds, and then she held up her phone, the phone she was supposed to use for emergency purposes only. "Don't tell Mom, but Brittany showed me how to set up a secret Instagram account."

This was serious. Albert set the ball down and walked over to the tent. Trying to keep it light, he joked: "I get it. Now you're addicted to cute cat photos."

He thought she'd laugh, but when she looked up, her eyes were wet.

"What's wrong?"

"Now I just see all her posts." She handed Albert the phone.

He scrolled through.

Brittany doing the splits on the balance beam, arms up, dazzling smile. Brittany in the middle of a flip, toes pointed, knees together. Brittany flying off the uneven bars, arms outstretched as gracefully as a bird. Brittany posing in a new gymnastics outfit, medals around her neck. Close-up of Brittany wearing sparkly eye makeup.

"She's perfect!" Erin cried. "She's a machine."

"She isn't perfect. Everybody has shawbles," Albert said.

"What?" Erin gave him a look. "What's a shawble?"

Albert's face reddened and he said quickly, "I meant flaws or

126

issues or challenges, you know. She just *seems* perfect. This is why Mom didn't want you to spend time looking at this stuff. It'll drive you crazy."

"But if I don't, I'm missing out," Erin said. "Everybody does it. And Brittany gets mad if I don't like and comment on everything."

"We need to throw a box over Brittany's head," Albert said.

Erin laughed and then looked as if she might cry. "She told me I couldn't come to her Christmas party unless I got twenty new people to follow her."

"She's a monster, not a machine, Erin! She needs to be stopped."

"I know! I don't want to go to practice today. I wish we were on different teams."

"Come on, let's get out of here, Erin. Come to the skate park with me this morning. It's fun. You can watch me fall. There's a flat rail, you can do some of your balance beam tricks on it and wow everybody."

She grinned.

As it turned out, Jessica showed up at the park again. She joked that Albert owed her a pound of chocolate, and then Erin teased them. But it was fun. Erin did her balance beam routine on the rail, and Albert could tell that Jessica liked the fact that Albert was the kind of guy who was nice to his little sister.

That afternoon, Erin went off to her gymnastics practice and Albert traveled to Jhaateez. He was excited for practice and surprised them all by showing more definite improvement.

"We're going to win this game," Doz said.

"For Kayko!" Beeda and Reeda said.

"And Giac is going to crack that code and find the evidence we need," Toben said.

Giac, who was sitting out the practice to continue trying to decode Mehk's encrypted files, smiled weakly. "I hope so."

127

10.0

The botmaker's first task, to take photos of the technician, had gone well, but this second task was going to be much more dangerous. As soon as lights were out, he began.

After signaling to the prisoner next door with their chant, Mehk opened the vent and removed the mirror fragment, the gum, and the data chip from the digital camera. Then he opened up his gheet, slipped the data chip inside, and tucked his gheet under his bem. The sensor-blocking coating on his gheet would keep the chip from being detected by his PEER. Once again, Mehk's gheet would play a crucial role.

"Here we go," Mehk whispered. With the mirror fragment, he sliced an ugly gash into his own arm. Then, as before, he used the gum to stick the mirror fragment on the ceiling, and he banged on the door.

Immediately the lights switched on, the door opened, and his PEER flew into his cell. "Behavior change. PEER on alert." In the next second, it detected the gash in Mehk's arm and sent an alert to the command center. "Minor injury. One arm wounded. Initiating prisoner-to-medic protocol," the PEER said.

Perfect!

The Zeenod next door then beamed the same code it had first used to keep the PEER from responding to threats or sending any security alerts. Once again, Mehk reached up to test it. The drone simply hummed. "Exit now."

Mehk followed his PEER out the door.

As he walked down the hallway, he hid his smile. His arm hurt, but it was so worth it.

Following the prisoner-to-medic protocol, the PEER led him to the medic office, announced their arrival, and opened the office door. Inside, the Z-Tev medic looked at Mehk from the eye in the back of her head. They had interrupted her nap.

While Mehk's PEER zoomed over to the wall and docked as he had hoped, Mehk showed off the gash on his arm, and the medic rolled her eyes. She barked at Mehk to lie down and then grabbed a bottle of cheap repair fluid and squirted it on the wound.

"Aren't you going to create a smartskin covering?" Mehk asked. "This is going to cause a scar."

The medic laughed. "Waste my resources so your arm looks pretty? Stay still. The bleeding will stop and the wound will close in a few minutes. Then you can clean up this blood on the floor and go back to your cell."

This was the point at which another Zeenod was supposed to

fake an even worse injury that would require the medic to go to that cell.

One minute went by, and Mehk began to sweat. If the medic didn't leave, Mehk had only one other option: to switch on the stun setting of his gheet and get the gheet to bite her. Knowing that the medic could discover and try to destroy the gheet before it bit her, Mehk wanted to avoid the risk.

Just when he was about to panic, an alert came in requesting the medic. The annoyed medic sent a message to the command center, took a laser gun and her medical pack, and left, assuming that Mehk's PEER was fully operational and in control.

The moment the medic left, Mehk hopped off the table, careful to keep his arm from dripping blood. He ran to the 3-D smartskin fabricator, withdrew the chip he had hidden in his gheet, and inserted it into the computer interface. Quickly, he pulled up the photos he had taken of the service technician and began making the expert adjustments needed to send instructions to the fabricator. He had done this kind of complicated work before, of course, but never under life-or-death circumstances—and never with one arm wounded. After he checked the levels for the smartskin liquid and the various tints in the machine's reservoir, he activated the command to begin.

As the machine began to create the smartskin mask, Mehk tried to imagine what was happening with the medic and the other prisoner. Thankfully, this was a high-speed, fast-dry fabricator, but if the medic saw through the other Zeenod's ploy, she might come back too soon.

The seconds ticked. The machine whirred.

After two more minutes, he heard the sound of footsteps in the hall. The mask was almost done. Just ten more seconds. He hovered over the machine. The moment it was done, he grabbed the mask, stuffed it down his prison uniform, and hopped back on the bed.

The door opened, and Mehk closed his eyes as if sleeping.

The medic walked in. "Wake up," she snapped. "Get back to your cell. This isn't a hotel."

Careful to hide his glee, Mehk had begun to walk to the door with his PEER when the medic suddenly yelled, "Wait!"

Frightened, Mehk froze in place. With his back to the medic, he suddenly became aware of the tickle of his gheet's feet on the back of his right arm. No, Mehk thought, go back under my bem!

"Gheet!" the medic yelled, and struck Mehk's arm. The bot-maker turned and saw his poor friend on its back on the floor, looking quite small and desperate as it worked to right itself.

Before Mehk could think of what to do, the medic picked up her laser gun and fired a shot. Within a nanosecond, the gheet burned to a crisp.

"Ha!" said the medic. "Got it."

The air seemed to disappear from the room.

"Get rid of it before you leave." The medic gestured to the trash can. "I'm not touching that thing."

Holding back tears, Mehk crouched down and collected the pieces of his beloved pet in his hands. He remembered the thrill he had felt when he had stolen time and materials during his old job to build and program this small robot. At the time, he had needed something he could call his own, something that the Z-Tevs, who controlled his life, couldn't control. He had chosen a gheet as his model because he knew that the Z-Tevs hated them, thought of them as pests, as insignificant creatures to squash underfoot. For years, Mehk had reaped the benefits. His gheet had kept him company and had helped him through stressful, sad, and scary moments.

"Move," the medic said.

With a heavy heart, Mehk let the charred pieces fall through his fingers into the trash and followed his PEER out the door.

When he arrived back in his cell, the Zeenod next door used the device to reenable the PEER's response protocol and return the drone to its usual nighttime position. Disabling it for a short time was risky enough. They couldn't keep it disabled for long.

Once the drone zipped back into position outside the cell and the door slammed shut, Mehk slipped the mask and the mirror fragment back into the vent. He knew the Zeenod was waiting to hear if he had been successful. A part of him wanted to tell him about the destruction of his gheet, but he was afraid he would lose control of his emotions. Voice shaking, Mehk chanted, *"Our work is done. We look forward to a better day."*

After a few moments, he heard the song of success being passed from vent to vent.

"Our work is done. We look forward to a better day."

11.0

By the time Albert arrived on Jhaateez for another Saturday practice in mid December, he was feeling on edge but upbeat.

As he and his team headed through the lobby toward their practice field, they passed Linnd, who was just leaving.

"Greetings, noddies!" she said with a wave of her sailwing. "Any news about Kayko?"

"No," Ennjy said.

"Yet the game goes on." Linnd's head bobbed sympathetically. "I admire you all for continuing without your tactician. And I hope this does not affect your team's ability to play well."

Albert could tell that she meant it.

She went on with a smile. "We want you to play your best game possible because we're definitely going to beat you. And we'd feel terrible if it was too easy!" With a cold strong hand, she gave Albert a pat on the back as she passed him.

"Don't count your chickens before they hatch," Albert called back with a smile of his own.

She stopped, her chin wrinkling as she struggled with the language translation.

"Chickens?" Toben asked.

"It's an Earth saying," Albert explained. "It means, don't be so sure you're going to win." Albert gave Linnd a pat on the back, and she laughed and said her goodbyes.

Feeb whispered, "Linnd is a friend of Zeeno. But she is desperate to win. The Jhaateezians can afford to be very generous to their winners, and they are offering Linnd a huge reward if they win. Linnd's family needs it, and she will fight with every fiber of her being."

Albert glanced back at his opponent, remembering her performance at the Skill Show, the intensity and perfection of each string pluck—all at a speed too fast to see.

Doz held open the door. "Let's roll and rock."

After their ahn ritual and before they started their physical warm-up, Ennjy called a huddle. "What's our greatest strength? We're not the fastest, the biggest, or the strongest in the solar system. So what do we have?"

"On-field responsiveness," Toben said. "We work together."

"We communicate," Beeda and Reeda said in unison.

Feeb nodded. "The Tevs are known for explosive runs and tend to send long balls. The Jhaateezians are known for their tricks and athleticism. We're known for our passing."

"Touch, touch, touch, touch," Heek said. "Up the field we go."

"Like Barcelona!" Albert said. "That's a team on Earth. Tight passing is called tiki-taka!"

Doz grinned. "Tiki-taka."

"The ice is our challenge," Sormie said. "The Jhaateezians are much more skilled on it than we are. They were born skating. They can skate and maintain ball control at the same time. We'll never have enough time to become that skilled."

"That's right," Ennjy said. "But we need to practice being more responsive on the ice. I want to try a new drill."

Splitting the team into groups of threes, she told each trio to skate in a chain by linking arms. She explained that when each trio reached a curve, the person who was closest to the field would naturally become a pivot, while the outside player would naturally pick up momentum.

"That's physics," Giac called out from the sideline, where she was still working hard to decode the botmaker's encrypted drive. "It has to do with centripetal force. The magnitude of the force on the skater farthest from the pivot is the greatest, so that skater will have the greatest speed."

Everybody smiled.

Giac would make a great science teacher, Albert thought.

"If you're the pivoter, then at some point quickly drop your arm to break the chain," Ennjy said. "Don't give a warning. Just do it. This will cause the other two to go flying. The job of the other two is to respond to the challenge in the best way possible. If one of you panics and starts to fall, you could take the other skater down. Use the ahn. Communicate without speaking. Work together."

Albert was paired with Beeda and Reeda. Beeda was the pivot. Albert was in the middle.

"You're separating us?" they asked Ennjy at the same time.

Ennjy laughed. "Go!"

Beeda linked an arm with Albert, who linked his other arm with Reeda. The three took off skating together on the straight section, picking up speed, the bems of both his teammates pulled in to reduce drag. Albert could feel himself tensing up, wondering when Beeda would break the chain, worrying that he was going to lose his balance and take Reeda down.

"Focus on the ahn," Ennjy said from the center of the field. "The goal is just to respond to the change without falling."

Albert felt Reeda on his right, felt her focus and her energy. Steady and ready, he told himself. Steady and ready.

And then Beeda unlinked. He tightened both his core and his elbow lock with Reeda. They sailed in an arc up to the top of the bowl, and he felt the panic rise. On Earth, he had been practicing hopping onto the deck for the past two weeks, but he still couldn't nail it every time.

Now he felt Reeda's muscular arm linked in his. He returned that strength and leaned into it and they both flew up and landed on the deck. He stumbled slightly, but Reeda was a rock. Then they turned and locked arms, and before Albert could even become nervous, they dropped in. Down they sailed together— strong and sure.

"Yes!" Ennjy said.

The ahn flowed through Albert and he could feel it flowing through Beeda.

"Yes!" Albert yelled.

Overall spirits were high for the rest of the practice. They played well, scrimmaging with the ball and practicing how and when to shift to the ice, bems flying like sailwings.

"All the December practices on Jhaateez have been productive, Albert," Feeb said as they moved into the cooldown.

"Thank you," Albert said. He had worked practice into every element of his day, and it was paying off. Every time he sat down on or got up from a chair or the floor, he did it on one leg with the other straight out in front of him to build up strength in his legs and core. Every time he went anywhere, he skated. And he looked insane because he never just skated in a straight line. He zipped up and down driveways, off curbs, somersaulting onto the grass, shooting the duck, jumping, stopping, skating backward. On and on. The only part he didn't like was when Trey would show up at the park with his skateboard. Competition between them would erupt, and Trey would laugh over every mistake Albert made. But during those practices, Albert would push himself hard, so those had been good practices, too.

Albert looked around at all the Zeenods as they finished up. On Earth, Albert found himself still uneasy about the death threat, watching over his shoulder. At least once a day, he would swear he was being watched or followed, but it would always turn out to be a false alarm. But here in the practice facility on Jhaateez, surrounded by his teammates, he felt safe.

12.0

At school on Friday afternoon, Albert received an alert from Unit D. Messages were only delivered in emergencies, so he was immediately alarmed. The atmosphere at school was already insane. The Winter Dance was that night, and the seventh-grade hallways were like the lanes of a pinball machine with all Albert's classmates bouncing around, too fast, too loud. By the time he found an opportunity between classes to read the alert, his stomach was in knots.

Ennjy would like me to inform you that Giac is missing. She did not arrive at her home after a routine errand in Zone 3 to obtain supplies for her family. Her work has disappeared as well. The team is anxious. No word of an arrest. The police have been informed but say they have no information. Please be on high alert.

A cold fear settled in. Albert couldn't imagine how distraught the Zeenods must be, not knowing if Giac was kidnapped or dead. The "work" that they referred to was definitely the material they stole from Mehk, the material they were hoping could provide the evidence needed to prove Kayko's innocence. This was terrible news.

He couldn't stop thinking about the team, Kayko, Giac, the entire planet. And he couldn't stop wondering if there was a target on his back.

After dinner, when his mom told him to get dressed for the school dance, he told her he didn't want to go. His nerves were frayed, although he couldn't tell her why.

"You're going to the dance," she said. "No arguing."

He tried arguing anyway, but Erin and Nana joined the effort, and he had to give in.

When he arrived, the dance floor was crowded with girls. Jessica and her friends were having fun, and Min Jee was right in the center, teaching them all a dance routine. It was completely surreal, Albert thought. One set of people in his life—his classmates—were having fun while another set of people—well, aliens—were facing life-or-death consequences.

Not knowing what to do with himself, Albert went to the snack table, where a group of boys were standing. "Hey, Albert!" said Freddy, whose lips were red from drinking punch.

"Hey, Freddy," Albert said.

"I saw you skating after school the other day," Freddy said.

Too exhausted to change the subject, Albert nodded. "Yep," he said, "I found some old in-line skates, and I've been skating."

"It gave me an idea," Freddy said. "I really like ice-skating and I was wondering. Do you think anybody would come if I invited them ice-skating on my birthday? I mean, it wouldn't be like a little kids' skating party. It would be more like a skating-on-my-birthday thing."

"I'd come," Albert said with a shrug. He couldn't afford to go to the rink on his own, but he knew his mom would cover his fee if it was for a party. Anything for more time on skates.

Freddy brightened. "Cool. Thanks, Albert."

Albert looked around. He tried to let go of his worries about the Zeenods and pay attention to what was happening.

The girls were dominating the dance floor, and Freddy's eyes were glued on Min Jee.

"Why don't you ask her?" Albert asked.

"Who? What?" Freddy quickly poured himself another cup of punch.

"Min."

"Ask her where? To my party?"

"Well, yeah. But I was actually thinking why not ask her to dance."

"Now?"

Albert shrugged. "Why not?"

Freddy gulped down his punch. "Why don't you go ask Jessica Atwater?"

Suddenly, Albert's face grew hot.

Both boys were silent for a few moments, and then Mr. Sam played "*Macarena*," and the energy on the dance floor erupted.

Freddy busied himself by piling cookies on a paper plate.

Albert watched Jessica and her circle of girlfriends on the floor. As they all did the old-school motions together, they were in a kind of happy trance. They were riffing off each other's energy and bubbling with a collective effervescence. He needed to join in and feel the joy of that connection. But he couldn't get his feet to move.

And then Trey walked out and started dancing, copying the moves with no inhibition. Everybody loved it.

Albert turned and walked out the door. Up and down the long, empty hallway he walked, stopping three times for a drink from the fountain, even though he wasn't thirsty. Then he went to the bathroom again and looked at himself in the mirror. He had on jeans and a button-down shirt, and he didn't think he looked too bad. He felt bad, though. He wanted to be the kind of person who didn't let fear overwhelm him, the kind of person who took risks, who didn't care what anybody thought, who could win a johka game and shred it on the dance floor. Albert the Amazing. Instead he was a loser hiding in the bathroom. His stomach growled. Worse—he was a hungry loser.

Checking his pockets for a granola bar, he pulled out an empty candy wrapper and a pebble. And then he realized that the pebble was the diamond he had smuggled from Jhaateez after his first practice. He had put it in his pocket after the Thanksgiving fiasco, intending and forgetting to sneak it back to Jhaateez.

Now he held the diamond up to the bathroom light and it glistened, its angles reflecting prisms of light. This little rock, so common on Jhaateez, was gorgeous. It was also proof that he was special. He wasn't a loser. He was a Star Striker. He wished he could slip the diamond to Jessica along with a note telling her that she was just as dazzling. There was no way he could take that risk.

Determined to do something, he grabbed a paper towel and wrote:

Dear Jessica, I remember when we were in the fifth grade and you said you sometimes felt like a black hole was in your soul. I thought that was so interesting because I have felt that way, too.

I just want you to know that I think you are an amazing dancer and skateboarder and sax player and artist and person.

Love, Albert

When he returned to the gym, he walked over to where all the coats were piled on the bleachers. Jessica's wasn't hard to find. She liked to wear her dad's old leather jacket, which had the image of a vinyl record on the back. Before Albert could lose his courage, he slipped the note inside the front right pocket of her jacket and turned to leave.

At that moment, Jessica was onstage, whispering something to her dad. Mr. Sam nodded, and when the song ended, he took the mic and said, "The next song goes out to Señora Muñoz!"

Everyone looked at the Spanish teacher.

"¡*Oye Cómo Va*'!" the teacher yelled. "I love this song!" She immediately started doing the cha-cha-cha. "Who's dancing with me? ¡Necesito una pareja de baile!"

Freddy and a few other boys by the table backed up, anxious that the teacher would pick one of them. Seeing Albert by the door, Freddy hustled over, calling out, "Albert, let's run for our lives!"

Onstage, Jessica spoke into the microphone, a huge smile on her face. "Hey, I see you back there, Albert and Freddy! You guys can't go! It's cha-cha-cha time!"

"Chickens!" another girl said.

Albert froze, mortified, and then Trey walked out on the dance floor. The girls started clapping and whistling.

Trey bowed to Señora Muñoz and then started cha-cha-cha-ing with her like a professional on *Dancing with the Stars*. The whole place erupted. He knew all the moves.

"¡Increíble! ¡Maravilloso!" Señora Muñoz yelled above the music. "Where did you learn this?"

"I watched a video after you mentioned it in class," Trey said.

Everyone gathered in a circle around them and started clapping to the rhythm. A group of loud girls were openly swooning.

"I need to learn that," Freddy said, openmouthed.

Albert felt every ounce of confidence he had disappear.

"Go, Trey!" Jessica was cheering.

Not wanting to look jealous, Albert stayed and put a fake smile on his face and clapped along until the song ended and Trey and Señora Muñoz took bows and blew kisses to the audience. Mr. Sam played a super-old-fashioned waltz next, and Trey knew all those moves, too, this time whirling Jessica around the dance floor as if he were a prince. The crowd loved it.

Freddy leaned in and whispered to Albert. "I'm doing it!" He headed straight to where Min Jee was standing, but instead of stopping to ask her to dance, he lost his nerve and headed back to the snack table.

In a fog of misery, Albert stood still, regretting the note. What was he thinking? Quickly, he made his way back to the pile of coats. Relieved that he had realized his mistake before it was too late, he found Jessica's jacket, pulled the note out of her pocket, stuck it in his jeans pocket, and turned around.

"What are you stealing, Albert?" Camila said. She and Gabby were walking by.

"Yeah, that's Jessica's jacket," Gabby said.

Standing near enough to hear was the principal. "I saw you take something, Albert. Is that Jessica's jacket?"

Albert started to sweat. "Honestly, I—I wasn't stealing," he stammered. "I—I put something in Jessica's pocket, and then I decided to take it back."

By this time, the girls had told Jessica, and, to Albert's distress, she was coming over.

"What's going on?" Jessica asked. "Gabby said Albert's in trouble for trying to steal my jacket."

"I wasn't trying to steal your jacket!" Albert's voice was louder than he intended, and the seventh graders standing nearby flocked over to listen.

"Albert says he put something in your pocket and then decided to take it back," the principal said.

Jessica smiled quizzically at Albert. "What was it?"

He pulled out the old candy bar wrapper from his pocket. "This!"

"An empty wrapper?" she asked.

He started laughing. "Isn't that hilarious? Yeah. Um, I put this wrapper in your pocket thinking it would be funny when you'd put your hand in your pocket and be like…*What's this?* I mean it would be nice if it were chocolate but it's just an empty wrapper! Ha ha!" He held up the wrapper and laughed louder. He knew he sounded ridiculous but he couldn't stop.

"I don't get it," Jessica said.

"Yeah, well, I figured you might not get it." Albert kept forcing himself to laugh. "So I decided to take it back."

"Jessica," the principal said. "Can you check your jacket pockets, please, to make sure nothing's missing?"

It was no wonder the principal didn't trust him, Albert thought. He was acting like a maniac. The seventh graders who had gathered to watch the spectacle were now laughing at him. Jessica let the principal know that nothing had been stolen and returned to the dance floor without another look at Albert.

Wishing he could crawl under a rock, Albert grabbed his coat and left. He'd have to text his mom and let her know he was coming home early. She'd want to know why. It was all a disaster.

13.0

Nineteen days and nights had passed since the imprisoned bot-maker's mask-making quest. Nineteen days and nights without his gheet to keep him company. Now all he could think about was taking the final step to escape, but a number of things kept getting in the way. First the Z-Tevs called in exterminators to deal with gheets because both the service technician and the medic had reported seeing them. That took several days and required extra surveillance. Worse, the service technician surprised them all by disappearing. Another Z-Tev took his place, a tall, thin female Z-Tev with smaller eyes and wider face markings. At first Mehk thought they would need another plan. But then one Zeenod overheard that the male technician was on vacation and was expected to return.

Finally, during the morning work session, Mehk received the message.

Under the sound of the work song, the Zeenod next to him whispered: "Zin heard two guards talking. The service technician is returning tonight."

Mehk's heart leaped. From Zeenod to Zeenod the news traveled, and as it did, Mehk could feel the lifting of spirits. They were imagining that Mehk would be helping Kayko to escape. They were imagining that Kayko would find a way to free them all. The work song grew louder and louder, bems pulsed, eyes turned gold.

Mehk blinked and looked down. In the metallic surface of the worktable, he caught a glimpse of his own reflection. His eyes were tight and tired. He looked thin. He thought about how Zin had said that the ahn was in him. He looked over at the old Zeenod, chanting and working, eyes full of hope.

Don't be an idiot, Mehk told himself. Focus on your goal!

For the rest of the day, Mehk felt on edge. He was anxious to take this final step, but his arms and legs and bem felt oddly heavy. When he was alone in his cell, he kept hitting himself on the side of his head, telling himself to cheer up, to be excited. This was not a time to question his purpose. What he needed to do was clear: take whatever the Zeenods were foolish enough to give him and offer nothing in return.

After lights went out, the procedure for the escape began. With the last piece of gum, again he stuck the fragment of mirror on the ceiling in front of the door.

Ready.

He began to pound against the door with one foot, and immediately the lights switched on, the door opened, and his PEER flew into his cell. "Behavior change. PEER on alert." The cell door slammed shut.

With the control device, his neighbor beamed the first command up at the mirrored fragment, the command to disable the response protocol. Then it sent the command for a service technician. Just as before, the drone hovered in place without responding to Mehk's movements.

Mehk removed the tranquilizer syringe from the wall space and readied himself for the next steps. After thirty seconds, the door buzzed open and the service technician walked in with weapon drawn. Mehk breathed a sigh of relief. Yes, it was the right technician.

"Hands where I can see them," the technician said, clearly suspicious to receive a second repair alert for the same unit—although that had occurred weeks ago.

As Mehk slowly raised his hands—one of which held the syringe—he quickly directed the technician's focus away from him and to the PEER. "See that leak? Definitely a problem." It was a trick that magicians used to keep their audience from seeing the sleight of hand, and Mehk was counting on it to work.

Sure enough, the technician looked up at the drone instead of at Mehk's hands, and Mehk took the opportunity to plunge the syringe into the Z-Tev's neck and then grab his gun.

The technician fell asleep instantly. Quickly, Mehk laid him out on his bed, pulled the communication device from his belt, and typed in the technician's password—one of the crucial pieces of information obtained from a fellow prisoner. Next, Mehk sent a message to the command center, trying to mimic the technician's gruff voice. "Rebooting PEER. No assistance needed."

Quickly, Mehk swapped clothes with the sleeping Z-Tev, stuffing his bem inside the coveralls. With the backpack on, the Zeenod appendage wouldn't be visible. Now for the disguise. Mehk rubbed the red chalk into his teeth, then pulled on the smartskin mask and snapped it into place, making microadjustments for the perfect fit. He smiled and felt the smartskin of his new face respond.

He covered the sleeping Z-Tev with his blanket and turned his attention to the PEER. He would have preferred to smash the thing into tiny pieces, but this wasn't the time or the place. Swiftly, he used the Z-Tev's badge to gain access to the PEER's system and programmed it to remain in normal sleep protocol. With satisfaction, he watched the drone fly out and lock into place in the docking station outside the cell door. No alerts. No alarms.

"Minor repair complete," he messaged the command center. "PEER and prisoner secure. No assistance required." Slinging on the backpack, he was about to step out of the cell when he heard the Zeenod next door whisper his name.

Mehk turned and stared at the vent.

"You have done so well, my friend," the Zeenod whispered. "Your parents would be proud. We will be sending you the ahn!"

Mehk gave one quick nod, rushed out, and then stopped. A cold rush of guilt was rising within him, and he suddenly felt weak in the knees. This was when he should have gone to Kayko's cell with everything in his pack. They would disable her PEER and then she would use the disguise to escape and he would return to his cell. He imagined Kayko ready in her cell on the floor above them and imagined all the Zeenods in their cells, waiting. He thought about how intelligent and courageous and patient the Zeenods were to acquire all this information. Each item, obtained separately, enabled the whole plan to work like a machine. The only way to accomplish any of this was to work together, and he admired this.

148

Snap out of it, he said to himself, hitting himself on the side of the head. No time to waste. Follow your plan.

Pushing down the guilt, he sent a new message to the command center. "Requesting first break."

Heart pounding, he waited. This was one part he could not control. After a few seconds the reply came back.

Break request granted.

Mehk walked down the hallway, past cell door after cell door.

At the end of each hallway, he swiped the technician's badge against an optical port, and the heavy doors swung open. He passed by the stairway that he was supposed to use to get to Kayko's cell, and he told himself to keep going until he reached the doors leading to the main hallway.

There would be four security guards here as well as a window into the warden's office. Blocck would be off duty, but the night warden would be sitting in his chair, looking out that window.

As Mehk walked through the double doors, he noticed three red cigars in the pocket of the coveralls he was wearing and pulled one out.

The two security guards by the first set of doors glanced at him.

Mehk nodded, waved his cigar, and kept walking. He had to pass the window next. Out of the corner of his eye, he could see the warden glance up. He kept walking. The final gauntlet was the inspection station flanked by two guards right in front of the exit.

This was the part he was dreading most. He handed them his backpack, hoping they weren't studying the bulging of his bem or noticing that the eye in the back of his head didn't blink. After he walked through, he turned around to see them staring at him.

One held out his backpack, but when Mehk was about to take it, the guard said, "Aren't you forgetting something?"

"Yeah, pay up," the other said. "You owe us."

Mind racing, Mehk took in the situation. Noticing that they both had reddish stains on their teeth, he reached into his pocket and withdrew the other two cigars.

One snatched the cigars and the other buzzed open the doors.

Mehk walked out. Free.

14.0

On Christmas day, after presents and breakfast, Albert's mom, grandmother, and sister settled into the kitchen to make a Yule log cake for dessert. Albert retreated to his room. He tried to listen to Kayko's sixth lesson, but he couldn't concentrate. With Giac and the evidence missing, the entire situation was critical. He wanted desperately to help, but he was afraid that his shawbles were too great. He was making mistake after mistake. Upset, he decided to write down his failures, careful, of course, not to reveal any secrets in case someone read it. Sitting with notebook and pen on his bed, he started from the moment his training for the Jhaateez game began.

What I Did Wrong
1. *I didn't read the guide carefully.*
2. *I thought I was Albert the Amazing and then I tripped.*
3. *I let embarrassment keep me from learning.*
4. *I refused good advice from a coach, from a girl at school, from Nana.*
5. *I let jealousy get in the way.*
6. *I didn't pay attention when I was listening to a lesson or review other lessons.*
7. *I took certain things too seriously—like noises in the night that turned out to be nothing.*
8. *I didn't take other things seriously enough—like thinking I didn't have to practice my clarinet or not being suspicious about the "gift" of candy. Every kindergartener knows not to take candy from strangers.*
9. *I betrayed my coach in public.*
10. *I didn't even dance at the school dance.*

He stopped and stared at the list, feeling overwhelmed. Desperately he wanted to go back and start again. Do things right this time. The mistakes he had made were so obvious. He knew he could do better, which was why he was so angry with himself.

If Kayko were here, she could help him work through this. Or maybe Lee. Had Lee made mistakes seventy-five years ago? Hearing about that struggle might help! Albert wished they could have another conversation like the one they had when he had been injured in the last game.

In the next moment, his nana walked in with a frosting-coated spoon. "Hey, kiddo, want a taste?"

He tossed the pen onto his desk and stuffed the spoon in his mouth, grateful for the chocolate hit. Chocolate. He had forgotten to give chocolate to Jessica! Another mistake.

"Things to do?" Nana asked, glancing at the notebook in his lap.

"Things I wish I hadn't done," he said.

She nodded with a smile. "My regrets list is way, way, way longer. It's on a scroll. In tiny handwriting. Last time I checked, it was two thousand, three hundred sixty-seven miles long."

He laughed.

"Writing down what you did wrong is not a bad way to learn. But if you stop there and just feel bad about it, you'll just be beating yourself up. Hold yourself accountable, but be kind to yourself. Sure, write down what you did wrong. But then turn the page and write down what you did right." She picked up the pen from his desk and tossed it to him. "And then come out and help us decorate the cake."

She left, and he turned to a blank page. What did he do right, he wondered? He went back to the moment he landed on Jhaateez, and at first his mind was a blank. Then he began to write.

What I Did Right
  1. *I got up after falling.*
  2. *I kept practicing.*
  3. *I listened to some lessons.*
  4. *I survived and even triumphed with the Ba Da Dee.*

It wasn't a long list, but when he looked at it and thought about the fact that he had persisted even though there were real things to be scared about, he started to feel better. His life and the lives of his teammates were in danger, and he hadn't quit. That was no small thing.

The fourth lesson came to him. *Everyone falls. If you are not falling, it means you are not trying anything new,* Kayko had said. *The only thing to know is that there is always more to know.* This whole Star Striker experience was new. Being a seventh grader was new, too. Of course he was going to make mistakes.

Feeling energized, he called up the sixth lesson and listened.

Welcome to the sixth lesson: What You Can and Can't Control.

Albert settled in and closed his eyes.

Take a few moments to focus on your breathing and to be present and we will begin.

Albert took in a breath. The cake in the kitchen smelled good. Really good. He thought about reaching over and picking up the spoon to see if there was any frosting still left on it. And then his eyes snapped open. He couldn't believe it. He couldn't even concentrate for one minute! What was wrong with him? He stopped. Okay, Albert…you screwed up…forgive yourself and focus. He took a breath, closed his eyes, and listened.

You can't control most things in life. You can't control the past. You can't control the future. You can't control the weather. You can't control what happens to your friends and family. You can't control the behavior or performance of your opponents or how they treat you or what they think of you. You can't control negative thoughts or emotions. You can't even control your own mind, keeping it from wandering during a short meditation.

Albert laughed. Well, leave it to Kayko to know his shawbles.

So what can you do? You can practice. What is the practice? The practice is to respond in positive ways to whatever challenges arise. Every challenge is an opportunity to practice. This practice strengthens ahnic energy within ourselves and each other.

A bell signaled the end of the lesson. Albert opened his eyes. He wrote down all the lessons he had learned since he had joined the team.

1. *Acknowledge thoughts and emotions without judgment.*
2. *Send kind thoughts to yourself.*
3. *Send kind thoughts to others—even your opponents.*
4. *Be open to learning.*
5. *Connect. The most power and the most joy come through connection.*
6. *Respond to challenges in positive ways.*

Okay, Albert thought. Time for cake.

15.0

A week after the escape from prison, Mehk sat waiting on a curb between two ITVs in the parking lot of the Zeeno capitol building. Still masked and disguised as the service technician, he held a bag of paranj seeds that he had stolen, and from time to time he poured a few from the bag into his mouth.

A gnauser had crept out of the shadows to beg for a nibble. Real gnausers weren't common on Zeeno anymore, and Mehk watched with fascination. In order to create his robotic gnausers, he had studied the creatures thoroughly, but there was nothing like seeing a real one. They were almost extinct. This creature was cautious, taking one step at a time and checking Mehk out just as steadily as Mehk was checking him out.

"Ha!" Mehk whispered. "We're both survivors, aren't we? The Z-Tevs and Tevs have tried to destroy us, but we're still here, outsmarting them."

The creature sniffed in his direction.

Mehk poured a few more seeds into his hand, considered sharing them, and then popped them into his mouth.

All week, he had lain low. The disguise had enabled him to exit the prison grounds without a problem, and the backpack full of tech tools and supplies had given him what he needed to break in and out of buildings—finding good places to hide each day for the past week.

A news update blared from a speaker in the parking lot, and Mehk stopped chewing.

"Tickets for the two upcoming johka games are now sold out," an announcer said. "The Tevs are expected to win against the Gaböqs, and the Jhaateezians are expected to win against the Zeenods. All eyes will be on the four Star Strikers…"

Mehk listened carefully as the announcer went on. Back when Mehk was arrested, Lat had told him she was going to kill Kinney. Clearly, she had failed. He would have to deal with the Earthling. Well, he was ready for that.

He pulled out a small container. In it was his newly made surveillancebot, this one in the shape of a flying beetle that was typical on Zeeno. He took a breath. Stealing the parts and making it had been the best part of the past week, had made him feel like himself again.

Now he went over the steps of his plan in his mind to make sure he hadn't left anything out. At any moment, Unit D would arrive in Kinney's ITV for its weekly service update, and Mehk would send his surveillancebot flying. Once the bot was in Kinney's ITV, Mehk would know where Kinney was at all times. Then Mehk would steal an ITV and leave Zeeno. That would be the riskiest part, but he had done it once and could do it again. In space, he'd intercept Kinney, kidnap him, and fake his death by crashing Kinney's ITV.

He paused.

It would be easier, wouldn't it, just to kill Kinney? Yes, but he would stick to this plan. Prove to himself and everyone else that he was not a murderer. A forced hibernation would take care of Kinney. He should have done that long ago. Once Kinney was out of the way, his masterpiece would finally, finally be called into play as Kinney's alternate. That was all he'd ever wanted.

Another news alert blared from the speaker. Mehk kept assuming he would hear something on the news about his escape from prison, but the alert was just a weather update. Perhaps a prison breakout would be too embarrassing for the Z-Tevs and for President Lat to admit, Mehk thought. No doubt they were looking for him, though. If they found him before he could leave, they'd make sure he kept his mouth closed. Permanently.

He glanced at the ITV parked in front of him and saw his reflection on its metallic surface. The mask of the Z-Tev service technician stared back at him, and his mind snapped back to the prison. Old Zin and all the Zeenods must be still grieving over his betrayal.

He felt a pang of guilt and hit himself on the side of his head to regain focus. Just then, an engine rumbled and the ITV pulled into the lot. Mehk peered out from the vehicle he was hiding behind. Ha! This was it! As soon as Unit D opened the door, Mehk released his microbot. While the robot began to walk toward the building entrance, the bugbot zipped over and flew inside the vehicle just before the ITV doors closed. Success!

16.0

By the time Albert arrived at the downtown rink, Freddy and the others were skating as the sound system played an old dance tune. Albert laced up and joined in, skating over first to say hi to Freddy. The evening air was the coldest yet, but Albert noticed that he felt completely comfortable. That high-tech frostbite treatment Unit D had given him meant that he had no need for a hat or gloves.

"You got your cast off!" Freddy exclaimed.

"Finally," Albert said, not mentioning how pleased the doctor was with the way the fracture had healed or how pleased Albert was that the doctor had no idea the fracture had been healed by alien fehkhahting weeks ago!

"I see Min's here," Albert whispered.

Freddy blushed.

Trey was already there, zooming around the rink, weaving too closely in and out of the other skaters, frightening the beginners while looking comfortable and smug. "Race?" he asked as he passed Freddy and Albert, grazing Albert's shoulder.

It was a Sunday, just four days after Christmas. Albert had spent the past four days in a trancelike state of productivity. Each day he had divided his time between reviewing Kayko's lessons, meditating, and training. Just yesterday at practice, he and the team had played their best scrimmage yet. And he had finally returned the diamond to Jhaateez, which was a relief. He knew that his preparation as Star Striker was the only important thing in his life right now. They had to win back support for the team. They had to win for Kayko and they had to find Giac. Yet here was Trey managing to make his blood boil.

Around Trey zipped again.

Jessica, Albert noticed with satisfaction, called out for him to slow down. "You almost knocked Gabby down!" she yelled.

Since the dance, Albert hadn't had the chance to talk to her, and he was dying to find a way to show her that he wasn't insane. He had a bar of gourmet chocolate in his pocket and just needed the right moment.

Camila unwound the long scarf she was wearing and handed the other end to Gabby. "Let's play Ice Limbo!" she said. "Whoever skates under without touching the scarf wins."

Jessica jumped right in. The music switched to a popular tune and she started singing along. One at a time the skaters ducked down and went under the scarf.

Raul, who was the tallest, was eliminated first. Every time

someone wiped out, everybody would laugh. Freddy was eliminated next, and then Trey, Jessica, and Albert were left. Jessica and Min tied and did a funny celebration dance.

"Shoot-the-duck next!" Albert suggested. "Longest shoot-the-duck without falling wins." After he demonstrated, most opted not to even try.

"I can't even do that for a second," Freddy said.

Jessica, Trey, Min, and Gabby wanted in. The rest skated out to watch from the sidelines. "Start skating and when I say go, shoot the duck!" Albert knew that his initial momentum would determine how long he could go, so he took off fast and put on speed. "Go!" Albert crouched in position, reaching out for balance and stretching one leg forward. Piece of cookie, as Doz would say. Albert made the first curve and saw Gabby wipe out. Then Jessica lost steam. Min lasted a little longer. Then it was just Trey and Albert. Trey's form was great, and he was strong enough to hold the position, but he hadn't gotten enough speed to start. With a grim look on his face, Trey puttered to a stop.

"We have a winner!" Albert stood up and grinned.

"Let's just skate," Freddy said.

"A race," Trey said. "Six laps. Fastest wins."

Freddy was about to object when Albert and Min said at the same time, "I'm in."

"Okay," Jessica said. "I guess I want in, too."

Camila played the part of the referee, using her hat as the flag to start the race.

Trey took the lead and held it for two laps, staying low and slicing forward like an Olympian. Albert dug deep and pushed himself, feeling the familiar heat of jealousy start to rise. Trey whizzed past Min, too close, and she had to veer, almost knocking into Jessica.

"Not cool!" Jessica called out. "It's not worth breaking a bone over this!" She skated off the ice, and Min followed her.

Albert knew that Trey had crossed a line, but it made Albert want to beat him even more. On the fifth lap, Albert finally caught up to him, but Trey zoomed ahead to win.

As Trey took a victory lap, Albert seethed. He was racking his brains, trying to think of a new challenge to propose, a way to beat Trey, when Jessica nudged him. "Look," she whispered.

Freddy was standing against the rink wall, a miserable look on his face, and Albert instantly realized what they had done. They had hijacked Freddy's party to play out their little competitive games. Trey had to prove he was better than Albert, and Albert had to prove he was better than Trey. It was ridiculous.

Gabby, Camila, and Min were back on the ice, and Freddy wasn't moving.

Albert had to do something. "I have an idea," he said to Jessica. "Grab on."

Jessica took his hand, and he steered them over to Min. "Min, grab on to Jessica. It's a game."

Min grabbed Jessica's hand, and now Albert steered their chain of three to Freddy.

"Freddy, grab Min's hand."

Freddy looked up.

"It's a game," Min said.

Freddy brightened and grabbed Min's free hand.

Four strong, they skated down the straight part of the rink, and everybody on the ice made way for them.

"Hold on!" Albert made a sharp turn and held on to Jessica's hand. With the momentum, Min and Freddy started flying faster, both of them laughing.

"Let go of Min," Albert whispered to Jessica.

Jessica let go of Min's hand, and Min and Freddy went flying, saving each other from falling by holding on to each other with both hands. Freddy looked deliriously happy.

Albert and Jessica skated apart, watching.

"Nice move, Albert," Jessica said with a smile.

Albert reached in his pocket and handed her the chocolate.

Her smile was dazzling.

17.0

President Telda Lat didn't choose to send an assassin to Earth on New Year's Eve for symbolic reasons and didn't even realize it was an Earth holiday. It takes time to plan such a radical and illegal operation, and it just so happened that on this night she was ready.

Unaware of any danger, Albert was busy doing what he always did on New Year's Eve. He and his family cooked a feast and played board games and went outside at midnight to bang on pots and pans during the countdown. The Kinney tradition.

After the countdown and the craziness, Albert told his family he was going to check on Tackle and then be right in. The Patterson tradition was to attend a party, so Tackle was always on his own.

"Tackle should be your dog," Erin said. "You take better care of him than Trey does."

"Thank you," Albert said. "I agree."

Delighted to see Albert, Tackle jumped up on him, and they spent a few minutes wrestling. Then they settled down on the Kinneys' front steps.

A new year, Albert said. He looked up at the treetops, bare now of all their leaves, and at the stars twinkling above them, wondering what his friends on Zeeno were doing. They could no longer enjoy views of their planet's once beautiful features. The near extinction of vacha trees, ahda birds, and so much else on Zeeno at the hands of the Tevs and Z-Tevs was something Albert desperately wished he could reverse. What a new year it could be if Zeeno could win back its freedom!

You ready for the big game? Tackle asked.

Albert nodded. *I've got six more practices before Friday. And then it's the ritual sleepover and then it's the game*—Albert rubbed Tackle right where he liked it, under his chin.

Nervous?

Yep. We have to show the entire solar system that we deserve their support.

You know I'm coming, right? Tackle asked.

Albert smiled.

Tackle shivered. *It's freezing out here.*

Wimp, Albert teased.

Tackle pounced, and Albert took off. They ran around to the Kinneys' backyard and then Albert dropped to the ground. Tackle stepped on his chest and puffed dog breath in his face. *Take it back.*

Okay, okay. You're not a wimp. Albert laughed.

Just then, Tackle's posture changed. His gaze snapped up. His hackles rose and his lips pulled back as a snarl emerged.

Albert was just about to ask what was going on when the top of his head grew icy and then warm. A szoŭ was occurring. But instead of Albert being beamed up, Unit D beamed down to Earth in front of Albert's eyes.

Perhaps it was the holiday excitement, but for a split second Albert assumed Unit D was making a friendly visit, which was, of course, ridiculous. First, no regulation robot would be authorized to appear on Earth. Second, the robot standing in front of him was a D model unit, but it was not Unit D3492778. And third, the robot was pointing a weapon at Albert's chest.

Just as the thing fired, Tackle pounced violently from behind, shifting the robot's arm so that the weapon fired directly into the ground. With an odd screeching sound, a golf-ball-sized sphere of blue fire flew from the weapon and hit the leaf-covered ground. In the next second a fire was burning at Albert's feet.

Albert was frozen in shock, but Tackle was in full hero mode. With a great chomp, he clamped his jaws around one of the robot's legs and swiftly pulled it off-balance as it was preparing to fire another shot. The machine fell face-forward, landing in the flames. The dog ran to push Albert out of the way and then turned to bark at the creature now engulfed in fire.

Albert snapped into gear and grabbed the nearest defensive weapon he could find—a garden rake. Together the boy and dog faced the fire, ready in case the creature rose up. But the fire acted quickly, not only burning the robot, but also creating a perfect crater in the yard, about three feet wide and two feet deep.

After another minute the fire seemed to fizz and sizzle like fireworks, and then it stopped. In the crater were the charred pieces of the robot.

Just at that moment, the light flicked on in the den—Nana's room—and she opened the door that led from the den to the patio.

"Albert?"

The boy and dog froze. It was dark in the backyard. They could see her clearly, but she could just see their shapes.

"Yes," Albert said.

"Everything okay out there?" she asked.

"Yep. Just playing with Tackle. I'll be inside in a second." The smell of smoke was clearly in the air, so he added, "I think somebody in the neighborhood is having a bonfire."

"Ah," she said. "Well, it's time to come in, don't you think?"

"Yep. Be right there. I need to get Tackle back. Good night, Nana."

The moment she closed the door, Albert dropped to his knees. Tackle rushed in for a hug. *You were amazing,* Albert said. *You saved my life.*

That was close. That was too close.

They both looked up, as if they could see anything but the usual night sky. There had to have been an ITV up there. Had the robot been alone? Was the ITV still up there or had it been programmed to return?

Do you think something else is coming? Albert asked nervously.

I will patrol all night, Tackle said.

With gratitude Albert hugged his friend again.

You will tell the Zeenods about this, right? Tackle asked.

Albert nodded. *Right now we have to take care of this hole. Maybe if we fill it with dirt and cover it with leaves...*

I'll move the dirt, you rake the leaves, Tackle said. Swiftly, Tackle stood with his back to the crater and pawed dirt behind him, moving around the circle until it was filled in. Then Albert raked leaves over it.

What do you think? Tackle asked when they were done.

It's fine, Albert said, knowing that the damage to the lawn was the least of his concerns.

18.0

The January days passed quickly. Although Albert and the entire Zeenod team were on alert, they made sure that each day on the johka field was a day of progress and purpose. They were astonished that a robotic hit man had been sent to Earth, they were worried about Kayko and Giac, and they knew they were all at risk of being murdered or kidnapped or arrested. But they had to keep training and stay connected as a team.

Albert wasn't afraid to initiate the szoŭ—Ennjy had assured him that his Z-da had not been hacked—so he looked forward to his practices. Being able to ditch school during lunch and beam up to play soccer on another planet for the Zeenods was an extraordinary honor and he remembered to be aware of it. He had a new mantra: Lunchtime? Launch time!

And then the big day arrived: the Friday before the game. On that day, Albert was skating home from school, already buzzing with anticipation about the sleepover on Jhaateez that he would be traveling to at midnight, when his phone vibrated: a text from Unit D.

Unit D here with a message from Ennjy: Giac has returned! Decoding is complete! Giac was being followed, so she went into hiding, not wanting to risk communicating until she was able to crack the code. We now have evidence to clear Kayko. It was President Lat who tried to kill you. Mehk wanted to scare you into quitting, but Lat wanted you dead. She blackmailed Mehk into creating the explosion. We believe she was working for President Tescorick of Tev. The Tevs and Z-Tevs are determined to keep Zeeno and to eventually eliminate all Zeenods. We have prepared a statement and have put all the evidence in one file. We don't want to send this electronically because we're afraid it will be intercepted and tampered with. Unit D has the file on board your ITV. We request that you leave now and go to Zhidor to make the statement and give the evidence to the Fŭigor Interplanetary Council in person. We cannot do this. Zeenods need permission from the Z-Tev government to travel to other planets and none of us would be able to gain permission to travel to Zhidor. We are asking that you leave as soon as possible and suggest you bring your dog as added protection. After you are done presenting the evidence, come to Jhaateez! Unit D can time-fold so that you can make it in time for the game.

Albert stared at the screen for a few seconds as the news about Giac's safe return and the president's guilt sank in. The Zeenod team must be celebrating Giac's courage and skill. The news about Lat was proof, finally, of what his team had been suspecting. He thought back to all the times Telda Lat had told them she was rooting for them, all the times she'd told them she could be trusted. She had been lying all that time.

Ennjy has requested that you receive the following final message: Telling the truth can be a dangerous action. What we are asking is for you to testify against someone in a powerful position. President Lat will either want to deny the charges or will confess that she was working for the Tevs. We believe you will be safe on Zhidor, and we believe that President Lat will be immediately arrested once you have presented the evidence; however, the Tevs and Z-Tevs will be furious. We understand if you feel the risks are too great.

Albert imagined standing in front of the interplanetary council giving an impassioned speech about Kayko's innocence and then showing the evidence. It would be like a movie! *Ladies and gentlemen, the real criminal is none other than President Telda Lat! And she was working for Tevs and Z-Tevs!* He imagined Kayko finally being freed from prison. Zeenods from all over the Fŭigor Solar System would be ecstatic. Finally, this crisis was going to end! He wrote back:

I am honored to be given this task.

Albert rushed to the Pattersons' house, found Tackle outside, and gave him the news. *Are you willing to come?*

I'm ready. The dog lifted his chin. *Backyard so no one sees us? Trey will be coming home soon.*

Albert nodded, grateful and relieved. *Meet you there. I need to drop off my backpack and call my mom.*

Leave my gate open so the Pattersons think I got out.

Good idea.

Albert ran inside. No one was home. His nana had left for a special birthday visit with an old friend in Baltimore—something she said she couldn't refuse. His mom's and Erin's suitcases were packed. The two of them were leaving soon for the Winter Invitational, which was Erin's big tournament in Delaware over the weekend. Albert was supposed to be having a special guys' night sleepover at a new friend's house, which was true in a way.

He called his mom and Erin picked up.

"Mom's driving. We just left my school," she said.

"Tell her I'm going to the sleepover early," he said. "I'll text Nana and let her know, too. Okay?"

He waited while his sister delivered the message. "She says okay," Erin said. Her voice sounded tight with anxiety. She had been training for this tournament for months and was clearly nervous.

"Hey . . ." He hesitated. He was going to say *good luck* but realized that *good luck* wasn't what he wanted to say. "Have fun."

"I won't have fun when I lose!"

He heard his mom's voice. "Erin! Don't say you'll lose."

Erin snapped back, "I found out that Brittany's mom let her skip school today so she would be rested. I'm going to be tired and I'm going to lose."

Albert took a breath. "Erin, I do the same thing. Sometimes I'm sure I'm going to fail. But I got some good advice from both Nana and Mr. Sam. Whenever you're doing something you love, remember that it's something you love doing. Just pick one thing in each of your routines that you love doing—like, I don't know, a certain move in your beam routine—and make a pact with yourself to actually enjoy it when you do it during the competition. Just that."

She was silent.

He went on. "When people see you loving it, I swear, they will, too. They'll be, like, *Whoa! That girl is amazing.*"

She laughed. "You're so weird, Albert," she said.

"See you, Erin."

"See you, Albert."

Albert put his phone in his backpack, put his Z-da around his neck, and ran out the door to initiate the szoŭ. Tackle was waiting in the backyard.

Come on! We need to go! The dog panted.

Ready, Albert asked.

To infinity and beyond, the dog said.

Albert laughed and initiated the szoŭ.

When they regained consciousness, they were on board the ITV and greeted by Unit D's mechanical smile. "Welcome, Albert. Welcome, Tackle."

Unit D handed Albert a smoothie and poured another into a bowl on the floor for Tackle. "Ennjy has requested that you have a nutritional smoothie and get as much hygg hibernation as possible so that you are ready. And Toben wants Tackle to do the same."

Albert hung up his Z-da and got to work on his smoothie.

Tackle lapped his up and looked at Albert. *Yum. Love this stuff,* he said.

Albert smiled. *Yeah, we should get the recipe.*

This was really happening. They were going to save Kayko and change the lives of Zeenods everywhere.

18.1

While Albert and Tackle were hibernating in the hygg and Unit D was piloting the spacecraft toward Zhidor, a text message from Giac came through. Unit D received it and set a reminder to tell Albert when he woke up.

This is Giac. Someone hacked into my files and has erased the copy of the folder containing the evidence. You now have the only copy. Please back it up. Also, whoever hacked my files could have gained access to the security passcodes for the ITV and for Unit D. Be on alert.

As Unit D began to follow through with the order to copy the evidence, the ITV alarm went off.

"Unauthorized vehicle approaching," the computer said.

Unit D switched its attention away from the folder and turned to investigating the new vehicle. And in the next moment, a figure beamed on board: President Telda Lat.

Registering the presence of the new life-form, the robot ratcheted up to its feet and swiveled. But with one quick movement, the president swiped a code over the optical port on the robot's chest.

Unit D's head tilted to one side, and then the robot walked to the nearest wall, folded into a seated position, and powered down. Telda Lat watched, holding her breath until the machine stopped moving. Then she exhaled and moved to the next step. She pocketed Albert's Z-da and the drive containing the evidence. After that she walked over to the system's control panel.

"Passcode accepted," the computer said.

Another breath in and out from Lat. "Prepare to set a new trajectory," she said.

"Would you like to choose from the most commonly used destinations or set a course for a new trajectory?" the computer asked.

"Set a course for Gravespace GJ7," Lat said. "And maintain the current speed for landing."

"At this distance, speed must be reduced," the computer warned. "Chance of complete destruction at this speed and from this distance is one hundred percent."

"Excellent," Lat said. "Maintain speed and course. Disable autopilot."

"Trajectory and speed are set. Autopilot is disabled. Warning. Code 13X. Complete destruction in eleven minutes."

The last sentence seemed to echo in the spacecraft.

Lat noticed with surprise that her emotions were flat. She had expected to feel satisfaction or relief or even joy. After all, a plan finally seemed to be working. She had tried so many ways to stop Kinney without having to physically do it herself. But, clearly, this was the only way. She stepped over to the hygg and peered in. The boy and the dog were curled up together, Albert's arm around the dog. He looked young. His Earthling skin was so smooth.

The headache that had been bothering her all day sharpened. She was supposed to get back into her spacecraft and set the course for Jhaateez. She was supposed to attend the game and pretend she knew nothing about what had happened to Albert. After the game, perhaps she would find Mehk and learn how he could have escaped.

She rubbed her temples. Suddenly, she had the fantasy of changing course, piloting her spacecraft far away, leaving the mess behind. She was tired of all the lies, tired of taking orders from Z-Tevs and Tevs, tired of planting evidence and faking

174

reports. She was tired of the Zeenods, too. Tired of their efforts and their desire to expose the Tevs and Z-Tevs. The Zeenods were no match for their aggressors. They needed to understand and accept that they were beaten.

"You should have quit, Albert Kinney," she said. "But you didn't. You kept surviving." She sighed. "That's not my fault. None of this is my fault."

She turned away from the hygg, and the ITV safe caught her eye. Albert's gold medal. Worth a small fortune. She could melt it down, and no one would be the wiser. She was owed something for all her trouble.

18.2

Tackle smelled it first, just as their hygg hibernation was coming to an end. He barked, fully waking Albert.

It's okay, Albert said. *Remember, we're just in the hygg.*

Someone is here, Tackle said, sniffing. *I don't like it.*

Cautiously, Albert peeked out of the tent. *I don't see anyone.*

They both crept out, Tackle sniffing the floor. *Someone was here.*

"Unit D, is anything wrong?" Albert stared at the robot sitting on the floor against the wall. The robot had taken a number of odd positions, but it had never looked inert before.

Tackle sniffed the robot and then nudged it.

Nothing.

The door to the safe was hanging open, its lock burned off.

A voice startled them both. "Albert Kinney is awake."

Tackle barked and spun around in a circle.

The videoscreen activated and President Lat's image appeared. "I'm riding next to you, Albert. We're on our way to a new location."

A cold prickle of dread went up Albert's spine. Out the side window, he could see a spacecraft. He ran to get the storage drive, but Lat's voice came through.

"No use, Albert. I took the evidence."

Albert's knees almost gave out.

"Now," she continued, "I have to make sure you don't talk to anyone."

The computer announced: "Approaching Gravespace GJ7. Warning. Code 13X. Complete destruction in four minutes."

Call Ennjy, Tackle whispered.

Albert turned to the see that his Z-da was gone.

"This will be your final destination, Albert," Lat said. "The ITV's system is set to make it appear to be a pilot malfunction. I'm afraid life-forms must be sacrificed sometimes to keep the peace."

"It isn't peace on Zeeno," Albert said. "It's an occupation. The Tevs and Z-Tevs have taken everything from the Zeenods and have used you. You don't want the Z-Tevs to throw you into prison so you keep saying yes to whatever they want you to do."

She didn't blink. Her voice sounded almost sad. "You made a mistake in saying yes to the Zeenods, Albert. You could have had a normal life on your little Earth."

Albert ran to the ITV control panel and pushed the green button, the one he knew from previous experience was supposed to activate the autopilot.

"Trajectory is locked," the computer said. "Autopilot cannot be used."

Tackle barked at the screen.

"There is nothing you can do, Albert," Lat said. Then the tone of her voice changed, and Albert realized she was sending a message. "Greetings—this is President Telda Lat. I am afraid I have terrible news. Please release the following statement to all media outlets: I regret to inform you that my office has just received word—the ITV piloted by Unit D3492778 carrying Albert Kinney and his canine companion to Jhaateez for the johka tournament has malfunctioned. The ITV veered off course and crashed on Gravespace GJ7. There are no survivors. On behalf of the entire planet, we mourn the loss of these two brave Earthlings."

Tackle growled.

Albert heard her tone change again. "Computer, set my trajectory to Jhaateez," she said.

Outside the window, Albert watched Lat's spacecraft zoom away.

We're going to crash, Tackle said, pacing. *We have to do something.*

Albert began suiting up, pulling on his uniform, pads, helmet, boots.

You think that's going to protect you from a crash? Tackle asked.

I don't know! Albert yelled, and sprayed the antifrostbite treatment on Tackle. *We need all the protection we can get. We need seat belts. No! Parachutes!*

The two of them raced around, pulling open every drawer and cabinet door.

"Warning. Code 13X. Complete destruction in three minutes."

Tackle stopped and looked at Albert, his velvety forehead wrinkling. *Three minutes?*

Albert crouched down, his voice breaking. *I'm so, so sorry I got you into this, Tackle.*

The dog nuzzled against Albert and then looked at him with his deep brown eyes. *My choice, my friend.*

Albert blinked back tears and hugged the dog close. He could feel his own love for Tackle streaming out and feel Tackle's love for him streaming in. The Lats of the universe could not win. He had to find a way. He thought about how often Unit D used the voice command feature to talk to the ITV's computer.

Albert stood up. "Computer, change trajectory to Jhaateez."

"Trajectory is locked," the computer said.

"Enable autopilot!"

"Password needed."

Tackle's ears went up. *What's the password?*

I don't know! Albert began running around again. "Computer, are there parachutes on board?"

"This ITV is not equipped with parachutes. Warning. Code 13X. Complete destruction in two minutes."

Tackle howled.

"Computer, is there any way to increase our chances for survival?" Albert asked.

"Would you like information about increasing the chances of survival of life-forms, survival of equipment, survival of the vehicle, or all of the above?"

"Survival of life-forms!" Albert yelled.

"Would you like information about increasing the chances of survival of life-forms in general or in this specific moment?"

"In this specific moment!"

"There are three possible ways to increase the survival of life-forms in this specific moment. Would you like to hear one, two, or all three?"

Albert wanted to rip his helmet off and throw it at the computer screen. "Just tell me all three!"

"The first would be to enable autopilot and—"

"I can't enable autopilot! What's the second?"

"The second is to use your Z-da to activate a—"

"I don't have my Z-da!"

"Warning. Code 13X. Complete destruction in sixty seconds."

"What's the third?" Albert yelled.

"Utilize the escape pod."

"You're kidding? There's an escape pod?" Albert screamed.

"To access the escape pod, lift the red lever in the rear of the spacecraft. This will open the access door to the pod. Once in the pod, activate the ejection sequence by pressing the button on the left."

Albert ran to the rear of the spacecraft and grabbed hold of a red lever. When he lifted it, a small door opened, and he peered in. No windows. No seats. Just an empty dome-shaped space about three feet wide and four feet tall. *Wow. This is small.*

Get in, Tackle said.

Albert scooched in backward, sitting down and drawing up his knees, smooshing himself as close against the walls as he could. *Okay. Come on, Tackle!* Albert opened his arms.

Tackle climbed in as the door began to close.

Pull your tail in!

Tackle shifted to pull in his tail and just then a small beetle detached itself from a seam in the ceiling and flew into the escape pod.

Did you see that? Albert asked.

What?

A bug followed us in.

A bug? The door closed.

Albert tried to see where the bug had landed, but neither of them had room to move. Tackle's face was against Albert's, his tongue out, his dog breath strong.

Where's the button to activate the ejection? Albert couldn't move his head to look.

Somewhere on the wall.

Albert knocked his elbow against the wall. Nothing. He shifted slightly and tried again. Nothing.

Keep trying, Tackle said.

Albert's knee bumped against something and the pod lit up.

"Ejection sequence activated," an alert blared.

Good job, Tackle said.

Hold on! Albert cried.

A loud sound came of metal shearing away from metal, and then they felt the force intensify as the pod shot out. Clinging to each other, they listened to the roar and hum for what seemed like an eternity.

Finally, they slowed down and then began to float.

In the distance, they heard the sound of an explosion— perhaps their ITV crashing on the surface of GJ7.

Albert tried to focus on his breathing. They descended steadily, rocked occasionally, and then the vehicle thumped twice, three times, and finally settled.

An alert rang out: "Landing successful. System is powering down."

The interior lights dimmed and the vehicle's hum grew softer.

We made it. We're alive. Tackle panted, his breath hot against Albert's face.

"Door opening…"

The bleak, white landscape of GJ7 was suddenly visible and

above it the view of a night sky. They were on a moon, and yet another moon was visible in the sky, lighting the black night and casting a soft bluish light over everything.

Tackle hopped out, but Albert froze. Lurking in his memory was a line from the guide about Tev creatures called haagoolts being present on gravespaces—something about haagoolts always being hungry.

18.3

Come out! Tackle said, sniffing. *It's not bad, and my breathing implant is working perfectly.*

Cautiously, Albert looked out.

The air was cold but not dangerously so and had a swampy smell. It appeared at first as if they had landed on a large, flat, empty plain—nothing visible but a low cloud of dense fog that clung to the ground, looking almost like snow. But then ahead—two Earth miles, Albert guessed—was a large building.

It's way bigger than a house. What do you think that thing is? Albert asked.

Tackle looked out and sniffed. *Too far for me to see. Should we stay or should we go?*

We need protection. We need to find someplace where we can get inside.

They stepped out and began making their way on the uneven

ground, walking in the tightly packed, ankle-hugging fog, their footsteps clattering. As they walked, Tackle sniffed, and then he stuck his snout down into the fog and came up with a bone in his mouth.

The color drained from Albert's face, and he quickly bent down and waved the fog away enough so that they could both look down—the uneven ground they were walking on wasn't rocky. It was bony.

Albert's stomach turned. *Drop it!*

Tackle dropped the bone. *What?*

The two looked at each other without saying a word as the reality sank in. Albert's stomach turned and he thought he would vomit. This wasn't like an Earth cemetery, a place where the dead were buried in neat rows and covered with grass and flowers. Bones were everywhere. Albert had a hundred questions. Whose dead was here? What planet would ship their dead off to be dumped on a distant moon?

What should we do? Tackle asked.

Albert closed his eyes and tried to take in a breath. His stomach was roiling, his knees were shaking, and a trickle of sweat was running down the back of his neck. *We don't have a choice. We have to keep walking,* he said. *Just pretend we're walking on rocks.*

They continued on, trying to ignore what was under their feet.

Does anybody actually live here? Tackle asked.

I'm not sure. Something, I think, called haagoolts.

Um..., the dog said. *What are haagoolts?*

I think they're creatures from the planet Tev. I remember something in the guide describing them as raylike. Not sure what that means. I think their hearing is weird or—I wish I had paid more attention! I wish Toben were here. He'd know.

If they came here from Tev, maybe it's because they only like dead things, Tackle said. *Maybe they won't be interested in us.*

That's looking on the bright side.

Tackle stopped and shook out his muscles. *I'm just saying—let's stay alive, okay?*

Agreed.

They walked on.

As they grew closer, they could see a collection of buildings in the distance, not just one. On either side of this compound were rock formations that resembled giant mushrooms. In fifth-grade science class, Freddy Mills had created a slide show on the hoodoos in Utah, and Albert thought now that these rock formations had a similar look.

Wouldn't Freddy be interested, Albert thought to himself. Just then the sky behind the buildings grew darker, as if a splotch of ink had spilled and was spreading.

They watched as the splotch moved toward them.

Is it a storm cloud? Tackle asked, sniffing the air.

I think it's ... an organism. It looks ... alive.

Suddenly, the inky stain separated into separate splotches, all moving toward them.

What's happening?

Whatever they are, they're fast.

One of the splotches suddenly shot closer toward them, gaining definition. In just a few seconds it was overhead, and then it flew over them and they could see it clearly.

A ray, Albert gasped. *Like a stingray, except ...*

With the grace of a sea creature, the large, flat thing sailed in the sky above them, low enough that Albert could see it clearly, its skin gleaming in the blue moonlight. Dark burgundy in color with strange slits in the silver belly and eyes that protruded out and swiveled down.

For a nanosecond, they were mesmerized as the creature passed, but then it turned and swooped back toward them. Instinctively Tackle and Albert took off running in different directions.

The ground was disorienting, not only because of the bones shrouded by the ankle-deep blanket of fog, but also because the moonshadows of a hundred haagoolts were now dancing on the blanket's surface.

Stop running, Tackle called. *There's nowhere to run to. We have to fight them off.*

Albert stopped and reached down and grabbed what he could find—a long oddly shaped bone—knowing it was no use. Overhead there were at least a hundred, and even more were coming.

We have to try, Tackle said. *Ray by ray, buddy. Let's do it.*

One of the haagoolts reached Albert first, and he swung the bone up at it. To his shock, a long tonguelike thing emerged from its underbelly, curled around the end of the bone, and snatched it out of Albert's hands. The creature sucked the bone up through its underbelly and then spat it back out. Albert had to jump out of the way. Out of the corner of Albert's eye, he saw another one swoop down toward Tackle, its long tongue emerging.

"No!" Albert screamed as the tongue wrapped around Tackle's hind foot and lifted him off the ground. Carrying Tackle, the haagoolt flew upward, passing over Albert. The two friends locked eyes for a split second, the boy standing on the ground and the dog dangling helplessly out of reach above him. And then Tackle howled, piercing and wolflike.

In the next moment, Tackle felt the creature jolt as if by spasm. The wings went limp and the tongue went slack. Both dog and haagoolt dropped to the bone-covered ground. Tackle hit first and rolled out of the way, and then the haagoolt came down with a clatter. At the same time, another creature fell from the sky, its limp wing grazing Albert's shoulder with enough force to knock him down.

The sound! Albert exclaimed. *I remember reading about how they can't tolerate certain frequencies of sound. Howl again, Tackle!*

Another fleet dove toward them. Tackle howled.

Haagoolts began dropping from the sky and clattering onto the ground, each sending a poof of fog outward for a brief moment. After a dozen seconds or so, each spot where a creature had dropped was covered again with fog, and the whole bluish-white plain stretched out as if nothing had ever disturbed it.

They looked up. Only the shapes that had been farthest away had escaped and were now retreating. Several seconds more and the sky was clear.

Are you okay? Your foot…

I'm okay. Hurts but I'll live. You okay?

Bruised. Ouch. Seriously bruised. But nothing's broken. My helmet and pads helped. We'll get your foot healed when we find our way back to Jhaateez.

Are the haagoolts dead?

I hope so.

Both boy and dog froze. After five or six seconds of silence, without speaking, they stood and began walking toward the buildings in the distance. Tackle limped. Albert gagged whenever his foot landed on the squish of a haagoolt.

When they arrived, they circled around the smaller buildings but found no way in, and no sign of life. The biggest building did have a dark, tunnel-like entrance on one side. Cautiously, they walked in and found themselves in a dim corridor with a series of doors on either side.

The oddest of sounds came from somewhere inside…Albert could swear it sounded like a radio or television…a play-by-play of a johka game? And then came the unmistakable sound of claws running on pavement.

Albert pushed open the nearest door, and he and Tackle ducked inside and leaned against it.

Within seconds a strangely familiar sound came. A bark. A nudge of the door. Albert braced against it. A panting and then, through the crack under the door, a snout pushed as far as it could and began to sniff.

Tackle sniffed back and barked with shock. *Dog?*

What did you say? the creature on the other side barked softly.

A voice came from a distance, and then footsteps.

Keeping quiet, Albert and Tackle listened to their conversation.

Laika, what is it?

Nothing. A gheet nest, Laika answered.

I hate those things. I swear they hitchhike in when the Z-Tevs do their dumping.

No worries. I squashed them all.

Good girl, the voice said.

The sound of footsteps retreated. Albert and Tackle waited. Just as they were wondering what to do, the sound of the dog's voice came again, softly. *I'm alone. It's safe. Open the door.*

Tackle nodded, and Albert stepped back.

The thing on the other side pushed the door open.

Standing in front of them, panting, was a dog...sort of. The creature was the size of a husky with a face that reminded Albert of a bear and a tail that was twice as long as any dog's tail on Earth.

The two animals sniffed each other.

Who are you? Laika asked.

I'm Tackle. Ridgeback. From Earth. We have been dumped here by someone who wants us dead. Who are you?

I'm called Laika.

A dim bell rang in Albert's mind. Something he had learned from his teacher Ms. Holly. *Laika the Soviet space dog!* Albert exclaimed. *Are you related? You must be!*

What are you talking about? Tackle asked.

Ages ago, a dog named Laika was sent into space from Earth, but everybody thought she died. Albert looked at Laika.

A rumor, Laika said. *She was rescued. I'm a descendant. We're called zawgs. I'm the companion of the crypt keeper.* She sniffed Tackle. *We're definitely related.*

Tackle sniffed her back. *Nice to meet you.*

We heard the ITV crash, she said. *Assumed no survivors.*

Escape pod, Tackle said.

But the haagoolts? Her eyes widened. *You howled, didn't you?*

I did, Tackle said.

A sound came out of the zawg, half snort, half laugh. *Certain sounds cause irreparable damage to any haagoolt within range. We dogs can make this sound and are useful here.*

Albert hugged Tackle. *I can't believe it. I'd have been slurped up if it weren't for you.*

Yeah, Tackle said. *I'm not bad to have around on a road trip.*

Who brought you here? Laika asked. *Who wants you dead?*

The presidents of Zeeno and Tev.

Laika shook her head. *Serious.*

Can you help us get out of here? There's more at stake than just our lives. Albert explained the situation as best he could, and the zawg listened.

We'll need to keep you hidden from the crypt keeper, she said. *She doesn't like attention. I think your only way out is to stow away on one of the transport vehicles that come and go.*

We need to go as soon as possible. We have to tell the Zeenods that Lat stole the evidence from this botmaker named Mehk—

Mehk? Laika's ears pricked forward. *There was a Mehk who came awhile ago. He paid the crypt keeper a bribe to store a life-form.*

You mean to dump a body?

No. To store a living being in our hibernation chamber.

Who is the being?

Don't know, said the zawg.

Wait, Albert said suddenly. *I know. It's not a human. It's the android—or robot—that Mehk made. It's the reason he wanted me to quit. He made a robot that he wanted to unveil at the johka tournament. He said it was completely realistic and it was supposed to be the alternate Star Striker for the Zeenods.*

Not sure about that, Laika said. *When the life-form arrived, it scanned as human DNA. The crypt keeper set it to be destroyed if it isn't picked up soon. The whole thing was illegal.*

It's not going to be picked up, Albert said. *Mehk is in prison.*

You want to see it? Laika asked. The zawg led them out the side door to one of the smaller buildings. She stopped and nudged a panel. A narrow door swung open and she trotted inside, Albert and Tackle following.

The room was small, dark, and empty. She trotted over and pressed with her head against a certain spot on the wall and then moved out of the way. About a foot off the ground, a large horizontal drawer with a plexiglass lid emerged from the wall.

Stretched out in the drawer was the body of Trey Patterson.

Albert gasped, and Tackle barked.

You know him? Laika asked.

Neither of them could speak for a moment, and finally Albert stammered, *I—I don't understand.*

Tackle began to sniff the body. *Smells like Trey,* Tackle said. *I don't think this is a robot, Albert. I think this is Trey.*

Let's find out. Laika nudged a panel on the drawer. Albert was about to stop her, saying he wanted to think, but it was too late.

The lid of the drawer opened, and Trey's muscles began to twitch. After a minute of involuntary shuddering, his eyes blinked open and closed a few times, and then his head turned and he looked at Albert.

Albert held his gaze, unable to comprehend what was happening. Trey sat up. "Albert?" A sudden smile.

A chill went through Albert. This was the Trey from his childhood. Trey, the old friend.

Tackle barked.

"Tackle!" Trey jumped off the platform and wrapped his arms around the dog.

This is the real Trey, Tackle said to Albert, balancing to take the weight off his injured foot, his tail wagging.

"What happened to your foot, boy?" Trey said with concern, and then turned to Albert. "What are you guys doing here? What's that uniform, Albert? It's so good to see…Wait…" Trey caught sight of Laika and the color drained from his face. "We're not—this is—" He began trembling, and Albert reached out to reassure him.

Trey's eyes snapped back to Albert with a spark of clarity. "I remember."

Albert and Tackle looked at each other.

"What do you remember?" Albert asked.

Trey staggered back and sat down, overwhelmed by the scenes rushing through his mind. "I was at camp, at camp…," he stammered. "It was after midnight, and I was in my bunk. Everybody else was asleep, and then I felt this sensation on the top of my head. It was scary. I thought—I thought something was wrong with my brain. Like seriously. Like a stroke or something. And then I woke up in a spacecraft and an alien was there." He looked up at Albert and immediately could tell that Albert knew what he was talking about.

Albert nodded. "Go on."

"The alien seemed to know everything about me," Trey said. "He told me I had been chosen by a team called the Zeenods as the alternate Star Striker and that he needed to borrow me. He said he had made a duplicate of me—a better me—and he was going to put me here just until he had the chance to show everyone his invention and then he would put me back on Earth. The whole thing was—I didn't believe it, at first, but then—it happened, didn't it? And now you're here. How did you know? How did you find me so fast? It was just yesterday." He began checking his body. "Nothing hurts. I was afraid he was going to kill me, but I'm okay. And you brought Tackle? Oh my God!" Trey crouched and grabbed Tackle in an emotional hug.

Both Tackle and Albert were struggling to comprehend what they were learning. Tackle kept sniffing and sniffing. *You are the real Trey, right?* the dog asked in a daze.

When Trey didn't respond, Laika explained that although Trey had been given a breathing implant, he hadn't received a language-translation implant so couldn't understand Dog or Zeenod. Mehk had communicated with him in English.

Tackle shook his muscles out, as if doing so could help him shed his earlier ideas and understand what was happening, and then he looked up at Albert with an amazed expression on his face. *Ever since Trey came home from camp, he hasn't seemed like the real Trey*, he said. *That's because he wasn't the real Trey!*

Albert, too, thought back over all the interactions he'd had with Trey—or the boy he'd thought was Trey. Since the beginning of September, the Trey who lived next door had been ridiculously good at everything…Spanish, saxophone, soccer, skateboarding. Albert thought back to how incredible it had seemed that Trey could watch a video of cha-cha-cha dancing on YouTube and then get out on the dance floor with all the moves memorized. No wonder Trey had seemed like a machine to Albert. He was a machine! All this time, the real Trey was here on Gravespace GJ7 hibernating in a pod.

"Albert. How did you find me?" Trey asked. "Where are we? What's going on?"

"It's—it's insane," Albert said. "Everything you described happened, Trey. This Zeenod named Mehk created a robotic version of you and swapped you out—except we didn't know it until now. But since August, the robotic Trey has been on Earth. He looks like you. He talks like you. He moves like you. Except he isn't you. He's more bulked up and conceited and obnoxious and we—we all thought you had changed, Trey. But it wasn't you, it was—your robotic twin. I can't believe it!"

I knew it! I knew something was off! Tackle said.

The Mehk guy must be a psychopath, Albert replied. *What a cruel thing to do to Trey.*

Trey was staring at them. "What are you guys doing? Don't tell me you're…talking to each other?"

Albert explained the language-translation implants, and Trey started pacing.

"This can't be true, Albert. I don't understand any of it. I don't know where I am. I don't know why I'm here. I don't know—"

"It's a shock to me, too," Albert said. "And I don't have all the answers. But I can tell you what has happened to me." The three friends sat down, and Albert went over the whole story from his point of view.

A flicker of confusion crossed Trey's face when he realized that

Albert had been chosen as the actual Star Striker. "But…if I was just the alternate, why weren't *you* abducted and replaced with a robot?"

Albert had been wondering the same thing. "Maybe it had to do with the timing," he conjectured. "You were at that camp when the swap was made. You were away from your family. Away from Tackle. Nobody there knew you. Maybe Mehk realized that if he replaced you while you were away at camp, it would be easier for him. He could have weeks to watch the robotic Trey and make sure everything was working. And then he probably thought he'd have no problem getting rid of me. He tried to scare me and then he tried to kill me."

Tackle put a reassuring paw on Albert's leg and Albert reached over to pet him.

"Wait, wait." Trey straightened up. "I just want to talk about the jokha thing for a second. Are you telling me that basically in the entire world, you were the top pick to play this johka sport and I was the next pick? Is that your Star Striker uniform?"

Albert nodded.

Trey grinned for a second, and Albert could see the twinge of envy in his old friend's eyes. But then Trey reached out and thumped Albert on the back. "That's so cool. I mean it's scary, but it's so cool. Congrats, Albert."

Albert felt a rush of affection. This was the old Trey, the friend Trey. Now that this Trey was here, Albert realized how much he had missed him. He smiled back.

Shh, Laika said suddenly, and the ears of both zawg and dog pricked. *A transport vehicle is coming.*

This is our chance, right? Tackle asked.

Don't ask first. They'll say no. Just hop on. Hide until you land and can escape.

"What's going on?" Trey asked.

"We have to get out of here," Albert whispered. "We can talk more later."

Cautiously, Laika led Albert, Trey, and Tackle between a series of buildings to a loading dock where a large transport vehicle had landed.

"Is that, like, a bus?" Trey asked.

"Shh," Albert whispered. "We're hitchhiking—secretly."

Stay back, Laika said. *Wait until they unload. I'll watch and when I bark, jump in. The doors will close and you'll taxi out to the launch dock, and then you'll be on your way. Good luck!*

Thank you, Tackle said.

Laika looked back with a smile, and then she trotted out to greet the truck.

They remained in the shadows of a doorway and peered out.

The doors at the back of the vehicle opened, and then the rear section of the craft tipped. Out rolled body-storage bins that were cinched together in rows, the bottom row on wheels. Ten across and three high. One set of thirty and then another and then another. They rolled out and came to a stop against the back wall of the docking alley.

Laika gave a short bark and Tackle took off. The rear of the vehicle was now empty, the back door still open.

Tackle hopped in first and sniffed around.

Albert and Trey ran next. "I don't know about this," Trey whispered, but Albert pulled him along and they climbed in the back.

As the vehicle door closed, they saw Laika trot away as if nothing unusual were happening. The vehicle rumbled and moved forward, and the three of them quickly sat on the floor, with their backs against the side of the vehicle.

After four or five minutes Trey asked where the spacecraft was going.

"First to the launch area and then to wherever their home planet is," Albert said. "When we get there, we'll ask the Fǔigor authorities to help us." He noticed a small access door just as the vehicle slowed and came to a stop. "I think it would be safer to get inside for takeoff." He stood up and pressed a button that looked as if it would open the small door. Instead, the large back door opened, and a lovely waft of fresh air blew in. For a moment, the three of them had a beautiful view of the sky and the moon.

And then the platform began to tip.

18.4

To keep from falling, Albert grabbed a metal ring on the wall, which happened to activate that small access door he had been trying to open. Trey managed to hold on to a rail that ran along the wall with one hand, scrambling to Albert's side. Albert pushed Trey through the door and then dove in. As soon as they were safe he turned to see Tackle scrambling and sliding down toward the open doorway, unable to get ahold of anything.

Tackle! Albert cried out. In a nanosecond, he could picture the whole of it, how Tackle would fall through the air and land on the moon's surface, how Albert would lose him.

By the small doorway, a coiled hose caught his eye. Quickly, he held on to the doorframe with one hand, reached out for the hose, and threw it out to the dog. The hose unspooled and dangled all the way down to the open doorway. Tackle managed to bite it, and Albert started to pull him in. Trey helped, and finally Tackle tumbled through. They all fell backward, and then Tackle's wet tongue was on Albert's face first and then Trey's.

A sound stopped them. Footsteps. All three turned to see that they were in a small corridor with a door at the end. The insignia on the door ahead of them looked vaguely familiar to Albert. Just as he was trying to remember where he had seen it before, the door began to slide open, and then he remembered. The Tev flag.

Stepping through the doorway, devices drawn, were two Tevs.

Tackle pounced.

From their devices, the Tevs fired three smartnets. One landed on Tackle, shrink-wrapping him completely in a netlike cocoon. Tackle went down on his back, helpless. The other two smartnets wrapped around the torsos of Trey and Albert, pinning their arms to their bodies.

Don't fight, Tackle, Albert said. *You'll make it worse and they'll kill you. Trust me, you have to calm down.*

The two open doors were secured, and the three Earthlings were dragged down a dark corridor and shoved through a doorway into the vehicle's cockpit.

Sitting with their backs to the doorway at the controls were two more Tevs, staring at the Earthlings with their rear-facing eyes.

"What's this? Stowaways?" the captain of the ship asked.

"We're not here to hurt you," Albert said quickly.

The two Tevs at the controls turned and laughed. "Obviously, you can't do that."

"We were dropped off at the gravespace by mistake," Albert said. "We're just looking for a way to get back to—"

"It's Kinney," one of the Tevs said with surprise, and then, glancing at Tackle, "And the dog! We've got celebrities on board."

All four Tevs began hovering around them like haagoolts.

Tackle growled.

Stay calm, Tackle, Albert said.

"We heard you died, Albert Kinney!" the biggest Tev said.

"Well, I'm here," Albert said. "We just need to get to Jhaateez."

"Big game tomorrow! Our game against Gaböq just ended. We won. Four to two." The Tev turned to his comrade. "This little Earthling thinks he can actually win the tournament."

"Doesn't look like he could score a goal against a gheet." His comrade laughed. "I know for a fact that the Tev team would be happy if we took care of them."

The other nodded. "Maybe even reward us."

"Definitely reward us."

Although his mouth was bound, Tackle tried to howl, hoping he could make these brutes thud like those haagoolts.

The Tevs laughed. One shook his head and said with mock concern, "Look how scared and sad they seem. They probably thought they were going to be rescued by Zhidorians or Zeenods."

"They probably thought they were going to get hugs and hyggs—"

"—and instead they got us!"

They all laughed even harder.

"Hilarious," Albert said.

The two in control stepped aside to debate whether to eject them into space or kill them and bring their bodies to Tev.

"What are they saying?" Trey gazed at Albert with incomprehension, tears forming in his eyes. "I don't understand any of this. I just want to go home."

The word *home* and the emotion in Trey's voice did something to Albert. Time stopped for a moment and Albert pictured himself in his comfortable bed, safe and sound, with his family sleeping in their rooms, and with Tackle sleeping next door, and with Trey, this Trey, his friend Trey, sleeping in his room. And then Albert's mind snapped back to the present, and he saw the Tevs through Trey's eyes, Trey who was seeing them for the first time—their muscular bodies, the fierce markings on their faces, the red eyes, the bolt-shaped pupils, the third eye in the back of their heads.

"I say we eject," one of the Tevs said, and the others agreed.

Two of the Tevs led the three Earthlings down a corridor. Trey began to panic, trying to loosen his arms from the net. Tackle tried to howl. Albert's stomach was churning with fear. None of Kayko's lessons had prepared him for this, he thought. Desperately, he wanted to save his friends, but he had nothing, no tool, no weapon, no trick up his sleeve.

The Tevs shoved them past a common room where a computer display was blaring the post-johka-game interviews. A reporter was congratulating Hissgoff and Vatria for a decisive win. Out of the corner of Albert's eye, just before the three of them were shoved into the ejection chamber, he noticed a johka ball sitting on the floor in front of the television.

The Tevs were about to secure the hatch and leave when a jolt of energy erupted in Albert. There was no way he was going to let these thugs kill him and his friends. And just like that, one of Kayko's lessons came to him: *Find ways to connect.*

Suddenly, an idea came to Albert. He cleared his throat and tried to keep the anxiety out of his voice. "You guys play johka?"

The two Tevs stopped and turned.

"You know you have two of the best johka players in the universe on this ship," Albert said. "I saw a ball back there. How about a little challenge?"

The Tevs grinned.

Albert looked around. "We don't have room to play here, but we could juggle. Whoever juggles the longest wins?"

Trey looked at him as if he were crazy, but Albert had guessed correctly. These guys grew up playing johka and they were stuck transporting dead bodies back and forth every day. Why wouldn't they want a chance to have a little fun?

A Tev ran back to get the ball.

"To make it fair, though, either you guys need to have your arms pinned or we get released," Albert said.

Albert and Trey, of course, were unarmed. The Tevs had two devices in hip holsters: one shot smartnets, the other shot bullets.

With a stern warning not to try anything, one Tev used a blade to make a small snip in the smartnets binding Albert and Trey and the nets sprang loose and landed on the floor.

They tossed the ball to Albert and told him to go first. He was more nervous than he had ever been in his life, but he knew that to make this whole thing work, he had to impress them, or it wouldn't be worth their while. He took a breath and focused on sending ahnic energy to his nervous core and legs. Knee to knee to foot to knee to head to back to knee, he kept the ball in the air, bouncing and bouncing, while the Tevs timed him.

How to use this to take over the ship or to free themselves wasn't exactly clear in Albert's mind, but he tried not to divide his attention at the moment. He just stayed with the ball. The Tevs were enjoying it, almost looking like ordinary sports enthusiasts if not for the fact that they were holding weapons. He was doing well and then fumbled.

"Not bad!" one Tev said. "My turn." He holstered his weapon, picked up the ball, and began.

An idea came to Albert. Moving back as if to give the Tev room, he deliberately placed one of his feet near Tackle, happy that he had thought to put on his official shoes before exiting the ITV on GJ7. While the Tev continued to juggle, Albert talked, choosing his words deliberately. "Not bad for a Tev. Of course, Jhaateezians can juggle while standing on a blade." On the word blade, Albert braced himself. His blades activated, and he had to balance on them without looking as if anything had changed. Ever so slightly, he tipped one foot forward to face the blade behind him toward Tackle. Sure enough, Tackle saw his opportunity. The dog moved his legs toward the blade and pressed the netting against it. With a ping, the net sprang open.

"Cleat!" Albert said. As he regained his cleats, Albert knocked down the Tev who was juggling while Tackle chomped onto the leg of the one with the gun. The gun dropped and Albert kicked it aside and grabbed the Tev's smartnet device. "Get back!" he yelled at Tackle, and then fired two nets, one at each Tev.

With their opponents immobilized, Albert cut Trey loose and handed him the second Tev's smartnet device. "We'll leave them here. Come on!"

Albert, Trey, and Tackle crept back down the hallway to the main control room.

"We'll have the element of surprise!" Albert whispered. "Trey, you go for whoever is on the right. I'll go for the left. Tackle, surprise them."

Tackle burst in barking like a beast, with Albert and Trey on either side, firing the nets before the eyes in the back of the two Tevs' heads could even blink. The two Tevs, wrapped tightly, thudded back into their chairs.

"I can't believe it!" Trey yelled. "This is amazing!"

While the Tevs cursed them, Albert walked in to look at the controls. His adrenaline was pumping and he wanted to celebrate, but he had to stay focused. "All I have to do is figure out how to set the trajectory to Zhidor," he said.

But before he could make another move, there was a change in the air. Tackle detected it first. Albert could tell by the shift in the dog's posture that something was happening. Then he felt a familiar icy prickle at the top of his head.

"What's—" Trey couldn't finish his sentence.

A szoŭ, Albert thought, and a split second later, he and his two friends blacked out.

18.5

When Albert regained consciousness, it took him a few moments to get his bearings. They were in a new ITV. Tackle was on his right. Trey was on his left. They both looked okay. Had they been rescued, Albert wondered? Or were they in more trouble?

A throat cleared and Albert looked up. From the shadows stepped a Zeenod, someone he had never seen.

Tackle growled, and he was hit with another smartnet. Whining, the dog squirmed on the floor.

Albert crouched down to help Tackle, and the Zeenod ordered him to step away.

Trey was standing, transfixed. "I remember you," Trey said. "You kidnapped me and left me for dead and—"

"This is Mehk?" Albert stared at the unfamiliar Zeenod.

A smile sliced across the botmaker's face. "I am famous."

Remembering Mehk's horrible betrayals, anger ripped through Albert, and then confusion. "You're supposed to be in prison."

Mehk held out his hands. "Apparently not."

From the floor, Tackle growled.

"You escaped?" Albert asked.

Mehk took one step back, lifting a weapon with one hand. With his other hand, he tossed the smartskin mask of the Z-Tev technician onto the floor in front of Albert's feet. "I have many tricks."

Mehk and Albert looked at each other, Mehk's eyes flashing with a complicated mix of emotions.

"How did you find us?" Albert asked.

Mehk leaned forward, plucked something off Albert's shoulder, and held it out. "Spybot. I've been watching every move."

Albert recalled the beetle that had been in the ITV and had flown into the escape pod when they were about to crash. "A miniature surveillance camera? Clever!" Albert said, and Mehk looked pleased. Buttering this guy up might be the way to go, Albert thought. He turned to his friends and gave them a quiet smile. "I'm sure Mehk doesn't want to hurt us. He's a genius and could have done so by now."

Mehk beamed and took a seat, gesturing with one hand that they should do the same. It was a small, beat-up ITV and the only other place to sit was a low metal bench. Albert and Trey sat down.

Cut me loose, Tackle growled.

Albert kept his voice calm and his focus on Mehk. "Tell us the whole story. Please."

Mehk leaned back, speaking to Albert in the Zeenod language almost as if he enjoyed finally having the chance to talk. "The moment I found out that the Zeenods were going to play in the tournament, I got the idea of showcasing my talent by creating a robotic Star Striker and tricking the entire solar system into believing it was real. So I began spying on the Zeenods." He held up the beetle spybot, pinched between his fingers, and smiled. "I've used these at various times and in various ways. I'm good at spying. I discovered that the Zeenods wanted you, Kinney, as their Star Striker, and that Lee was keeping a close eye on you on Earth. They didn't want anybody but you, but they had to choose an alternate and picked the person you grew up training with— Trey Patterson. I realized that it was safer and easier to duplicate Trey rather than you."

"You discovered that Trey would be leaving his family for camp"—Albert was connecting the dots—"and that was a chance to get your robot into place without his family around."

"Yes! It was a perfect plan!" Mehk said. "At great risk, I stole all the resources to create a robotic replacement for Trey, and then stole my first ITV. You cannot imagine the effort, the creativity, the courage it took to do all this. Extraordinary! Impressive beyond measure!"

"Then you kidnapped Trey at camp the way I was abducted," Albert guessed. "By beaming him up to your ITV?"

"Yes. I put him in hibernation on GJ7. My plan all along was to swap him back the moment the Zeenods recruited him to replace you." Mehk looked at Trey and then back at Albert. "I'm no murderer!"

"And in the meantime you were able to watch your robot on Earth—"

"Yes! I had a surveillance system in place. And everything was going according to plan. But there was one thing I didn't predict." Mehk stopped, almost out of breath. "I thought it would be easy to make you quit, Albert Kinney. But you wouldn't step down." There was a trace of admiration in his voice.

"We admire each other," Albert said, holding his anger toward the botmaker in check. "Your inventions are remarkable. None of us suspected that the Trey on Earth wasn't the real Trey."

Tackle growled, and Albert leaned forward and put a reassuring hand on his head without taking his eyes off Mehk.

Mehk's anger was softening. Albert's strategy was working.

"The language, the movements, the facial expressions," Albert went on. "I didn't think anything like that was even possible."

"The Tevs and Z-Tevs have made some progress," Mehk said. "But I have integrated features they haven't even dreamed of. Sophisticated artificial intelligence and the most realistic visuals. I even added an aroma and a way to pass DNA testing."

"You are a genius, and I know you're not a murderer," Albert said. "Bring us to Jhaateez! We can win—"

Mehk leaned forward. "There is no 'we.' Lat has told the Zeenods that you died in an accident, Kinney. Everyone in the solar system thinks you and your dog are dead. That's what I have wanted all along! With you gone, the Zeenods will recruit their alternate, and when my masterpiece gets called into action—"

"But it's too late for the Zeenods to call up and train an alternate for this game." Albert tried to keep his voice calm. "And so—"

"I know that!" Mehk snapped. "It's too late for this game. But not for the next! I can't let you return."

Albert's mind worked through what Mehk wanted from Mehk's point of view. "I understand why you need to get your invention on the field," Albert said cautiously. "If the Tevs or Z-Tevs get it before you do that, they'll claim it as their own—"

"Yes!" Mehk said. "That's what they always do!"

"And they'll use your technology in ways you never intended," Albert went on. "They'll use it—"

"My intentions were always good!" Mehk stood and began to pace, agitated. "I see inferior robotics and inferior life-forms, both riddled with either technical flaws or internal shawbles, and I know that I can offer perfection."

"Surprise them, Mehk! Bring me to Jhaateez in time to play against the Jhaateezians. It will be like bringing me back from the dead!" Albert smiled. "You know how angry that will make Lat and the Tevs and Z-Tevs?"

Mehk began to pace. Albert could tell that his idea was taking hold. "You're smart, Mehk. You know that if I don't play in this game, the Zeenods won't have a chance. Do a little time-folding. Take me to Jhaateez, and then take Tackle and Trey to Earth. After the game, I'll quit." Albert's heart thumped. He had no intention of quitting, but he couldn't say that. "You can pick up your robot and hide somewhere until this game is over and—"

"Stop and let me think." Mehk's voice cracked out like a whip.

Albert's mouth closed. The three friends sat in frightened silence as the botmaker stood and began pacing. Albert wanted much more than to be dropped off. He wanted to see for himself that both Tackle and Trey would be returned safely. He wanted Mehk to help free Kayko and to join the movement to end the occupation. But he couldn't ask for all that.

Mehk looked out the window. Finally, he initiated a voice command. "Set trajectory to Jhaateez." Then he turned to Albert. "After the game, you quit, or else we're right back here."

Cautious hope swept in. Albert explained to Trey and Tackle what was going to happen, and then Mehk gave them orders to remain quiet. They rode to Jhaateez in silence.

When Mehk gave him the cue, Albert stood and waited for the familiar sensation of the szoŭ.

"Don't go, Albert!" Trey said, scared.

"I have to," Albert said. "You'll be okay."

I want to go with you, Tackle said.

Albert looked into Tackle's deep brown eyes. *I need you to be with Trey.*

The dog's brow wrinkled. *Can we trust Mehk?*

We have no choice.

For Albert, the cold prickling came next, then the strange warmth and the falling upward. Everything went black.

19.0

When Albert gained consciousness, the dazzling light made it difficult for him to see, but after a few seconds he realized he was on a snow-covered slope, a crater on each side. The Fŭigor sun was up. A new day. Game day.

"*Breeeet. Breeeet.*"

A furry white six-legged creature, goat-sized, turned to look at him, bright blue eyes suddenly visible through a face covered with fur. The thing had strange ears, two hard little scoop-shaped things that swiveled on top of its head. "*Breeeet. Breeeet,*" the creature said.

There was another and another, Albert now noticed. The hillside was dotted with the furry things. He turned to get a full look at his surroundings and there was the johka stadium, about two hundred meters downhill. For a moment, he was stunned by the sight of it, the sunlight bouncing off the huge geodesic dome, each clear panel studded with diamonds.

"You're Albert Kinney!" a voice said, and Albert whirled around to see a Jhaateezian standing there. Twenty yards away was a sled covered with a clear bubble of protective plexiglass. "What are you doing here?" the Jhaateezian asked. "You're supposed to be dead."

Albert stammered out the quickest version of the story possible. The Jhaateezian lifted the bubble off the sled and invited Albert to jump in. As soon as he was behind the wheel, the bubble popped back into place. Immediately, warmth began radiating from the sled's seat.

The Jhaateezian tapped the glass. "Wait!" She pulled out a camera and took a selfie with him and then yelled, "Go!" and gave him a push.

Stunned, Albert grabbed the wheel as he took off, zooming down the hill. On either side were craters and between them, a path about six feet wide, about half the width of a car lane on Earth. He wanted to try looking for a brake, but he was terrified of turning his focus away from the wheel. At top speed, he struggled to stay on the path, gripping the wheel and gritting his teeth until finally the slope emptied out into the parking area in front of the stadium. As he navigated his way through the parking lot, trying desperately to avoid crashing into parked ITVs, his feet frantically searched for a brake. Just as he rounded the corner and was heading straight for the main doors to the stadium, his foot found a pedal. He slammed it and the sled skidded into a spin. One, two, three, four, five times, Albert saw the main entrance pass by in a blur. And then the sled slowed to a stop. Automatically, the bubble roof opened. Albert jumped out and raced inside in the stadium lobby.

A Jhaateezian stopped him.

Albert could hear the faint sounds of the Jhaateezian anthem. "The opening ceremony started?" he asked in a panic. He had been hoping he would arrive in time to rest and prepare for the game. Instead he was arriving just as it was about to begin. If the Jhaateezian anthem was being played, it meant the Zeeno anthem had already been played. The exchange of crests would be next and then the introduction of the Star Strikers.

"Ticket, please," the Jhaateezian said.

"It's me," Albert said. "I'm Albert Kinney. I'm—"

The Jhaateezian looked frightened for the first second and then jumped into action. "Clear the way!" She grabbed Albert by the hand and led him through the entrance to the deck. Choking with gratitude, he ran with her, knowing that if he had landed on another planet, a robotic ticket-taker would have been programmed to block any life-form without a ticket. Lucky for him, Jhaateez relied on genuine Jhaateezians.

As they ran onto the wide deck that circled the entire stadium, vendors passed back and forth, and the smell of food from the carts made Albert dizzy with hunger. He reached out and grabbed a Jhaateezian sandwich, calling back to the Jhaateezian, "I will pay you later. I promise."

The vendor broke into a grin. "It's Albert Kinney!"

Albert took a bite, moaning with pleasure. "Thank you!"

Below, the field stretched out like a dream with the curved oblong ring of flawless ice around it. The starting players for the Jhaateezians and Zeenods were standing on the turf in lines as the last notes of the Jhaateezian anthem played. Up here on the deck at the center-field line the rest of the Jhaateezian team stood at the benches in front of the doorways to their locker room. The bench for the Zeenods was empty, of course. No subs. And rising above the deck were the stands full of fans from all over the solar system.

Suddenly, the johkadin of Albert was being projected onto screens throughout the stadium and onto the glistening, diamond-studded geodesic dome.

A Zhidorian's voice rang out over the loudspeakers. "The Zeenods would like to dedicate this game in memory of—"

"Wait!" Albert yelled.

The entire stadium, it seemed, turned to look at him on the deck. Out of the corner of his eye, Albert saw an official FJF surveillance drone approach, scanning his face.

Albert's mouth suddenly went dry and his heart seemed to stop.

"It's Albert Kinney!" the Jhaateezian ticket-taker yelled out, her voice echoing throughout the stadium. "He's alive!"

Albert snapped back to the moment, activated his blades, and dropped in. The sound of his descent onto the ice cut through the silence as all eyes followed him down. When he reached the bottom and slid onto the turf, the players stared as if he were a ghost.

Eyes wide, Ennjy walked up to him and put a hand on his shoulder, as if she had to feel him to believe he was there. "Albert," she gasped.

Albert nodded, not quite able to believe it himself. He noticed the sandwich, still in his hand, and, unable to help himself, he took another bite.

The Zeenods and the Zeenod allies all began to cheer. Albert looked up and joy rushed in. There were Zeenods in the stands! More than he expected, more than had dared to come to Zeeno. They were waving and jumping, their bems responding.

The Zeenod team was about to move in for a group hug, but

the FJF official stopped everything and announced that a DNA scan had to be complete—they had to make sure.

As the stadium fell silent, not one, but two medical drones scanned Albert.

There was a pause and then the announcement was broadcast. One hundred percent Albert Kinney.

A cheer went up and his team piled in for a group hug.

"Albert!" Doz said, squeezing in. "Albert! Albert! Albert! Albert!"

"We heard that you died," Sormie said. "We thought it was true."

"I have so much to tell you," Albert said, feeling giddy at being suddenly surrounded by these familiar faces. Their eyes were turning gold, and Albert felt another wave of gratitude. Their emotion was for him. He was loved and valued. He was a part of this amazing team.

"The evidence to free Kayko?" Giac whispered. "Did you make it to Zhidor?"

"Lat hijacked my ITV," Albert whispered back, and watched the faces of his teammates fall. "She has the evidence." He wanted to tell them everything, but it would have to wait. There was a commotion in one of the VIP boxes, and the team looked up.

Albert couldn't see President Lat's face, but he knew she had to be shocked. The presidents of all the Fŭigor planets were present, and the presidents of Tev and Gaböq were demanding that Albert be disqualified from playing.

A trio of FJF officials consulted the rule book while the players and fans waited anxiously, and then the announcement was made: "There are no grounds for disqualification. Albert Kinney may play. The Star Strikers will be introduced and the game will begin."

The opening ritual resumed, and he was called forward.

"Introduction of the Star Strikers," the loudspeaker boomed. "Albert Kinney and Linnd Na."

To the sound of cheering, Albert stepped up. Above him, the fans from Jhaateez, Liöt, Fetr, and Manam stood along with all the Zeenods who had come.

"Nice idea coming back from the dead, noddie," Linnd whispered to Albert as she put a hand on his shoulder. "I think even my family now wants you to win!"

Albert gave her a fist bump and the crowd cheered even louder.

After they said their official FJF tournament vows to play to the best of their abilities, to respect each other as competitors, and to uphold the rules of the game, Albert added his own meditation aloud: "May we both play well, Linnd."

"May we both play well, noddie." She smiled. "But I still intend to win!"

Funny, Albert thought, how different that would sound coming from Vatria.

The ref tossed the coin in the air and Jhaateez won the first kick.

19.1

Mehk felt strangely light as they approached Earth's orbit. What was the reason for this feeling, he wondered? Relief? Happiness? Yes, he was close to being reunited with his robotic masterpiece. But there was more to it. He was glad that he had returned Albert to Jhaateez.

Wait. Glad for Albert? Was that it? Or was it fun to imagine the look of shock on Lat's face? If the Zeenods did win, the Tevs and Z-Tevs would be furious—and that thought made him giddy with delight.

The dog and boy waiting for their release sat side by side. Well, not exactly side by side. More like entwined, Mehk noticed. The boy's arms were around the dog. The dog's chin rested on the boy's shoulder. Mehk had agreed to release the dog's netting. The dog had to behave. After all, Mehk was the only one who could deliver them to Earth.

Mehk thought back to the way his gheet's eight footpads felt as they crawled up his arm. The boy was being comforted by the dog, Mehk could tell. What would it feel like, Mehk wondered, to be comforted by something so large and warm and alive? Mehk had watched the way Albert, Tackle, and Trey had all tried to comfort each other in different ways, and he felt a pang of envy. Life-forms were capable of spending time and energy cooperating voluntarily. His gheet had only completed comforting actions because he had programmed those actions.

His mind flew back to the Zeenods in prison and how they had cooperated so willingly and so cleverly. The Zeenods were intelligent and capable. What the Tevs and Z-Tevs were doing to them had to be stopped. For a moment, Mehk thought through the possibility of going to Zhidor and working with the authorities to expose the Tev occupation.

"Approaching szoŭ range for planet Earth," the ITV's alert rang out.

Trey and Tackle both straightened up.

"What's going to happen now?" Trey asked. "You promised to return us to Earth."

"I'm keeping my promise," Mehk said in English. "But first—a necessary but unauthorized memory wipe. For your own good. And to protect me."

"You don't have to do that," Trey said. "I won't tell anyone about you or about all this."

The botmaker shook his head. "I can't trust you." He activated the stolen ITV's medical drone and began programming it. "I have to take you all the way back to when I abducted you. That means when you regain consciousness, the last thing you'll remember is being at camp. Months will have gone by that you will be unable to account for. Earthlings do lose their memories sometimes. A concussion will do that. Yes, a concussion will be a plausible explanation." Mehk glanced at Tackle. "No need to wipe your memory. No one on Earth could understand you even if you wanted to talk."

Before Trey or Tackle could respond, the drone flew to Trey and swept a laser across the left side of his head. While Trey was stunned, Mehk initiated the szoŭ for both the dog and Trey at the same time. After the two disappeared, Mehk took a breath.

The spacecraft felt sweetly empty. He was happy to be rid of the responsibility of these Earthlings at last. As a smile spread across his face, he found and locked onto the coordinates of his robotic creation on Earth and activated the szoŭ to retrieve it. Heart pounding, he counted one, two, three . . .

Nothing happened. Mehk waited a few seconds and tried again.

It should not be taking this long, he thought. He was within range. The szoŭ had worked to send the two to Earth. Something was wrong.

19.2

"Albert," Ennjy said as the ref prepared the ball for play. "Are you ready for this? You missed the ahn ritual. Have you had a chance to rest and hydrate?"

"I'm ready," Albert said.

"Roll and rock!" Doz called out.

Albert took his place across from Linnd in the center of the field.

As the rest of the players assumed their positions, Albert's mind spun. Visually, he was taking in the magnitude of the crowd, the beauty of the field, the sight of his teammates and his opponents. But he was also in another world, imagining Tackle and Trey back on Earth and hoping everything was fine. And he was thinking about Kayko, still in prison, and all the other Zeenods who weren't free. The evidence that could have exposed the injustice was gone; what Giac had worked so hard to deliver was gone. He glanced up again at the VIP boxes, wondering how all the issues with Mehk and Kayko and Lat would be resolved. He figured he had one thing in his favor—Lat hadn't expected him to show up, so most likely had not planned another explosion on the field.

Ennjy, at the left wing, had her eyes on him. As if she could hear his thoughts, she called out, "Albert, it's time for one thing only. Johka."

Albert nodded.

The ref released the ball, the trumpet blared, and it was game on.

Linnd sent the ball to a teammate, and for the first few minutes, the Jhaateezians dominated. Albert knew that Linnd and the Jhaateezians used their sailwings in an almost theatrical way, but experiencing it on the field while he was already struggling with fatigue and hunger was distracting. Everywhere on the pitch and on the ice, it seemed, the iridescent wings were flashing. The Jhaateezian defenders and attackers stayed loose and relaxed, as if there were nothing to it, and yet they kept throwing little tricks into their basic runs, like leaps and slides and flips, using their sailwings to propel themselves in various directions. They moved swiftly—one moment using the ice, one moment owning the field—and each Jhaateezian seemed to catch Albert's attention, pulling his gaze away from where it needed to be. For what seemed like an eternity they possessed the ball with no discernible desire to score, just a desire to show off to the crowd. And the crowd loved it.

Finally, they misplaced a pass, and Doz won the ball. He passed it to Feeb, who was defending on the right. Nice and easy, he passed it up to Heek, who ran with it. Although the Jhaateezians put the pressure on, the Zeenods kept passing the ball, nice tight passes on the turf, the tiki-taka they were so good at, working toward the goal.

Albert, who was marked closely by two Jhaateezian defenders, was annoyed that he wasn't receiving any action. Eager to show Lat—and the entire solar system—what he could do, he ran off to the side, activated his blades, and hopped onto the ice to skate toward the goal.

"Ball!" Albert yelled.

Seeing that Albert would be in a good position for a strike, Sormie passed. Albert angled down to slide off the ice, intending to receive the ball on the turf, but when he hit the ground, he forgot to retract the blades, and he wiped out.

A Jhaateezian defender swooped in, intercepted the ball, and started the counterattack.

Embrace the fall and get up quickly, Albert thought. But exhaustion slowed him down. As he watched with a sinking heart, Linnd made the same skating run toward her goal that he had done toward his. The defender played a long ball behind the Zeenod defense. And as the ball was sailing through the air, Linnd jumped off the ice toward the box, scored a diving header, and somersaulted out of it in style.

Goal!

1–0 Jhaateez.

To celebrate, Linnd did a standing backflip, which was repeated in a chain reaction by all of her teammates. This was the Jhaateezian ritual for scoring.

The crowd went wild. The Jhaateezians and the many Liötians in the stands who had come to cheer Linnd stood and flapped their sailwings, causing each of them to rise slightly off their feet and then float back down. The magical effect of their joy deepened Albert's regret and shame.

19.3

As consciousness prickled back into Tackle's mind and body, a rush of smells came first: the particular, cold smells of a typical January day in his neighborhood. A nanosecond later, the feeling of familiar pavement under his paws. Earth-style road pavement.

Nice…but then a smidge of disappointment popped in: how uneventful the next stretch of time was going to be. He wished he could be protecting Albert on Jhaateez. He was just about to let loose with a *grrrr* and shake out his muscles when the final fuzziness of the szoŭ cleared from his brain and the full menu of smells and sights and sounds around him coalesced. In one blindingly clear moment, Tackle realized that instead of landing in the yard or the driveway, he and Trey had landed in the middle of the street in front of his house…and a mail truck was headed straight for them.

Through the windshield he could see the wide-eyed shock of the woman at the wheel as she slammed on the brakes.

Tackle rushed at Trey, head-butting him over the curb, where he face-planted in the grass.

The truck swerved and screeched to a stop. The driver jumped out, and Tackle stood by Trey's side.

"You—you both just appeared in the middle of the street," the driver said, shaken by the close call.

"I think I'm fine," Trey said, dazed and a little scraped up.

Mrs. Patterson was hustling out of the house, beside herself with worry. "I saw it from the window! Trey, are you okay?" As she knelt by Trey, the driver rushed to talk with her, letting her know that the dog had acted fast to get Trey out of the way.

"Good dog, Tackle!" Mrs. Patterson said, giving Tackle a hug and checking Trey for broken bones.

Amazing, Tackle thought, how often people talk to dogs even without translation implants, and, yes, I am a good dog.

In the next second, a familiar smell hit the air. Tackle sniffed and looked up and saw something he did not expect.

Walking toward them from the direction of the park was the robotic Trey, the strong smell of him wafting in Tackle's direction.

Tackle's ears pricked. The szoŭ must not have worked right! There were two Treys on Earth. And this one was headed straight for home.

19.4

With Zeeno down one, Albert was shaken but determined not to show it.

Ennjy approached, her violet eyes full of concern.

"It was my boots!" Albert said. "They didn't work right."

"Albert, when was the last time you slept? Or ate?" Ennjy asked. "You can't play if you can't even think. It will be dangerous for all of us."

"I'm fine. I've got this," Albert said, quickly taking his position before she could say more.

The ball flew to the center spot. The trumpet blew.

The match resumed, and Albert passed the ball back to Doz, but the pass fell short. The Jhaateezians got possession and immediately took to the ice. Once on it, they were unbelievably fast.

The fact that the play never stopped, not even for an out-of-bounds ball, meant that the Zeenods could barely catch their breath. Whenever they got on the ice, their energy was sapped by the effort to stay in control. The Jhaateezians, meanwhile, seemed to receive energy from being on the ice.

Soon enough, their midfielder managed to split through the Zeenod defense and skate the ball down to Linnd. With no problem balancing on one skate, Linnd took a shot from the ice, perfectly aimed. Albert winced, but Toben parried the shot safely to the right. Feeb gathered the ball and the Zeenods worked it up the field.

The Zeenod fans in the stands cheered.

The way his teammates were passing with their bems billowing told Albert that the ahn was flowing. But he couldn't feel it, a fact that was rattling his confidence. Determined to overcome it, Albert forced himself to push ahead, making a diagonal run behind the Jhaateezian back line. Although the turf felt good under his feet, he wanted to prove that he could handle the ice, so he went for it.

After landing well, Albert felt his spirits lift, and he skated toward the goal. Heek saw him and sent the ball in his direction. Albert veered toward the field, remembering to retract his blades. With perfect timing, he shifted from ice to field, receiving the ball as soon as he was running. For a split second, he felt like a superstar. This was what all that training, all that practice was for! The Jhaateezian goalie was crouching, ready for Albert's strike. Albert was going to get a goal, he could feel it!

And then a Jhaateezian defender was in his face.

"Drop it!" Ennjy yelled.

Albert could feel the open space behind him. But instead of passing the ball back to Ennjy, he took a shot. The second he kicked, he knew it was ridiculous. Two Jhaateezians were there to block the ball before it even got to the keeper.

The Zeenod fans in the stands groaned.

With blinding speed, the Jhaateezian defender with the ball dribbled past Albert, hit the ice, and sailed down toward their goal. Doz and Feeb hopped on to try to stop the advance, but the

Jhaateezian was too fast, careening toward their goal. In the net, Toben squatted, arms out, knowing that the ball was coming.

But on the ice, the Jhaateezian didn't shoot as he approached. Instead he whipped around behind Toben.

Expecting the player to zoom around to the other side, Toben and the Zeenod defenders shifted to defend that side. And then, a complete surprise—the Jhaateezian with the ball stopped abruptly right behind the goal.

For a moment, the Zeenods were confused. Toben actually turned to look. And just then, with an almost nonchalant elegance, the Jhaateezian put his toe under the ball and lifted it over the net. Linnd, waiting in front of the net, headed it in.

Albert collapsed to his knees.

Goal! 2–0.

Again Linnd began the chain reaction of backflips to celebrate, and the home-team fans and Liötians went wild.

Ennjy gave the ref a signal that a teammate was leaving the field and ran over to Albert. "Go to the locker room. Get in a hygg."

"You're kicking me off the field when there aren't even any subs?" Albert stood up, blood boiling.

Ennjy straightened, her violet eyes steady. "Go get your mind right, Albert. Right now, you're hurting us."

As the crowd roared, Albert turned away from his team. He knew he wasn't angry at her. He was angry at himself. The thirtieth minute of play and he had given up two goals. Albert the Awful. Albert the Atrocious. Albert the Abominable. He didn't even know if he had the strength to skate up the bowl and onto the deck, which was where the door to the locker room was.

"Do you need to use the emergency exit?" Ennjy asked softly.

He summoned every ounce of strength, ran, jumped onto the

220

ice, and skated up the bowl. Not quite making it all the way, he had to grab onto the deck and pull himself up. Once he managed to stand, he stormed into the locker room.

Inside, his strength drained, his mind flooded with negative thoughts, and he collapsed onto a bench.

A security drone approached and began to scan him to make sure he was authorized to be in the space, and he spat at it. A dozen hyggs were floating about two feet off the ground, ready for any player who needed a quick rehydrating rest. Unable to get up, he reached out and punched the hygg that was closest.

Then came the sound of the door opening. Albert turned, and in walked a fully cloaked and masked figure with arms outstretched. "Albert!"

At the sound of Lee's voice—distorted by a disruptor in the mask—Albert stood. The security drone did a DNA scan, and, since Lee had authorization, didn't send an alarm. But Albert felt rocked by paranoia and confusion. "Wait," he said, stiffening. "How do I know you're Lee? You could be anyone."

The figure in front of him stepped forward. "The last conversation we had was in the medic tent at your last game. We talked about attitude and how you could either be a help or a hindrance. It's me. I'm here."

The mistakes Albert had just made on the field were like invisible weights pushing him down. Although he kept standing, he felt as if he were caving in on himself. "You came to tell me my attitude sucks," he said, staring at his own feet, so suddenly exhausted he could barely get the words out.

And then he heard Lee take a breath.

"Albert, I came here to tell you how overjoyed I am that you're alive. When I heard the news about the gravespace—" Lee choked up, and then dove to embrace Albert.

Albert stiffened, but Lee didn't let go. For a long moment, the two didn't move, and slowly Albert felt something brittle inside him begin to soften. What he and Lee had talked about in their last meeting came back to him. To be a star meant to be a part of a constellation, a team. He wanted that.

"I made a huge mistake," Albert said, tears springing to his eyes. "I thought I could muscle my way through. I shouldn't have played." Overwhelmed, he had to sit down.

Lee picked up a smoothie and handed it to Albert. "We all make mistakes. You must be exhausted. And hungry and thirsty."

Albert took the cup and drank it down. Almost immediately he could feel the nutrients and hydration doing their work. He looked up. "What do I do now?"

Lee pulled a hygg toward him. "Rest. Join your teammates at the halftime break for the ahn ritual. You'll know then if you're ready to get back in the game."

"Get back?" Albert choked. "They're not going to want me. Ever again."

"You made a mistake. You can learn from it."

"I lost the game!"

"The game isn't over."

"We're down two." Albert groaned. "The Jhaateezians are going to win."

"Albert, do you believe you can see into the future?"

Albert looked up. "What?"

"Avoid assumptions. The Zeenods are strong," Lee said. "The ahn is strong."

Albert broke down. "I know, but I couldn't feel it. At all. It's like I'll never connect to it again."

Lee's hand touched Albert's shoulder. "Albert, you tried to force it by relying on yourself. You forgot that power comes from connection."

"But I shouldn't have forgotten that!" Albert cried. "You told me at the last game. Ennjy and Kayko told me. I listened to the lessons. How could I have forgotten? There's something wrong with me. I have too many shawbles. I can't remember what I learn."

"Albert, we don't learn something once and then respond perfectly for the rest of our lives. We learn something and then sometimes we get it right and sometimes get it wrong. Don't try to be perfect, because you can't control that. When you make a mistake, try to acknowledge it and then remind yourself what you can do to respond positively."

"I haven't done anything right!"

"Albert, you survived! Somehow you got yourself here alive. That is huge."

"It doesn't help Zeeno."

"Being here can help Zeeno. What is one constructive thing you can do right now to move toward that?"

"There isn't anything I can do."

"Albert. Is hitting yourself constructive?"

Albert closed his mouth.

"Is saying that you know the Zeenods will lose constructive?"

Albert let out the breath he was holding.

Lee took Albert's empty cup. "You drank your smoothie. That was constructive. Name one other constructive thing you can do right now."

"The hygg."

Lee nodded. "I wish you could see me smiling behind this

mask. That's it, Albert. Rest and see how you feel when your team comes in for the break."

"But I shouldn't ask to play, should I? I mean, even if I'm rested."

"I can't answer that, Albert. Be honest with yourself and honest with your team." Lee turned to leave. "I will be with you no matter what you decide to do."

Albert took a breath and crawled into the hygg. While his teammates were playing for their lives on the field, he did the only thing he could do at the moment to help them: he fell asleep.

19.5

Tackle turned to face robotic Trey, who was walking toward him down the street. Thankfully, Mrs. Patterson was focused on getting Trey into the house, so focused that she forgot about bringing Tackle inside.

"Hey, boy, who let you out?" robotic Trey called out.

The dog stared. It really was remarkable how close a duplicate the robot was and how lifelike this Trey's voice and actions were. Mehk was a genius. The dog stopped himself and focused on what was at stake. To protect Albert, he had to make sure that no one on Earth found out about robotic Trey, which meant that this Trey could not walk through the Pattersons' front door now that the real Trey was home.

He barked a warning, but robotic Trey kept approaching.

Grrrr.

Tackle could bark the birds out of the trees and this Trey would not understand him. Mehk had not bothered to install Dog in the robot's language-translation processor because Mehk had completely underestimated Tackle's intelligence.

If Tackle couldn't tell robotic Trey to get lost and if robotic Trey wasn't afraid of him, how was he going to keep this machine from entering?

An idea came to him. Tackle knew that the robotic Trey had been programmed to follow the basic rules of home, and one of the basic rules was not to let the dog run off leash. So he took off running, wincing at the pain of his injured foot.

Behind him he could hear robotic Trey's voice. "Tackle! Stop!" Tackle kept running down the block and turned onto a side street. Robotic Trey was following.

Ignoring the pain in his foot, Tackle picked up speed, leaping over a low hedge, darting up a sidewalk, dashing around a group of kids walking home from school, jumping over another hedge, knocking over a garbage can—*Mmm*...chicken bones...

Grrrr. Don't stop, dog! He tore down the sidewalk.

"STOP!" the robot ordered.

After another block, the dog realized that no matter how fast he managed to run, robotic Trey would eventually catch him. The thing had precision. The thing had speed. The thing had awesome batteries. In its "brain" three commands were flashing: *chase dog, catch dog, bring dog home.*

Tackle, on the other hand, was getting tired. He recognized where he was and turned toward his favorite park. Maybe there he could just stop. Turn on the charm. Convince Trey to hang out and just play for a while, at least until Mehk figured out what had happened and straightened this mess out.

"BAD DOG. I SAID STOP!"

BAM! Robotic Trey pounced from behind. Tackle hit the ground and quickly wriggled free. Valiantly, the exhausted dog jumped up and took off again.

19.6

The locker room was filling up when Albert stepped out of the hygg. His teammates, beaten, were streaming in. The sight of them made him feel ashamed all over again. But he took a breath and reminded himself that the shame didn't have to control him. He cleared his throat. "Guys," he said. "I'm sorry. I know what I did was wrong."

Ennjy sat down to catch her breath. The sadness in her voice was heartbreaking. "Thank you for apologizing, Albert. We're all exhausted."

"Still two to zero," Giac added.

"They're outrunning, outskating, outdefending, and outattacking," Doz muttered. "On the tops of all those outs, they are outentertaining. The crowd loves them."

"Did you all feel it?" Sormie asked, her eyes wild with despair. "Even our fans in the stands stopped sending out the ahn. They have given up on us, haven't they?"

Albert looked around, feeling their defeat and fatigue. "Guys," he said, fetching smoothies and handing them out. "We cannot give up. I know this is going to sound ridiculous coming from me, the one who basically handed our opponents two goals on a platter. But listen, I wasn't open to the ahn during the first half. I am now. I'm rested. I'm ready. I will not be a hindrance. I will be a help. Even if you don't want me to play on the field, I will be on the bench sending you the ahn." He gave a smoothie to Ennjy, who looked up, her eyes filling.

"Let's bring Albert back in," Doz said.

Albert wanted to hug him.

Ennjy stood. "In for the ahn." They huddled in and began to breathe. Albert closed his eyes and let his breath rise and fall. Doz on his right. Ennjy on his left. Toben directly across from him. The rest of the team in between, links in the chain. Albert began to sense that shimmering thread, the vibrations of energy connecting them. He focused on sending his energy outward toward each of his teammates, and, as effortlessly as inhaling, he felt energy returned to him. The positive intensity of the energy increased and increased until Ennjy, renewed, gave a long, loud whoop and they all jumped forward, arms around each other's shoulders. Albert opened his eyes, and it seemed as if the entire room had turned a beautiful shade of gold.

"Let's show the solar system what it means to be a team," Ennjy said. "And why we love johka."

Albert brightened. "Let's give the crowd something unexpected and fun. Let's make an entrance."

Normally, the routine on Jhaateez after halftime was for each player to run out of the locker room onto the deck, skate down one by one, and take their positions. Home team first.

At the doorway, while the Jhaateezians were taking their places, Albert and the Zeenods devised their plan. When it was their turn, instead of coming out and skating down one by one, the Zeenods ran out, singing the Zeenod anthem, spreading out on the deck until they were all out of the locker room, all standing with their arms around each other's shoulders. Already the fans were loving the change, standing and singing along. Then, on a signal from Ennjy, they slid down on their rears, still holding on to each other, yelling, "Woohoo, Zeeno!"

The crowd roared with delight, and the team and the stadium buzzed with ahn energy.

"Crazy-good idea, Albert!" Doz said, and fist-bumped Albert as they ran to their places.

Albert grinned, feeling so good to have this second chance. With a sweeping look up at the fans in the stadium, he put his hand to his heart and bowed, hoping they could feel both his apology and his determination to make things right.

The ball zoomed into place. The trumpet blared. And the game was on.

Caught off guard by the burst of lighthearted positivity from the Zeenods, the Jhaateezians fell flat, and the Zeenods came out strong.

Albert stayed on the turf, where he felt most confident, and focused on connecting with his teammates and keeping an eye on the big-picture view of the game. As his teammates worked the ball up the field, Albert ran to find an opening near the top of the box. Expecting to be attacked, he was surprised when two Jhaateezian defenders split apart. With lightning speed, they skated up the ice on either side, turned, and stood on the deck, each waiting like a vulture. They were setting up for an epic slide tackle. Sure enough, as Doz dribbled up and passed to Albert, the Jhaateezians swooped down—both heading straight for Albert. Knowing he was going to be clobbered by the incoming challenge, Albert saw Sormie making a run to the top left corner of the box and delivered a one-touch pass to her feet.

Doz yelled, "Jhaateez on, Albert!"

One of the flying Jhaateezians slid into Albert, knocking him off his feet and sending him sliding on his back across the field.

The other Jhaateezian, sliding onto the field, lifted his sailwing, changing his trajectory toward Sormie. Valiantly, Sormie took aim and fired a shot toward the goal. The keeper was ready and prepared to dive to the right to make the save, but at the last second, the incoming Jhaateezian made what would turn out to be an accidental move. Rather than taking out Sormie, his body deflected the shot. Luckily for the Zeenods, the ball still sailed toward the goal—just at a different angle than Sormie had intended. The goalie had no chance. The ball whizzed past him into the net.

The Jhaateezians and Liötians in the stands groaned, and the Zeenods and their allies cheered.

"Goal!" Albert screamed, so excited he felt as if he might shatter the ceiling with his joy alone. It wasn't a beautiful goal, but it was a goal.

"We're luckies!" Doz yelled.

Albert and the Zeenods had planned what they would do to celebrate their goals, and now was their first chance.

At Ennjy's signal, they sped from their individual positions to the ice. In unison, they quickly zoomed up, did a 180, zoomed back down, and then slid out onto the turf on their knees with their arms out.

The crowd cheered.

Jhaateez: 2. Zeeno: 1. They had thirty-seven minutes to get two more goals.

Albert's eyes filled as he looked up to the VIP box, searching in vain for a sight of Lightning Lee.

They had to do it.

19.7

"BAD DOG!"

On the grass by the pond, robotic Trey pounced again, but Tackle darted sharply to the right just in time. The robot went down, and Tackle ran a few feet away, turned around, and panted.

Okay, Tackle thought, let's calm down. No need to keep this ridiculous chase up. Just show him you want to play and keep him distracted.

Robotic Trey stood slowly. "Stay, Tackle. Sit."

Tackle sat and gave robotic Trey his *let's play* face. He stuck a paw in the air, which he knew humans always liked. And he added a little sneeze, even though he didn't have to sneeze, because, in the past, Trey had always thought that was so cute.

The irises of the robot's eyes flickered, although the stare was intense. "Bad dog."

Tackle tensed up, alarmed. Something wasn't right. He sniffed, hoping to detect a clue, but that was the thing about this Trey—the smell of the robot didn't change. Mehk had said that he had programmed the robot to give off an aroma. Now Tackle realized that the aroma was one of the things he had found confusing. This Trey had old Trey's aroma, but the scent never changed. When the old Trey was scared or mad or even really happy, the aroma would change, depending on the emotion. Those differences in scent had helped Tackle know what was going on with Trey.

Robotic Trey took a step toward him. "Bad dog."

Grrrr. Fight or flight, Tackle wondered?

Robotic Trey took another step toward him.

Tackle sat and put both paws up. See? I'm sitting. I'm staying. I'm being a good dog.

Still glaring, robotic Trey crouched, his muscles rippling.

This thing is going to kill me, Tackle thought, panting. Was Mehk in the shadows, operating it with a remote control? Or was the thing glitching, and was this why the szoǔ hadn't worked? Freaking out, Tackle took off and raced to the pond, sending a team of ducks flying.

Since it was a Friday afternoon and most adults were at work and most kids were just getting home from school, there weren't many people in the park. But there was an old couple sitting side by side on a bench on the dock.

Tackle ran the length of the dock and jumped in, splashing the poor couple. He thought for sure that the robot would avoid getting wet, but it ran to the dock and copied Tackle's jump, belly-flopping onto the water and sending a second wave over the couple.

Tackle paddled, looking back. And as robotic Trey swam closer, Tackle realized his mistake. Of course the robot was designed to swim. He was designed to be the perfect athlete.

Frantically, Tackle paddled back to shore and scrambled out just as Trey reached for his tail. Tackle felt the brush of metal, and he whipped his tail, found his footing, and ran.

19.8

The Jhaateezians and Liötians in the stands were now chanting for their team to take control.

As Linnd ran to the center, she did a series of cartwheels and flips, as if to tell the fans not to worry. The game resumed. After several minutes of even play, Linnd and her teammates got down to business. They had a different energy. Their passing was sharper, and they quickly hustled the ball toward the goal. A Zeenod tried to steal, but the Jhaateezian kicked it onto the ice. Another Jhaateezian, who was already on the ice, launched into the shoot-the-duck position, neatly receiving the ball. As she zoomed around behind Toben, two Jhaateezian defenders hopped on and flanked her, skating on either side and pushing her along even faster—a completely legal move.

Albert felt his newly won confidence begin to melt. So intent was he on watching the Jhaateezians, he hadn't noticed that Beeda and Reeda had hopped onto the ice on the other side and were on their way to greet them from the opposite direction. The twins linked arms, their bems spreading behind them, forcing the Jhaateezians to react.

The Jhaateezian defender closest to the field threw up his sail-wing to make a sharp turn toward the field, pulling the Jhaatee-zian with the ball along with him. Those two headed toward the field while Beeda and Reeda crashed into the other Jhaateezian. The three of them went tumbling, Beeda sliding onto the field and Reeda crushed beneath their opponent.

The Jhaateezian with the ball passed it to Linnd, who was in a goal-scoring position. Linnd launched a shot. As the ball sailed to the goal, the entire stadium seemed to hold its breath. It was a beautiful kick.

Ahn to Toben, Albert thought. Ahn to Toben.

Toben leaped up and caught the ball.

The Zeenods cheered. But Beeda screamed for help. The Jhaa-teezian defender had untangled himself and stood, but Reeda wasn't getting up.

"Medic!" Beeda cried out, and ran to Reeda's side. She was out, blood streaming from her forehead. The Jhaateezian defender ran to apologize and offer his help.

The ref stopped the game and the medics came onto the field. A medical team moved Reeda carefully to a stretcher and then rushed her toward the emergency door that was opening on the field. Beeda was following, calling at Reeda to wake up.

"It was a fair collision," Ennjy said, trying to pull her away. "Calm down. Take a breath."

The stocky defender's eyes were wild. "Why isn't she wak-ing up?"

There was no time to process anything. Without knowing if Reeda was going to be all right, they had to resume play.

Toben had the ball, and the tension was thick.

The first pass went to Beeda. She charged forward, dribbling the ball and fending off the Jhaateezians. Doz was open, but she couldn't see it. She just kept dribbling up. Doz fell back to defend, and Albert felt his heart sink, worried that Beeda's emotions would make her hold on to the ball and miss the passes that could pay off. Quickly, the other Zeenods moved in to defend her.

Too far from the goal, Beeda played it long. It was a bad move. A Jhaateezian easily jumped up and headed it back. Over Beeda's head it flew, and she winced.

But Doz ran in to win the ball and send it back to Beeda. Somehow she snapped out of it and made a successful pass. In a series of quick touches, the ball moved up the field to Giac. Albert ran to receive the ball in the box but was suddenly surrounded by defenders. In the meantime, Ennjy had hit the ice and skated behind the goal to the other side.

Giac crossed the ball to Ennjy. The trajectory was a tough one. To connect with the ball, Ennjy had to turn sharply and kick while on the ice, something the Jhaateezians could do without a doubt. Using her bem for the turn, Ennjy managed a kick but then wiped out, sliding on the field. The kick wasn't bad, though, and the ball went flying back to midfield. Beeda, playing with the strength of two, was there. She headed it to Albert, who passed it back to Ennjy, who had already popped up into position. Albert's pass made it over the head of a Jhaateezian whose timing was off, and Ennjy received the ball. She sent it flying toward the goal, slicing it in just under the crossbar. Their keeper dove for it, but the ball brushed past his hand and hit the net.

Goal for Zeeno! A tie at 2–2.

Joy erupted. The Zeenods took to the ice, skating up, doing

their 180s, and sliding back onto the field with arms outstretched. "Zeeno!"

Albert looked at his teammates. Their bems were extending. Their eyes were shining.

Five minutes left in the game. His arms, his legs, his core were charged with energy. They had to score one more goal.

19.9

In a series of lucky breaks, Tackle managed to dodge Robotic Trey long enough to run to the area of the park with the restrooms and the hot dog truck. The smell of food was enough to reduce the dog to tears. And then he saw his opening. Literally. Tackle dove under the parked truck, pressing his body low and squeezing to safety.

Robotic Trey hit the ground and tried to crawl under, but he couldn't fit.

"Trey! What's up?" a voice called.

Tackle's ears pricked up.

The back door of the truck creaked open. "Trey, what are you doing?"

It was Freddy Mills, holding a set of tongs. He walked around to the front of the truck where Trey was belly down.

Ignoring Freddy, robotic Trey glared at the dog. "Tackle! Bad dog! Come out right now."

Tackle growled.

"That's your dog? What's he doing under there?" Freddy asked.

The fact that Freddy had left the back door of the truck open meant that more hot dog aroma was spilling out. Tackle squirmed, sniffing deeply, wishing the aroma alone could fill his empty stomach. He felt as if he hadn't eaten for days, and perhaps he hadn't. He had completely lost track of time.

"I'm working here now. Isn't that cool?" Freddy said. "The owner is my uncle. He's not supposed to leave me in charge because I'm not sixteen, but he takes these really long cigarette breaks, even though he knows he shouldn't smoke. And, as you can see, it's really dead around here and—"

Tackle couldn't stand it any longer. He darted out the other side of the truck and faked running to the right. Robotic Trey jumped up and headed to the right, and then Tackle cut to the left and zipped into the open back door of the truck. Once inside, he tipped over a tray of waiting hot dogs, clamped as many as he could in one bite, and took off.

Yum.

The charbroiled flavor of the hot dogs! The crispy casing! The soft and juicy meat! The—

"Those cost money!" Freddy was screaming. "My uncle is going to kill me!"

Then Robotic Trey pounced on the dog. Around and around the two rolled.

"G-guys! Whoa!" Freddy stammered. "That looks rough— yikes—I mean…"

Something had glitched in the robot's programming. With one hand, Robotic Trey grabbed Tackle by the throat and lifted him off the ground.

Freddy screamed and tried to hit Trey with the tongs. "Trey! Let him go!"

Every muscle in Tackle's body screamed *Fight.*

Tackle swung his hind legs forward and punched the robot as hard as he could in the stomach.

Although Tackle didn't know it, the robot was designed with a secret emergency On/Off button behind its synthetic belly button. The only way the button could be activated was with a small pointed object, and, luckily, Tackle hit this spot dead-on with one of his nails.

Robotic Trey collapsed like a rag doll.

Freddy gasped and jumped back.

Without thinking, Tackle clamped his mouth on the robot's throat and dragged him behind a bush. And then he turned and saw Freddy.

Freddy, who was frozen with his mouth hanging open, took a breath and then let out the loudest, highest scream possible while running back inside the truck. *Bam!* He slammed the metal door shut.

Trouble, Tackle thought. Trouble, trouble—wait! Hot dogs on the ground. Tackle ran over and began eating the hot dogs he had dropped. O. M. G. Nothing had ever tasted this good.

"Help!" Freddy yelled out the window as he fumbled for his cell phone to dial 911. "Help!"

Tackle raced to the truck's window to calm Freddy down. He sat and put his paws up and panted. See? Nice dog. Good dog.

"I just witnessed a murder!" Freddy yelled into his phone. Panicking, he picked up a handful of hot dogs and threw them at Tackle.

Tackle jumped up to catch them. Okay, dude! Tackle thought. Keep 'em coming!

Freddy threw a ketchup bottle next and then the mustard bottle.

Tackle dodged them and barked for more hot dogs.

"I'm in the truck," Freddy was saying to the police. "I'm defending myself from a wild dog." He picked up a gallon jug of water and heaved it out.

Water! Tackle ducked and the jug landed on its side. The cap flew off, and as the water started gurgling out, Tackle lapped it up. Oh, water! He hadn't realized how thirsty he was.

19.10

With only five minutes left in the game, Albert saw it clearly. Their last play had been clunky and strained, accomplished with more luck than skill, and they all knew it. They needed to stay on the field where they were comfortable and avoid the ice completely. If they kept tight possession of the ball on the field, it would also mean that the ice would be less useful to the Jhaateezians. They needed to play Earth-style soccer, and they needed to connect.

"Tiki-taka," Albert said to Doz.

Doz's eyes lit up. "Tiki-taka," he said to Beeda, and the message was quickly passed along.

As soon as they got the ball, the team pulled in. Immediately, Albert could feel a shift in energy. The ahn started flowing freely again, as if it liked them being close together on the field. Working together, the team began to carry out a series of tight passes, pinging the ball from player to player with control. From the defenders to the midfielders, every Zeenod got a piece.

The Jhaateezians pulled out all their tricks to distract, trying to swoop in and steal. But the Zeenods now had that seemingly effortless control, the flow. As soon as the Jhaateezians focused on trying to extract the ball from Doz, Doz would pass to Wayt, and as soon as Wayt got it, the ball was sailing to Sormie. With swift grace, the Zeenods were working their way up the field, almost as if in rhythm. And that was when the singing in the stadium began. The Zeenod fans could feel the flow of ahn and they responded, standing and letting their voices stream out.

Suddenly Giac took off for the ice, and two Jhaateezians immediately zipped after her. Albert and all the Zeenods knew without speaking what a spectacular move this was, spectacular because the Zeenods had no intention of using the ice, and Giac knew it. Like a magnet, she was deliberately drawing the opponents toward her—and away from the real action. The departure of those defenders left a lovely hole for the Zeenods to fill.

Happy to respond, Albert rocketed to the box. Sormie passed him the ball, and with one lovely left-footed kick, Albert fired it over the keeper's head. With a satisfying force, it slammed into the net. It was a beautiful, soul-satisfying goal, but before Albert could enjoy it, he saw the Jhaateezian defender sliding toward him. It was going to be a late, crunchy tackle, a takedown, a bash, a wallop, a bad, bad bruising. Time seemed to freeze, and Albert thought, No way, not now! Summoning his strength at the last moment, Albert dove, somersaulting over his opponent and landing back on his feet.

The crowd cheered, and then Albert could feel the reality of the goal sink in: 3–2 Zeeno! Almost in shock, Albert looked at Sormie and his other teammates. "We're in the lead!"

"Woohoo!" Doz shouted. "Full steam in the head!"

"We can't celebrate yet!" Feeb warned. "Two minutes left on the clock. They could still get one back."

"Focus, team!" Ennjy cried out.

Holding back their joy, the Zeenods took their positions and faced their opponents. The sounds from the crowd were deafening, and Albert felt slightly dizzy, adrenaline pumping through his system. Then the ball was in play, and the Jhaateezians leaped into action.

Desperate with two minutes left, the Jhaateezians set up a risky shot. One of them sent a long ball toward Linnd, who was positioning herself nicely to receive it, and the stadium erupted. Fans on both sides were stomping so vigorously, the glass ceiling above them seemed to rattle. But as the ball descended, Doz leaped into the air and headed the ball away. Giac was there to win it, and immediately, the Zeenods moved in and began passing.

The Zeenods in the stands started singing again. Albert felt a smile spreading on his face. The clock was ticking and they were doing their tiki-taka with style. All they had to do was keep the Jhaateezians from scoring and they would win.

"Albert!" Doz called, and passed him the ball.

And just as the ball came sailing toward Albert, just as Albert was thinking to himself how much he loved his team, how much he loved this game, the final trumpet blew, signaling time.

The ball stopped in midair.

Game over!

The crowd went wild.

"Zeeno wins with three goals!" The game-over announcement blared from the loudspeakers.

Albert sank to his knees. Everything he had done to arrive at this moment—training, performing in the Skill Show, dealing with his shawbles, facing the haagoolts with Tackle, escaping with Trey, outsmarting the Tevs, negotiating with Mehk, piloting the sled down that crazy snow-covered hill, making those mistakes in the first half—it came rushing back in a surreal jumble of images. With help, he had survived it all. With the help of Lee, Tackle, and his team, he had been able to deliver what he most wanted: his best effort to help his friends win.

Relief and gratitude flooded him, and then came the joy.

19.11

From the cloaked, hovering ITV, the botmaker worked feverishly to make adjustments. It had never occurred to him that the szoŭ wouldn't work, and he wasn't sure if the problem was related to his system or if a flaw had developed in his creation. He hadn't been able to monitor the robotic Trey ever since he had been imprisoned.

Casting another search to pinpoint the robot's new location, Mehk received an alarming alert. He knew exactly where the robot was, but the robot's system appeared to have gone dark. No functions available. He tried to activate the szoŭ again. Nothing.

His entire body began to shake. There was no way he could leave without knowing what had gone wrong. If he couldn't bring his creation up, he had to go down.

His mind was swimming. Beaming to Earth had not been a part of his plan. Was it too reckless or was it possible?

He installed a breathing implant, programmed the ITV to continue hovering in its current cloaked position, adjusted a manual override code, and initiated the szoŭ for himself. The moment he materialized in the park, he took in the situation. His robot lay at his feet. Beyond the bushes stood a vendor cart, and beyond that, he could see the dog eating. Quickly, he picked up the robot and fled, running behind the restrooms and into the shadows of the nearby woods.

19.12

Tackle was lapping up the last of the water when the police arrived.

Freddy called out to the officer from the truck window. "The dog bit my friend in the throat and he dragged him behind these bushes. I saw the whole thing with my own eyes."

Tackle looked up. He had been so focused on food and water, he had forgotten where he was or what was happening. Suddenly, his ears snapped up. He sniffed. Something was not right. That smell! That szoŭ smell was in the air. Tackle ran toward the bushes. The robot was gone. Lingering on the bushes and in the air was a complex set of aromas. The szoŭ must have worked to beam the robot up, Tackle thought.

The officer drew her gun and began slowly approaching Tackle.

Tackle knew he was not a killer dog, but the officer didn't know that. Tackle also knew there was no murdered body to see, but he couldn't explain that to the officer, either. Taking a chance, he decided to make a run for it.

Using the bushes as cover, he took off, zooming away before the officer could even react.

In no time, he was making the turn onto the Kinneys' street. By the time he arrived, Mrs. Patterson and Trey were getting into the car.

"Tackle!" Trey was the first to notice him.

Tackle slowed to a trot and tried to look natural. Wagging his tail, he headed for Trey, who crouched and gave him a hug.

Trey smelled terrible. Stinky clothes. Stinky pits. Stinky skin.

Tackle smiled. The real Trey.

But the lovefest didn't last long. "Bad Tackle!" Mrs. Patterson took him by the collar. "Don't reward him for running off, Trey! Bad, bad dog! Worrying us at a time like this!"

She was about to pull him inside when a police car pulled up. Freddy's wide-eyed face was in the back window. The officer got out. "I'm Officer Tanner. I'm looking for the Patterson family. Trey Patterson?"

"I'm Cynthia Patterson and this is my son, Trey. I was just about to take him to the doctor. He fell when he was almost hit by a truck. I assumed it wasn't bad, but he keeps saying he just returned from camp. I think he may have a concussion."

The officer looked at the boy and the dog standing next to Mrs. Patterson.

"He wasn't just attacked by that dog at the park?" the officer asked.

Tackle sat obediently and gave the police officer his sweetest look.

19.13

With the johka ball still suspended in its game-over position in midair, Albert glanced around. All the Zeenod players stood motionless in shock. And then Doz yelled, "We won!" and they all ran toward each other, hugging and yelling.

Reeda appeared at the top of the deck with a medical sleeve around her ribs and a smartskin bandage around her head. "We won!" she exclaimed, and skated down to join them.

The geodesic dome above them suddenly lit up with a dazzling array of lights, and the Jhaateezian ritual to celebrate the winners began. Laser beams were projected across the ice, and one hundred or so Jhaateezian musicians took to the slopes. Around and around the musicians skated, amplifying different notes as they passed through the laser beams, making music with their movements, a symphony of Jhaateezian sound.

Albert thought back to the Zeeno ritual after the first game, that moment when the vacha-blossom petals fell from the sky like snowflakes and when the ahda birds sang a song so ethereal, it lifted them off their feet.

"Two games," Feeb said, stunned.

The Jhaateezians and Linnd joined the Zeenods and Albert on the field to offer their congratulations. They looked sad to have lost—no doubt about it. But it was a fair game.

When the symphony ended, the Zeenod anthem was announced and everyone in the stands stood. As the Zeenods on the field and in the stands began to sing, Albert felt the energy of the ahn expand. He looked around. Bems were extending, eyes turning gold.

They had played without subs. They had played without a coach. And they had almost played without a Star Striker, Albert thought. Against the odds, they had won. The ahn filled him and made him feel more alive than he'd ever felt. He had completed his second game on his second planet in the Fŭigor Solar System, and he still couldn't believe it.

The medal ceremony came next, and the presidents took their places on the field. It was then that Albert's mind snapped back to President Lat, to Mehk, to Kayko, and to the occupation. Anger quickly replaced his joy, and he felt the tension rising in his Zeenod teammates, too. There was the Zeenod president smiling and waving at the crowd, acting as if nothing were wrong.

"We must have evidence before we confront the authorities," Ennjy said. "For now, we focus on this johka triumph."

Bowing to the president of Jhaateez, President Lat said, "The planet of Zeeno humbly thanks the Jhaateez players for a game well played."

The Jhaateezian president bowed and gave his congratulations.

The Zeenod fans cheered, and President Lat began placing a new victory medal around the neck of each Zeenod player, smiling but avoiding eye contact. A media drone followed her, recording and projecting the video footage up onto the geodesic dome.

When President Lat put Albert's medal on, his eyes drilled into her. He flashed back to the moment he woke up from his hygg to see Unit D crumpled on the floor and the safe door swinging open and his first medal gone. President Lat refused to look up, moving on to the next player and the next.

After the victory lap, robotic reporters flooded the field.

"How does the medal feel?" a Jhaateezian reporter asked Albert as Lat stood nearby, getting her photo taken with the president of Jhaateez.

Albert smiled. "Amazing! I plan to make sure this one never

gets lost or stolen!" Out of the corner of his eye, he could see Lat's entire body stiffen, and then she began to walk away.

Albert couldn't stop himself. "Excuse me, President Lat!"

She turned.

"You'll be shocked to hear this, but someone broke into my ITV and stole my first game medal—and also my Z-da." Albert tried to keep his face neutral.

"Really? How disturbing," she said, the corners of her mouth twitching. "I'll be sure to look into it."

"Thank you!" Albert smiled.

Ennjy pulled him away and led the whole team into their locker room.

There the team celebrated again, slurping down smoothies and trading fist bumps.

They agreed that they wanted to talk through the high points of the game but first wanted to hear Albert's story.

He told them about Lat and Mehk, the haagoolts, and the Tevs. He told them everything.

"We are back to where we were before," Sormie said sadly. "After all Giac's hard work and all the risks, we have no evidence."

At the word *evidence,* a new thought entered Albert's mind. "Wait!" he said, and everyone looked at him. "There might be new evidence. Mehk planted a surveillancebot shaped like a beetle in the ITV. He said he watched footage of Lat entering the ITV. The whole thing must have been recorded! It would prove that Lat stole that drive with the evidence and that she sent me to the gravespace and then lied about my death."

"But you escaped in a pod," Sormie said. "And the ITV crashed on GJ7. That means the surveillancebot was destroyed with it."

"Mehk had the bot follow me in the escape pod," Albert said.

246

"It was on my shoulder and I didn't even know it. He took it from me."

"Mehk has footage in that spybot!" Giac's eyes lit up. "All we have to do is find him!"

"If we can show the interplanetary council that Lat tried to kill you, Albert, then maybe Lat will confess what the Tevs and Z-Tevs have been doing," Feeb said. "Maybe Kayko can be released and the truth about what's going on will be believed."

"And we'll build even more support if we can win our next game against the Gaböqs—" Toben said.

"We *will* win," Albert said.

Sormie winced. "Albert, you are not going to like Gaböq. It's terrifying."

But Doz refused to let fear have the last word. He jumped up on a bench and held out his arms, his bem rippling behind him. "Dudes, we just won! So let's enjoy it!"

Everyone cheered.

19.14

In the woods that bordered the park, the botmaker sat with his back against a tree. Cradled in his arms was his robot. He was thinking through everything he had done wrong. And then he stopped and hit himself hard on the side of his head.

You have two options, he said to himself. Focus on what your next step will be. You could take the robot back to the ITV and find a place in the Fŭigor Solar System to hide. Or…

He looked around. A squirrel scampered down the trunk of a tree and began to search for acorns. A live squirrel! For a moment Mehk was completely distracted. He had studied Earth life-forms, and here he was on Earth seeing the real thing.

What about staying right here? he thought. He would have to hide his bem and find a way to make a smartskin mask of an Earthling. Maybe he could break into a robotics-engineering facility and fix his masterpiece and start creating again.

No one in Fŭigor Solar System would expect him to be on Earth. And as for Earthlings? Mehk had a feeling they'd be very easy to fool.

19.15

The time-folding calculations brought Albert back to Earth close to dinnertime on the same Friday he had left. He reappeared in his backyard, which was already dark. He could sense that the January air was cold, but he didn't feel uncomfortable. There were no lights on in his house—and for a moment he was confused. Then he remembered that Erin and his mom were at her Winter Invitational competition and his nana was in Baltimore. He was supposed to be at a sleepover.

He stood for a moment in the dark and drank in the silence. No fans cheering. No johkadin projected against the night sky. No moon or stars, in fact. Just the shadowy presence of his house and the trees and the fence. And then—*thwap*—the sound of the dog door came. It was followed by the jingling of Tackle's tags and then the sound of the dog jumping up, paws against the fence.

Albert?

Albert ran to the Pattersons' house, and by the time he had opened their front gate, Tackle was on top of him.

Hey, it's so good to see you, Albert said. *Did you rip up any teddy bear packages while I was gone?*

Tackle laughed. *No, but I ripped up a robot!*

They told each other everything, cuddling up together on the Pattersons' front steps. Trey and his mom were still gone, and Tackle had been waiting for Albert to return.

After every detail of their stories had been shared, Albert explained his next goals. He had to help the Zeenods find Mehk and get the evidence to free Kayko. And he had to train for Gaböq, which had the most dangerous terrain yet. Albert paused and looked at the glow of the streetlamp and said the next sentence like a birthday wish. *I hope I can stay strong.*

Tackle nuzzled in and pushed his head into Albert's hand, hinting for a behind-the-ear scratch.

Albert pulled Tackle close for a hug and then gave him a full-head rub. Then, while the dog panted with contentment, Albert closed his eyes. He saw himself sitting on the steps, in Silver Spring, on Earth, and he pictured his teammates in the Fŭigor Solar System heading home to Zeeno. He hoped his team and all Zeenods everywhere were able to celebrate. He hoped Kayko was learning about the win and was feeling the ahn and would know that they were still fighting for her. He hoped Lee was proud of him and somehow watching over him. He hoped his sister's tournament was going well and that she and his mom and his nana were experiencing joy—even if it was something small. He hoped the real Trey was feeling happy to be back even if he couldn't remember where he had been. He hoped Lat was feeling remorse and would come to the realization that she could help rather than harm. He hoped Mehk was realizing that the evidence he had was crucial and that Albert and the Zeenods were not his enemies. He hoped Freddy wasn't too freaked out. And then he thought about Jessica. He hoped she was looking out her window and eating some chocolate...thinking of him.

He took a deep breath and exhaled. And then he opened his eyes and gasped. *Tackle, look!*

From the depths of the black sky, the first snowflakes of the year were falling. He knew they were just tiny crystals of frozen water, glistening in the glow of the streetlamp, but that didn't make them any less miraculous.

What a universe to live in, Albert thought, a universe where you can be sitting with a friend in the hushed darkness, sitting on a rock in space, and suddenly you can be surrounded by specks of ice that sparkle like diamonds.

Beautiful, Tackle said.

Albert agreed.

ACKNOWLEDGMENTS

Thanks to Simon Amato for inspiration and help on every level, to Ivan Amato for support and science advice, to Karen Giacopuzzi for brainstorming, to Kenzie Hart for dog info, to Christine Ellis for her knowledge about gymnastics training, and to Tyler Cauvel at the Rink Family Fun Center for answering my call about skating. I'm also grateful to Simon Mundie for his *Life Lessons From Sport and Beyond* podcast, to Jeff Warren for his *Daily Trip* meditations, to Joanna Axtmann for lighting so many candles for me, and to my editor Mary Cash and the team at Holiday House for continuing to cheer for Albert and the Zeenods.